THEFT
of an
IDOL

DANA STABENOW was born in Anchorage, Alaska and raised on a 75-foot fishing tender. She knew there was a warmer, drier job out there somewhere and found it in writing. Her first book in the bestselling Kate Shugak series, *A Cold Day for Murder*, received an Edgar Award from the Mystery Writers of America.

Contact Dana via her website: www.stabenow.com

The Kate Shugak series

A Cold Day for Murder
A Fatal Thaw
Dead in the Water
A Cold Blooded Business
Play with Fire
Blood Will Tell
Breakup
Killing Grounds
Hunter's Moon
Midnight Come Again
The Singing of the Dead
A Fine and Bitter Snow
A Grave Denied
A Taint in the Blood
A Deeper Sleep
Whisper to the Blood
A Night Too Dark
Though Not Dead
Restless in the Grave
Bad Blood
Less Than a Treason
No Fixed Line

The Liam Campbell series

Fire and Ice
So Sure of Death
Nothing Gold Can Stay
Better to Rest
Spoils of the Dead

✳

The Eye of Isis series

Death of an Eye
Disappearance of a Scribe

✳

Silk and Song

DANA STABENOW

THEFT
of an
IDOL

An Aries Book

First published in the UK in 2022 by Head of Zeus Ltd,
part of Bloomsbury Publishing Plc

Copyright © Dana Stabenow, 2022

9 7 5 3 1 2 4 6 8

A catalogue record for this book is available from the British Library.

ISBN (HB): 9781800249820
ISBN (XTPB): 9781800249837
ISBN (E): 9781800249806

Cover design: Ben Prior

Printed and bound in Great Britain by
CPI Group (UK) Ltd, Croydon CR0 4YY

Head of Zeus Ltd
First Floor East
5–8 Hardwick Street
London EC1R 4RG

WWW.HEADOFZEUS.COM

for
Nic Cheetham
and the rest of his wonderful team at Head of Zeus,
who produce the most beautiful books in the business.
(With a special shout-out to Liz H.,
the copyeditor who has saved my bacon
too many times to count.)

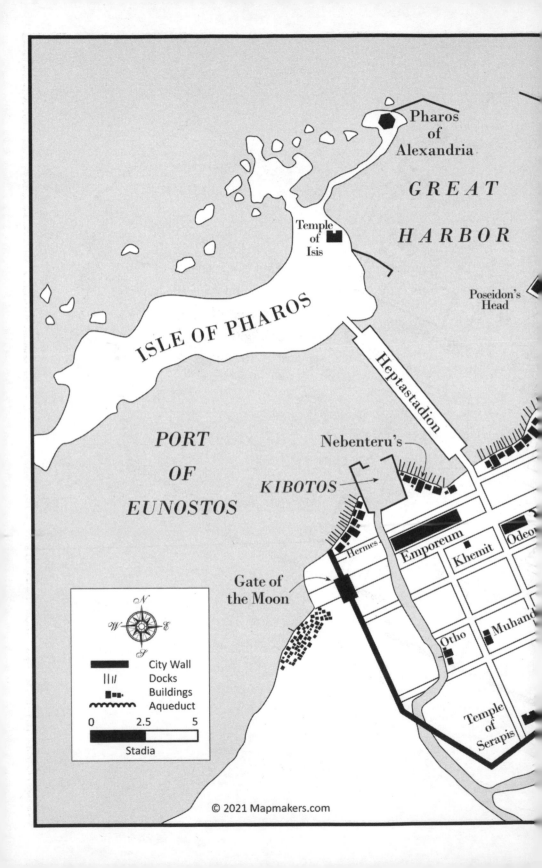

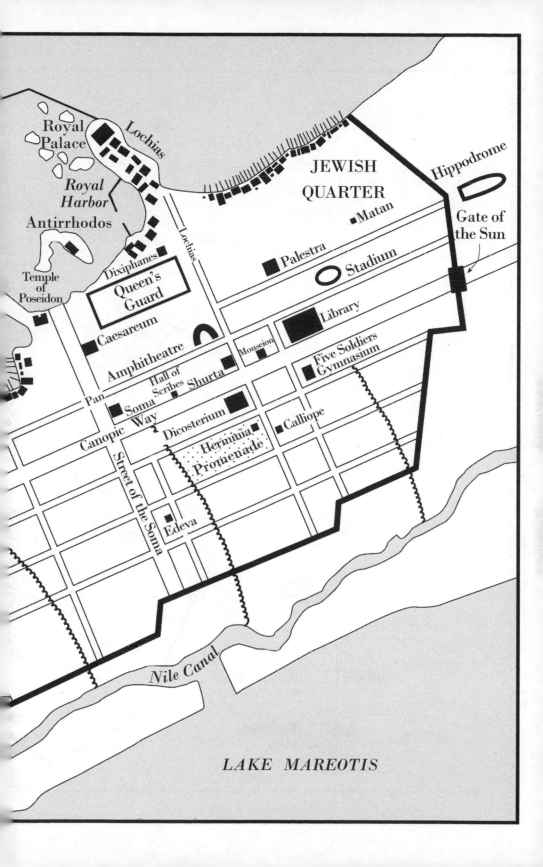

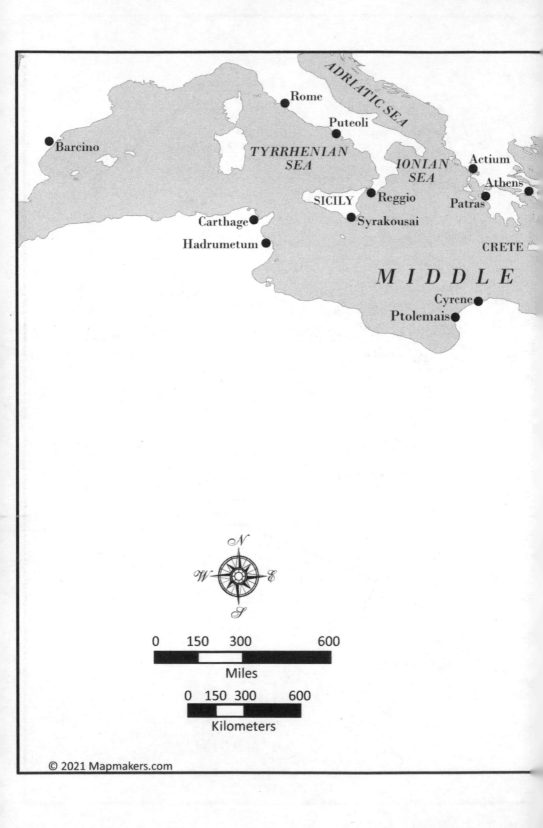

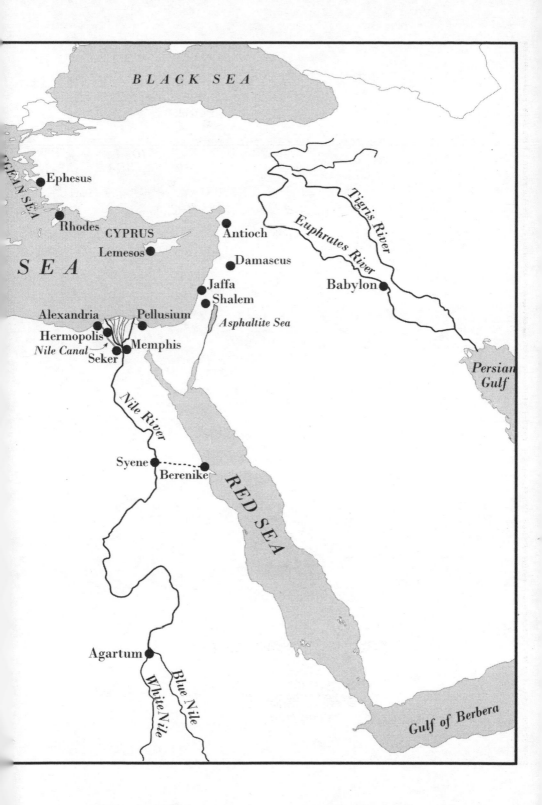

CAST OF CHARACTERS

Agathe	Novice at the Temple of Seshat
Amenirdis	A resident of Syene
Apollodorus	Partner in the Five Soldiers
Aristander	Head of the Shurta, the Alexandrian police (wife Merti)
Arsinoë	Cleopatra's sister
Aurelius Cotta	Roman legate to Egypt
Babak	Head of the Order of the Owl (in company with Roshanak, Agape, Narses, Bradan)
Basil	Stage manager at the Odeum
Caesarion	Son of Cleopatra VII and Julius Caesar ("Little Caesar")
Calliope	A hetaira
Castus	Partner in the Five Soldiers
Charmion	Cleopatra's personal servant and administrative aide
Chloe	Herminia's cook

Cleopatra VII	Queen of Alexandria and Egypt
Crixus	Partner in the Five Soldiers
Dejen	A member of the Shurta
Demetrius	A builder of ships
Dubnorix	Partner in the Five Soldiers
Eua	Herminia's steward
Euphrasia	High Priestess of the Temple of Seshat
Fulvio	Cotta's manservant
Fuscus	High Priest of the Temple of Serapis, Alexandria
Hagne	Tetisheri's mother
Henu	A farmer
Herminia	An actor
Heron	A scholar and a son of the Nomarch of the White Walls
Hunefer	Tetisheri's husband, deceased
Hypsicles	Amenirdis' steward
Idu	A novice at the Temple of Ptah
Iras	Cleopatra's personal servant and head housekeeper
Isidorus	Partner in the Five Soldiers
Julius Caesar	General, Senator and Consul of Rome
Karis	A stylist
Keren	A physician and a member of House Nebenteru
Korinna	Calliope's cook
Linos	Advisor to Ptolemy XIV

Markos	Captain of the *Nut*
Matan	A lapidary and jeweler
Merimose	A retired soldier
Min	The Master of Acolytes at the Temple of Ptah in Memphis
Myrto	Herminia's maid
Nakht	A scribe
Natasen	High Priest of the Temple of Ptah
Nebenteru	Tetisheri's uncle and partner in Nebenteru's Luxury Goods, owner/captain of the trade ship *Hapi*
Nebet	Hunefer's cook, now a member of Tetisheri's household
Nephilim	Matan's house guard
Nike	Hunefer's former slave, now a member of Tetisheri's household
Ninos	Producer/director at the Odeum
Phoebe	Cook for Uncle Neb's household
Phryne	Calliope's housekeeper
Ptolemy XII	Cleopatra's father (Auletes)
Ptolemy XIII	Cleopatra's brother, deceased (Theo)
Ptolemy XIV	Cleopatra's brother, husband, and co-ruler (Philo)
Ptolemy XV	Cleopatra's son by Julius Caesar (Caesarion)
Rhode	Cabria to House Nebenteru
Tabe	A novice at the Temple of Ptah

Tetisheri   The 28th Eye of Isis
Thaïs   A dressmaker of Memphis
Timon   Nomarch of the White Walls
Vitruvius   Roman engineer and architect

Honestly, I think historians are all mad.

—Josephine Tey

PRÓLOGOS

"How deep is it?" In spite of every effort to keep it steady, Henu heard the tremor in his voice.

"If you fall in you won't care because you'll be dead, and if you don't fall in you won't care because you'll be rich, so what does it matter how deep it is?"

The darkness of the tomb was stifling, the light cast by the flickering torch negligible, and the depth of the shaft seemed endless. Henu rested his forehead against the rope he was clinging to and felt as if he were entering the realm of Anubis well before he was expected. "Are you sure we entered by the correct door?"

"There is only one door to this kind of tomb!" The reply was somewhere between a groan and a hiss. "And would you, for the love of Ra, the giver of all that is bright and good in this world, please stop asking me that!"

"Would the both of you shut up and keep moving? It's no fun down here, either, with Henu's feet smelling of pig shit!"

The wavering light of the torch Nakht held above them cast moving shadows that had faded to black by the time they reached Merimose, who was moving steadily down the rope. Henu, just above him, didn't want to move out of the light of the torch but it was either that or Nakht's feet in his face as his were in Merimose's. The torch that they had dropped down the shaft before they began their descent had begun to sputter, casting grotesque shadows that in Henu's imagination took on the shape of the jackal god himself, manifesting outrage at this desecration of his realm.

The shaft was made of smooth granite blocks that seemed to press in on him ever more closely with every course of stone that rose above him. At least the pig pen on his father's farm was out in the open, where there was air to breathe. His heartbeat thundered in his ears and every labored gasp tightened his throat. But there was nowhere left to go but down, and so he loosened one reluctant, sweaty palm at a time. Beneath him came a steady, low-voiced cursing. Henu wondered how Merimose had the breath for it.

"I'm at the bottom!" The old soldier's voice was hoarse with excitement.

Henu himself was nearly delirious with relief and his sweaty grip loosened of itself. He slid the rest of the way, uncaring that the rope was burning his hands. His feet touched the floor and his knees gave out and he landed in a clumsy heap. Merimose was shouting up the shaft. "Throw down the other torch, Nakht!"

Henu raised his voice. "Yes, throw it down!"

"I heard him the first time! Watch your heads!"

A moment passed, another, and there was the sound of something whistling through the air, followed by a thump. "Ouch!"

"Sorry. I meant to catch that."

Merimose didn't sound very sorry. Henu rubbed his head and tried to be charitable. They were all stuck in this tomb together and everyone was scared. He took a deep breath, trying to suck in air from what felt like an airless and, at this point, eternal existence. There was the scrape of flint, a crackle of flame. The atmosphere and his spirit lightened when the torch caught and began to burn. Merimose's intent face coalesced out of the darkness.

"Will the ladder reach?" Nakht's voice from on high.

Merimose raised the torch and they both looked up to see a pale and distant smudge staring down the shaft. "I think so! Send it down!"

Wood scraped on stone and one of the ladder's feet hit one of Henu's. "Ow!" He hopped around, holding the injured foot, and bumped into Merimose.

"Be still, you fool," Merimose growled, and thrust the torch into Henu's hands. He muscled the ladder against the shaft. Henu tried to flatten himself against the wall and mostly failed, but he was past complaining, especially since— if!—they were almost at their goal. He watched the flame of the torch leap and fall and thought dreamily of the riches that awaited them, and what he would do with them when they at long last regained the living world.

3

His were modest ambitions. Pay off the debt on the family farm so that the Nomarch of the White Walls would never again have cause to take half a year's grain for back taxes, leaving the family to slowly starve through eight long months until the next harvest. Even better, his father-in-law would have no further cause to bemoan his daughter's choice of husband, especially when he saw the new house Henu would build for her. No mud hut this; it would be made of the finest Syene granite in meticulously quarried blocks polished to such a shine that it would hurt the eyes to look upon it when Ra's golden chariot was at its height in the sky above. And never again would he have to watch his wife go hungry in order to spare their sons a bite of bread.

The ladder creaked and groaned. Henu hoped it wasn't going to disintegrate beneath Nakht's weight before they had a chance to collect the wealth he had already spent in his imagination.

"What's the holdup?" Merimose said, looking up the shaft. "It's damn close in here, I can hardly breathe!"

"Sobek's balls! I can't see a hand in front of my face and the ladder doesn't reach the tunnel edge so I have to feel around with my feet for the top of it! If you think you can do any better, Merimose, get your ass up here and change places with me!"

Defeating both speed and silence, the two essential things Nakht had grimly emphasized to both his co-conspirators. Again Henu held his tongue. He wanted nothing more than for them to complete their task and get out of this accursed

4

place. He rested the back of his head against the stone shaft, closed his eyes, and concentrated on breathing in and breathing out.

Merimose had served a full sixteen years with the Roman army, including with Crassus at Carrhae, and could go on at tedious length about Crassus' total lack of ability to successfully prosecute any action bigger than a fistfight. The old soldier had a taste for wine, women, and gambling, and he had frittered away most of his pension indulging himself in these activities, a common story among veterans. If this mad gambit paid off, Henu could see Merimose moving to Alexandria in search of bigger game on all three fronts. The danger being that the sharps in Alexandria were even more adept at fleecing their prey than the ones in Memphis.

He knew what Nakht needed the money for, or what he said he did, although he kept the details so vague as to be invisible. The law forbade marriage between Greeks and Egyptians. Unless, of course, one knew a friendly judge with flexible ethics who might be willing to look the other way when issuing a license in exchange for a fat purse. As a professional scribe, Nakht probably knew many such judges.

More scraping of wood on stone, a slip, a flurry of movement, and a series of panicked oaths as Nakht slid the rest of the way down the ladder, ending in a loud thump and more curses. Henu opened his eyes to see the scribe in a heap on the floor of the shaft.

"Are you hurt, Nakht?" Merimose said with a concern belied by the wide grin spreading across his face.

Henu thought he could hear Nakht's teeth grinding together, but the other man saw something behind Merimose and his expression changed from annoyance to intense excitement. He scrambled to his feet and pointed, forcing the other men to turn to look. Henu thrust the torch forward and the light picked out rocks and mortar formed into a solid wall dividing the base of the shaft and what lay beyond. "That will lead into the serdab."

"Are we going to be able to get through it?"

"It's already crumbling. Look." Nakht snatched the torch from Henu and held it close to the wall, showing a small pile of rocks beneath a growing hole. "The mortar is so old that it has dried out entirely."

Merimose stepped up beside him and kicked at one of the larger rocks. Under the force of the blow the stone dislodged easily and flew backwards out of sight. There was a crash and a tinkle of something falling and possibly breaking.

"You idiot! Stop that! You may have broken something valuable!" Nakht looked around. "Henu! Another torch! Quickly!"

Henu fumbled for the torch they had dropped from the top of the shaft and lit it again, and the three of them went at the wall with a concentrated intensity. Nakht was right; the mortar crumbled at a touch and mostly they had to catch the rocks before they fell on their feet. Soon there was a ragged, gaping hole, like the menacing maw of a great beast, but it was big enough for them to scramble through and that was all that mattered. Henu and Merimose pushed their torches inside and all three of them stared, barely breathing.

The chamber was small and square and occupied chiefly by a stone sarcophagus, richly carved and painted. Crowded around the walls and tucked into shelves as high as the hand would reach were boxes and bags and bundles and the four canopic jars containing the dead man's organs. There was enough room for a thin man to walk between the shelves and the sarcophagus and not a finger's width more.

"It's intact," Nakht said, a note of wonder in his voice.

"Didn't you say it would be?" Merimose said, gloating. "You're the one who found the reference in those old records. You said no one had looked at them for hundreds of years."

"Yes, but…" Nakht pulled himself together. "Henu, start looking for jewelry and art. Small pieces, the most valuable and portable and easily sold, as we discussed. Merimose, help me move this lid. Let's see just how rich this priest was."

The bags deteriorated at a touch along with their contents, bread and meat and fruit and the like. Henu ran his fingers lightly along a shelf lined with tiny statues carved from wood and painted in bright colors. Ushabti, servants made to serve the dead in the next life.

He heard the grinding of stone on stone and looked over his shoulder to see the lid of the sarcophagus pivoting open. The wrapped body of the mummy lay within, and Henu was relieved to see there was no death mask. He didn't know how they would have managed to get something that large up the ladder and he was certain both Merimose and Nakht would have insisted that they try.

There was a broad collar with large gold terminals in the shape of Seshat. Merimose made a purring sound and removed the collar with more haste than care, tearing the gauze wrappings. Nakht lost no time in searching for the amulets the priests had folded inside the shroud when they wrapped the body. Such amulets were usually made of gemstones, especially if the dead were wealthy enough to pay for a tomb as rich as this one.

Henu continued around the chamber, passing a stand hung with spears and swords, all marvelously intact, and a small table topped with a chessboard and an exquisite set of chessmen carved of ebony and ivory. The ebony ones were shaped like Nubian warriors, the ivory as Egyptian soldiers. He scooped them up and put them in the sack he had tied around his waist. The board was too bulky and probably too heavy; he left it behind, not without a pang.

He came to a wooden bureau shaped to look like a tree trunk, with shelves formed from spreading branches. Each shelf bore a small box. The first one he opened held a full set of matching bracelets in what looked like gold. The contents dropped into the sack with a satisfyingly solid clank. He hoped they hadn't broken any of the chessmen.

"Ah, you found the jewelry, then," Nakht said at his shoulder. "Good. What are you staring at?"

The wall above the bureau was covered with carvings of every imaginable creature living on, in, or around the Nile.

A fat crocodile with a long-jawed smile curled his tail over an ibis with a beak as long as her legs, next to a vulture with a topknot. Cobras raised their hoods, jackals their ears, bulls their horns, snails their tentacles. It was an entrancing fantasia of the animal kingdom, beautifully carved and richly colored in red and blues and yellows that glowed even in the dim light of the torches, still vibrant centuries after their creation.

"They knew how to draw back then," Henu said, hardly knowing he spoke.

"Yes, yes, obviously done by a master's hand. Now, what's in the rest of these boxes?"

The bureau proved a treasure trove: six separate tiny, exquisitely made chests filled with collars and bracelets and earrings.

"Quite the dandy," Merimose said with a snigger. "Well, he won't be needing them now."

They were all three of them sweating profusely even though the air of the tomb was dry and chill. "That's enough," Nakht said as they emptied the last box. "We have to be able to carry all this up the ladder."

"A problem I am happy to have," Merimose said. He hoisted his bag over his shoulder and fastened the strap in a secure knot.

"And we can always come back for more later," Henu said.

Something bright caught his eye. He paused, raising the torch higher. Tucked into a corner was a small tiered shelf, each of its three layers occupied by a small statue inlaid with gemstones. They depicted the three manifestations of Seshat: the goddess of wisdom with the cheetah's hide worn as a cape, the goddess of writing with palm leaf rib and stylus in hand, and the goddess of knowledge with the knotted surveyor's cord at her side. They were made of ebony, alabaster, and gold respectively. The craft of their makers was manifest down to each individual toenail, and each statue was as exquisite as it had been the day it came from the artisan's hand. He realized he hadn't taken a breath since seeing them and huffed in a great lungful of air before he stuffed all three figures in his sack. He knotted the strings firmly against further temptation. The sack was heavy enough, and his new house had acquired a tiled roof.

He edged around the sarcophagus and the lid that remained askew. The mummy, stripped of valuables, stared faceless at the tomb's ceiling, oblivious, past need or care.

Henu didn't believe in ghosts. Not even in gods, not really. His closest relationship was with the earth, with the dark, rich soil of the banks of the Nile, not with omnipotent beings who by all accounts proved capricious and malicious and vengeful with each other and even more so toward all those less powerful than themselves. Those distant rulers in Alexandria who paid homage to the gods by assuming their appearance on earth were no better. When did they ever forgive a tax when the harvest was bad? When did they open the granaries when the people were hungry? They'd rather sell it to the Romans, whose armies marched on Egyptian grain.

No, Henu believed in the Nile and that it flooded every

year, except when it didn't, and when it didn't, in finding other ways to feed his family. Such as this one. If the sack he carried held what he thought it did, and if he managed the proceeds wisely, he would never have to fear the absence of a flood again.

"You go first, Henu," Nakht said. "I know how much you hate the dark. Be first out."

Henu had lost his fear of the dark and of traps laid by the tomb's builders with the first sight of the treasure within, but he didn't argue. He cinched the sack's straps tighter around him and almost scampered up the ladder without once looking down. At the top he took the guttering torch he had left in the ring socket on the wall and kindled the last remaining torch they had left behind. He looked down into the dark shaft that no longer seemed so bottomless.

Nakht picked his way up with the same care he had shown going the other direction, slowly, steadily, making sure of his footing. In the flicker of the torch he looked like a giant camel spider, pale, all legs and arms, the engorged bag on his back resembling a sac full of eggs. He reached the top safely and turned to crouch at the edge of the shaft, Henu behind him still holding the torch high. Far below, Merimose began to climb. He was bigger than the other two men and the ladder creaked loudly but held. His progress was slow and steady. Henu could see him quite clearly over Nakht's shoulder.

Midway, the wood creaked again. "Hurry!" Nakht said.

Merimose, his face a sweaty grimace, increased his speed. He had very nearly reached them when the ladder gave another ominous crack and the ladder seemed to shift beneath his hands and feet.

"Hold on!" Nakht said, bending forward, his hands on the ladder's ends, out of Henu's sight.

But the ladder shifted and tilted up. Merimose yelled, "Grab my hand! Grab my hand, Nakht!"

"Here, Merimose, right here!"

But it was too late. The ladder was falling into the dark and Merimose with it. Frozen with horror, all Henu could do was listen to Merimose screaming as he fell, the sound ending abruptly with a thud of flesh hitting stone.

"Merimose? Merimose!" Henu shoved Nakht to one side and hunched at the edge of the shaft. He screamed down into it, repeating Merimose's name over and over again. His voice was swallowed by the darkness, like Merimose had been, who made no response.

"He's gone," Nakht said. He put a hand on Henu's shoulder. "It's awful, I know, Henu, but we have to leave." A pause. "We'll recover his body and bury him decently when we come back."

And retrieve the contents of Merimose's sack, Henu thought numbly.

All he could do was think of Merimose's last, furious cry.

And wonder whether he had truly seen Nakht's hands shove the ladder away from the wall of the shaft, or if it had only been his imagination.

1

House Nebenteru was bubbling over with excitement. This was the afternoon Herminia would be performing a preview of her Lysistrata at the Odeum. The entire house had been invited as guests of Queen Cleopatra herself, from Nebenteru right on down to every single member of the Order of the Owl, Tetisheri's personal band of underage spies.

They weren't of the house per se, as they lived over the stable in what Nebenteru had jocularly dubbed "the Mews." The smaller apartment across the landing had been claimed by Rhode, the house's new personal cabria. Rhode's cabrio alone wasn't going to be large enough to bring them all to the Odeum in one trip so she had gone forth that morning and hired two more carriages, and was currently occupying herself with chivvying their respective drivers to neaten their livery and clean their vehicles.

"We shall arrive in style," Uncle Neb said with satisfaction.

Tetisheri laughed. "If you don't hurry up and get dressed we won't arrive at all."

He winked at her, the large teardrop pearl woven into the point of his beard standing out proudly. "You should talk," he said, and strutted off to his rooms.

Tetisheri, grinning, hurried off to her own room, there to find Keren, Phoebe, Nebet, and Nike debating over what she, Tetisheri, was going to wear. Bast, the night-black cat with the blue eyes that matched her own, was of course also present to offer commentary. Apollodorus was meeting them at the theater and the entire female contingent of the household was united in their determination to see that Tetisheri looked her very best. It was their not-so-secret wish that they weren't going to see her again until the following day.

Tetisheri was not herself averse to this goal. Apollodorus had been out of the country—again—on what she assumed was the business of the queen—again. Between his travels and her work—in both of her occupations—there had not been a great deal of time to pursue a relationship. She was, she admitted only to herself, growing a little impatient. All she knew of romance she had learned from various books, for certainly her marriage had taught her nothing of it. She glimpsed herself in the silvered mirror hanging on her wall and saw that her mouth had flattened into a grim line. Hastily, she reshaped it into a smile. "Well? What is the verdict?"

During the next fifteen minutes every single garment in her clothes press was yanked over her head and off again at least once, as her dressers universally found fault with each article. In the end Keren prevailed, chiefly by force of manner, and Tetisheri stared into the mirror at a slim woman of medium height dressed in the Greek style: a tunic of sunflower yellow beneath a stola of mint green, beneath a palla of sky blue so deep of hue it looked carved from lapis. Each of the three layers was woven of the same fine sheer linen.

Nike, among the other and many duties she had assumed since she'd taken up residence in House Nebenteru, had also arbitrarily taken unto herself the title of hairdresser. Tetisheri's straight black hair had been pulled in a smooth cap to the nape of her neck, there pinned into a nest of curls. A thin gold ribbon circled her brow, and earrings of carnelian and lapis hung from her ears.

"Well?" Keren said.

Tetisheri's straight black brows drew together as she surveyed herself in the mirror. Even she could see how the blue of the palla brought out the blue of her eyes, and how her skin gleamed beneath the tunic. "It's a good thing there are three layers to this dress, otherwise there wouldn't be much between me and the eyes of every dirty old man in Alexandria."

"And not a few young ones," Keren said cheerfully. She was dressed in her favorite deep red with a gaily striped palla draped artfully around her shoulders. Her hair stood out around her head in its usual lustrous black cloud of natural curls. Nike was dressed in yellow with her hair wrapped in a matching yellow cloth in the Nubian fashion. Phoebe and

Nebet wore traditional white, strapped sheaths and all the jewelry they owned.

"You might not be the only one not going home alone," Phoebe said, surveying them all with a satisfaction to match Uncle Neb's.

As if on cue Neb's voice was heard from the hall. "Where are all my women! Stop that infernal primping and get out here or we're going to be late!"

They gathered around him at the door and his smile nearly split his face in two. "Never has a gentleman of Alexandria been surrounded by such a collection of beauty and charm."

The great thing about Uncle Neb was that you could always feel the absolute sincerity behind his compliments. Tetisheri stood on tiptoe and kissed his cheek. "Thank you, Uncle." She stepped back to subject him to her own survey. "You do us justice."

"I'll say," Keren said.

Uncle Neb, resplendent in green tunic and green-and-purple striped toga, beamed at them. "Shall we go?"

The pearl at the tip of his beard led the way out the door and around to the stable yard, where Rhode and the two hired cabrios waited, along with all five members of the Order of the Owl, scrubbed clean by the merciless hands of Phoebe and Nebet and looking self-conscious in their new dress clothes, each with their owl brooch pinned to their left shoulder. Rhode herself was very fine in her new livery, sporting a brooch featuring House Nebenteru's sigil of a trading ship in full sail.

Apollodorus was there, too. Unconsciously Tetisheri's step quickened, finishing up in what she would later blush to acknowledge was nearly a run, both hands outstretched. "I thought you were meeting us at the theater."

He clasped her hands in his own and smiled down at her. "I couldn't wait."

She drank in the sight of him, tall, broad of shoulder and narrow of hip, fair of hair and green of eye. His features weren't handsome, precisely, but there was a self-assurance in the way he held himself that Tetisheri found even more attractive than good looks. He had the carriage of a Roman soldier, which he had once been, the arrogance of the partner in a successful business which owed no debt, and the confidence of a man entrusted by the Lady of the Two Lands herself to carry out the most private and sensitive of tasks.

Uncle Neb greeted Apollodorus with the grateful air of one man welcoming another into a woman-heavy establishment and made a fuss out of handing the two of them up into Rhode's carriage. There followed a considerably larger fuss as he and the rest of the household crammed themselves into the other two carriages.

Apollodorus grinned down at her. "Subtle isn't exactly their middle name, is it."

The laughter that had been growing beneath Tetisheri's breastbone tumbled out to fill the courtyard. Apollodorus joined in, and laughter led the way across Hermes Street, through the Emporeum, and onto the broad magnificence of the Canopic Way.

The Odeum was one of Auletes' more ambitious attempts at building a venue in which he could coerce Alexandrians into enduring his solo flute concerts. Modeled on the theater in Skias in Sparta, although on a mercifully smaller scale, it sat on the south side of the Canopic Way near the Street of the Soma. The capitals of the columns were inlaid with colored glass placed in intricate patterns, lacquered over for protection from the elements. Inside, it seated 2,500 in a series of curved tiers, and the massive wooden beams holding up the roof were works of the sculptor's art, featuring scenes to rival those on any pharaoh's tomb, continuous, sinuous, almost sensual representations of lotus and papyrus, stem, leaf, and bloom. It went without saying that each and every one of the carvings was painted in the brightest possible colors, with tracings of gold and silver for added sparkle.

The three stuccoed interior walls were also lavishly illustrated, the most recent one hastily created following the conclusion of the Alexandrian War and the installation of Auletes' daughter, Cleopatra, as queen of Egypt. Her brother, Ptolemy XIV, known familiarly as Philo, was in the mural as well but was represented as being much smaller in height and removed to the distant left, one of a group of lesser nobles, priests, and administrators. The painters had known where the real power in Alexandria and Egypt lay. Cleopatra herself appeared in cloth of gold, wearing the double crown of Upper and Lower Egypt as she gazed across the Middle

Sea at the city of Rome, where stood a Roman soldier in a general's cloak, a wreath of laurel leaves crowning his combover. Caesar himself, lest anyone be ignorant of where the real power in the entire known world lay.

The fourth wall was the stage, fronted by slim marble columns and flanked by paraskenion made of more marble. Here the artists' hands had been restrained and the marble was allowed to gleam in its original creamy splendor, a relief to the eye and an invitation to watch what was happening on stage.

The theater was nearly full, the tiers of seats teeming with Alexandrians in all their variety of ethnicity, nationality, and dress, emitting a noise like a gigantic hive of bees. Ninos stood just inside the doors, a short, rotund fellow with thinning, flyaway hair and an air of perpetual harassment. He saw them and uttered a small shriek and scurried over to cast himself on Nebenteru's bosom, nearly sobbing. "Neb, Neb, how glad I am to see you! This is going to be a disaster, I swear, would you believe that the actor playing Myrrhine was caught by her husband in bed with the actor playing Koryphaios and now she has a black eye and he sprained his ankle jumping out the window and neither of their understudies could even find their marks in the dress rehearsal. Jumping out a window, I ask you! Actors are the least original people in the world. I should have gone with men in masks and no music and especially no Isis-damned musicians who are more trouble than all the rest of them put together, there is nothing wrong with following tradition and none of those old idiots at the Dramatists' Academy would be so up in arms if I had, there's talk of them marching in protest, with placards no less, let's hope they don't drown out the cast. You have your tickets, yes, not that it matters, you're seated directly behind the queen."

He swooped down on Tetisheri. "Tetisheri, you look stunning, no one is going to be looking at Herminia with you in the audience." He cast a furtive look over his shoulder, probably to make sure Herminia, the star of the show, wasn't within earshot. "Apollodorus, well met, Keren, I don't suppose you'd mind popping backstage to check on the sprained ankle and the black eye?"

"They're here?"

"Good lord yes, you couldn't keep either one of them off the stage at spear's point, Myrrhine with a black eye and a limping policeman, may Thespia forgive me."

"Well, at least they'll both look like they've been in the wars," Uncle Neb said.

Ninos gave a laugh that sounded more like the bray of a nervous donkey.

Keren disappeared obligingly behind the stage to inquire after her new patients. Ninos himself led the way to their seats, where it appeared he had stationed an aide to fend off any attempts to preempt them. "Thank you, Straton, very good of you, now go and see what Ezer needs because he will undoubtedly need something, he's never done asking, and when he does ask tell him no, I said no and I meant no, he absolutely may not change that business with the dildo in the fourth scene, it's the only laugh in ten lines and it won't do the rest of the cast any good to change things at the last minute anyway, and none of those awful Assyrian flutes, I don't care what Nirari says about their blasted tone!

"Here are your seats, second tier center, my goodness there are a lot of you, Phoebe! I didn't see you there, am I never to eat of your lamb dish again, the one with the plums? Never mind, we'll squeeze you all in, who, I ask you, are all these children, Tetisheri, is there something you haven't told me, there, I told you we'd manage, you all should have a cushion, I made sure the best ones were specially provided, Straton was commanded to defend them with his life, well nearly the best, the very best are reserved for herself." He gave another bray of a laugh and almost as if it were signal all heads turned up toward the main door and every single person present rose to their feet and bowed.

Except for Ninos. "She's here!" He scurried back up the aisle, there to bow so low before his sovereign his back gave out on him and he couldn't stand up again. Cleopatra, dressed simply in tunic, palla, and stola, with only a gold fillet marking the place where the royal cobra usually stared threateningly down on the masses, smiled kindly upon him and raised him upright again with her own hands. He stepped back and bowed again, although not quite so deeply this time, and made a sweeping gesture reminiscent of the great Nericius playing Dionysus in *The Bacchae*, from whom he had undoubtedly stolen it. With the greatest possible deference he escorted the queen, her maids Iras and Charmion, and Rome's legate to Alexandria and Egypt, Aurelius Cotta, down the aisle to applause and cheers and saw them safely into their seats located at exactly and precisely the center of the front row. Her personal guard remained outside, an impressive act of faith in her people's affection for her. Certainly no Ptolemy before her could have had that kind of confidence.

As Cleopatra was seated she turned her head and winked at Tetisheri. Tetisheri winked back. From the corner of her eye she saw the members of the Order of the Owl transfixed by their proximity to Cleopatra VII Philopator, queen of Alexandria and Egypt, Lady of the Two Lands, and many more titles, some of them complimentary, others definitely not. Babak was doing his best to look nonchalant, as, after all, he had been in the presence of their sovereign lady once before, just last month, in fact, and this was business as usual for him.

More seriously, Tetisheri thought it was good for them to be made aware of who it was they were really working for when they'd agreed to their employment as pages to the Eye of Isis. She felt for the pendant at her breast before she remembered that on this one public occasion she had left it at home, largely because the linen of her dress was so diaphanous that no matter how many layers thick it was her badge of office would be clearly seen through it.

A slight movement on her right made her turn her head, and she saw Apollodorus looking at the hand between her breasts. Only the expression on his face told her he was not looking at her hand.

He leaned over to whisper in her ear. "That is a very attractive ensemble you are wearing."

Her heart skipped a beat. "Thank you." Her voice sounded breathy to her own ears.

His green eyes smiled into hers. "I suppose Keren picked it out, as usual?"

Her gaze dropped to his mouth, so near her own. "She had help."

He leaned closer, albeit not kissing-close because that would have been a scandal from the Sun Gate to the Moon before the play even started and they were, after all, personal advisors to the queen, and as such, behave with decorum, at least in public. But she could feel his breath on her lips as he spoke. "You have never been to my home here in the city."

She drew in a swift breath. "I—I wasn't entirely sure you had one."

"I do. Would you like to see it?"

A totally involuntary flush began somewhere between her knees and swept up over her body in a rich, warm flood. She swallowed. "Yes."

The word was barely a whisper of sound but he heard her. "Good. After the play, then."

"Yes. After the play."

His smile was slow and satisfied. He looked like nothing so much as a lion certain of his prey, and for one panicked moment Tetisheri didn't know if she were aroused or terrified. Given the predatory look on his face, probably she should be both.

Between them his hand closed briefly over her own, and one finger tickled her palm. Her eyes flew to his but his gaze was trained on the stage and his expression so noncommittal it was almost insulting.

She straightened in her seat, trying to remediate her body's determination to fall back and let him do whatever he wanted with her then and there. She looked down, pretending to fuss with her dress, and saw that her nipples were hard enough to be seen clearly even through three layers of linen, something Apollodorus had clearly observed as well, and which had evidently told him everything he needed to know. She gave up and looked at the stage, too.

Everyone was looking at the stage, waiting, as the queen's arrival was all that was needed for the play to begin.

They were still waiting fifteen minutes later. The vendors, delighted to have more time to make sales, were doing a rousing business with their trays of drinks and snacks and amulets in the shapes of the cast of characters.

Keren leaned over and said in a low voice, "Who's that?"

Tetisheri followed the jerk of Keren's chin and saw a dark man with a severe expression sitting five rows back on the left. He was handsome, with wide, dark eyes, high, chiseled cheekbones, and a square, firm chin held very high. His hair was clubbed into a neat knot at the nape of his neck. His attire was traditional, if erring a little on the opulent side for such an occasion, especially the elaborate citrine and lapis collar that extended shoulder to shoulder and nearly to the gold cord girdling his waist. He was surrounded by a group of young men similarly but more modestly attired. To a man they wore their hair combed away from their faces and clubbed into a knot at the back in the same style as his own. It made them look oddly alike. "I don't know. I've never seen him before."

Phoebe, who spent a lot of time in the Emporeum and was therefore privy to all the choicest bits of gossip running rampant across Alexandria every day, leaned across Keren. "That's Natasen, the High Priest of Ptah."

"Of the temple of Alexandria?"

Phoebe shook her head. "Of the Great Temple of Ptah in Memphis."

"Ah." Tetisheri's glance wandered. "And who is that gentleman a few rows behind him?"

Phoebe followed Tetisheri's gaze. "You mean the man who looks as if he'd like to separate Natasen's head from the rest of him? As slowly and painfully as possible? That would be Fuscus. High Priest of the Temple of Serapis here in Alexandria."

She was whispering and Tetisheri understood why. Fuscus had been imported direct from Rome by Aurelius Cotta, the man sitting in front of them to the immediate right of the queen. The high priest had arrived on the same ship upon which Caesar had afterward departed, which argued that he had some standing. His god, Serapis, had been the deliberate construct of Ptolemy I Soter, an empyrean meld of Osiris, Hades, and Dionysus created in an effort to bring together Soter's Greek and Egyptian subjects beneath one temple roof.

A vain effort, as Egyptians had rebelled against every single Ptolemy since.

Except one.

Tetisheri looked at the back of Cleopatra's head.

So far.

"They say Natasen is bringing Ptah back into favor with the noble families from White Walls to Land of the Bow. The rumor is the nomarchs are sending their extra sons to Ptah instead of Serapis."

"Fuscus feeling the competition?"

"Evidently."

Tetisheri abandoned the back of Cleopatra's head for the High Priest of Serapis' choleric expression, before shifting back to Natasen. He, on the other hand, surveyed the increasingly restive audience with an undeniable smirk. "He looks very pleased with himself."

Phoebe snorted. "All high priests look like that."

When not enraged by a rival, Tetisheri faced forward again. Cleopatra and Aurelius Cotta were engaged in an animated chat conducted in hushed voices.

Apollodorus nudged her. "What's all that about, do you think?"

"Oh, just the personal representative of the Colossus of Rome and the Colossus' personal banker parceling out the world between them."

He nodded. "The usual, then."

Half an hour after the play was meant to have begun the vendors retreated to replenish their trays and pitchers. They had not anticipated quite such a drain on their resources this early in the afternoon. The refreshments and cheap souvenirs had kept the crowd's annoyance at bay but now with nothing to occupy them the commentary was becoming louder and vaguely threatening. But so long as the queen remained in her seat, chatting apparently amicably with Aurelius Cotta, no one left.

Ninos appeared at center stage some twenty minutes later. He looked, not to put too fine a point on it, upset. One might even go so far as to say terrified. Nevertheless, consummate showman that he was, he raised a hand that did not tremble to call for silence, and when he spoke the engineered acoustics of the Odeum made the voice he consciously deepened heard all the way to the cheap seats in the wings of the last tier. "Majesty, good citizens of Alexandria, my most profound apologies. Due to unforeseen circumstances, this evening the part of Lysistrata, meant to be performed by the glorious Herminia, will be performed instead by the illustrious Valeria, unknown, perhaps, to some of you, but—"

The cries of outrage were immediate and from every section of the theater.

"What!" "You must be joking!" "I paid to hear Herminia, not some unknown girl I've never heard of and who probably sounds like my mother's old goat anyway!" And, fatally, "I want my money back!"

Ninos faltered for a moment before coming back louder and stronger. "Now, my good ladies and gentlemen, I am certain that the fair and just spirit of the citizens of Alexandria is such that you will want to give this newcomer to our shores a chance—"

"Refund!" "I want a refund!" "Give me my money back!" "I want my money!"

Cleopatra rose to her feet, took five steps forward, placing her exactly midway between row and stage, and turned to face the audience.

The spate of complaint ceased as if someone had thrown a lever. All eyes focused on the queen.

Her words were clear and calm and the Odeum's acoustics did as well by her as they had Ninos. "Good Ninos, you rightly speak of the spirit of fair-mindedness that is the pride of the citizens of the great city of Alexandria, and of her queen." There might have been a slight emphasis placed on the final word in that sentence. "Of course we will be pleased to hear the illustrious Valeria play the part of Lysistrata, in this most original and innovative production of that storied play. Our good Ninos and his company continue to bring a fresh look to the classics of traditional theater, making them as relevant to modern audiences today as they were to audiences at their first performance. Aristophanes himself would be proud and delighted to be among us this afternoon."

Ninos bowed so low his nose touched his knees. By a miracle he regained the vertical without assistance, although Tetisheri was certain she heard his bones crack from where she sat.

"Let the play commence," the queen said, and resumed her seat.

The audience perforce subsided. Although the resentment felt by everyone present was palpable, no one was going to offend Cleopatra by leaving after she had declared such whole-hearted support of the theater, its manager, and his production.

Ninos retired backstage and after a moment Lysistrata entered, to pace up and down and give voice to her frustration at having her summons to the women of Athens ignored. If there was a low growl of displeasure from the audience she took no notice.

She was a slender girl with a good voice, but she lacked the robust figure and the mobile features that lent word and gesture the infectious bawdiness Herminia brought to every comic role. But most of the jokes landed, especially the business with the dildo, and the musical interruptions were surprisingly good, Assyrian flutes or no. The ire of the audience was at least in part soothed by the exodos.

"At least no one is calling for Ninos' head."

Apollodorus' shoulders shook.

As the last actor vanished backstage Cleopatra rose to her feet, applauding. The rest of the audience followed her and waited for the cast to reassemble on stage, beaming, to take their bow. Cleopatra waved for Ninos to come forward and congratulated him warmly, lightening his obvious misery, and turned to go.

At which she paused, and since everyone was on their feet very few saw her lean forward to speak in Tetisheri's ear, and only Tetisheri heard her words.

"Find Herminia. Report back to me only. As soon as possible, my Eye."

Tetisheri, who had bent her head to hear her, pulled back, startled, to see if Cleopatra was serious, but the queen was already departing, Cotta at her side lending his arm. In a display meant to awe and no doubt intimidate, the queen's guard, resplendent in their dress uniforms and at a quick count almost half of them Egyptian, trotted down the aisle to form an honor guard in two rows on either side of the aisle.

She nodded and smiled and greeted citizens by name, not hurrying, but progressing steadily up and out the doors.

"There are days," Keren said, "when I am very happy in our queen."

"And this would be one of those days," Nebenteru said. "Come, let us away to home, where I'm as certain as I'm standing here that Phoebe and Nebet have orchestrated a feast for us."

"Bring Ninos," Tetisheri said.

Apollodorus gave her a sharp look—he hadn't missed the royal whisper in Tetisheri's ear—but Uncle Neb said, "An excellent idea," and sent Babak backstage to find the producer.

2

Babak returned with Ninos in tow, who looked uncharacteristically quenched.

"You are exhausted, good Ninos, and no doubt hungry and thirsty, too," Uncle Neb said, and bustled them into the three cabrios. At home they found the promised feast laid out by the servants, who were all agog to hear every detail of the production. Uncle Neb had promised them tickets to the first formal performance but they were still envious of missing the human drama of The Night of the Missing Idol.

For indeed, Herminia was a living idol, from Alexandria right across the Middle Sea. The young poet Horace had praised her in hexameter after a private event in Rome, saying she "pleases from every view and in every musical note." She had returned home, trailing clouds of glory, to cement her position as Alexandria's darling with a command performance before queen and court. Her lavish beauty was held to be without equal, her voice a lyric gift from Apollo himself, her comic timing such as to make Sophocles wish he wrote comedy.

None of this explained Cleopatra's interest in her disappearance.

As the family crowded around the dining table Tetisheri slipped from the room, conscious of Apollodorus' eyes upon her. In the kitchen the Order of the Owl sat at the table with the maids, retelling the events of the afternoon with embellishments, and who could blame them? "And then the queen—the queen herself! not a foot away from us!—stood up and said with a voice like thunder that had us all shaking in our seats—"

Across the table Roshanak was making a hideous face at Babak, who was speaking. Narses, sitting next to him, looked over his shoulder and saw Tetisheri. He elbowed Babak and jerked his head in her direction. Babak turned and saw her. "But it's true, isn't it, lady? Everyone was yelling about Herminia not being there and demanding their money back and the queen herself shut them all up and the play went on and it was good anyway! Wasn't it?" He appealed to the other Owls, who nodded vigorously. The maids sighed with envy and the Owls preened.

"The performance was good," Tetisheri said diplomatically. "Babak, may I speak to you for a moment, please?"

He followed her into the hallway. He was black and slim, a Nubian whose father had been a casualty of the Alexandrian War and whose mother had died soon after. He and Nike could have been twins in both appearance and intelligence.

"As soon as you finish your supper I want you and three of the others to seek out Herminia's home."

His eyes widened. "The singer who wasn't there?"

She nodded. "When you find it, fan out around the neighborhood and find out as much about her as you can. Who were her friends? How often did they visit? Did she have any disagreements with her neighbors? Did they see her earlier today? And be discreet. I don't want this talked about."

He nodded crisply. "We'll go now, lady. It will be dark soon, with few people on the streets to ask questions of."

She smiled. "Finish your dinners first. Oh, and Babak? Not your dress tunics, but not your old clothes, either."

He grinned broadly, looking even younger than his ten years. "I get it, lady. You think she lives in an upscale neighborhood and you don't want anyone chasing off the beggar kids."

"Exactly."

"Should we go to the theater as well? It's where she works, after all. Usually."

"I will be going to the Odeum tomorrow morning to talk to the cast and crew and see if they know anything useful." As he hesitated she said, "What?"

He looked at his feet for a moment and then looked up to meet her eyes. "I saw the queen whisper to you. Is this for her? Are we working for the queen?" He looked awestruck at the prospect.

She bent a little so she could meet his eyes at his level.

"Babak, you work for the Eye of Isis, and the Eye of Isis is in service to queen. You are always working for the Lady of the Two Lands."

His grin was blinding. He threw her a salute. "Yes, lady!"

She help up an admonitory finger. "You can't say so."

"No, lady. Of course not."

"To anyone. None of you can."

She didn't threaten him but she could have and he knew it. Until a month ago the Order of the Owl had been a group of street urchins sleeping in alleys. Their luck had changed when they had helped Tetisheri escape a kidnapper and she had taken them into her service, ostensibly as pages to House Nebenteru. "No, lady," he said soberly.

"Go finish your dinner."

She slipped into the seat next to Apollodorus—which of course had been left vacant for her by her matchmaking household—and filled her bowl with savory lamb stew. Apollodorus passed her the bread and she took it with a smile of thanks. Something in her expression made his eyes narrow. He waited for the conversation around the table—a dissection of that afternoon's play, with editorial commentary and the occasional moan from Ninos, and speculation on the whereabouts of the absent actor—and leaned over to say in a low voice, "Why do I get the impression I'm going home alone tonight?"

His face was very close to hers and she wanted nothing more than to fall into those green eyes and drown her cares there. Her instincts told her that Apollodorus knew his way around a bed and that the experience would be nothing compared to what she had suffered at the hands of her husband, the late and unlamented Hunefer. Surely Herminia, an actor after all, a class known for their less than conventional behavior, could have... what? Forgotten that she was starring in an old play made entirely new as a means of showcasing her own renowned talents? Was husbanding her energy for the opening instead of wasting them on the preview?

Tetisheri thought of Myrrhine with a black eye and the limping policeman, both determined to stagger on stage in their assigned roles, and dismissed the thought. No, Herminia would not willingly miss the role of a lifetime, especially not in her own city, and especially not in front of her own queen.

Apollodorus was still staring at her. "I'm so sorry," she said, low-voiced.

"So am I," he said, equally low-voiced, "but I knew when she whispered to you that I was probably not going to get lucky tonight."

She flushed right up to the roots of her hair and he laughed, a deep, rough sound that rippled across her entire body in a warm wave of sensation.

"What's so funny?" Uncle Neb said.

Apollodorus sat back. "A private joke between the lady and myself." By his tone they knew not to pursue the topic, although every one of them was dying to.

"Too bad," Ninos said drearily. "I could use a good joke."

"Come, come," Uncle Neb said bracingly. "It was a fine performance, Ninos, if not one for the ages. Of course people were disappointed when Herminia did not appear, but there will be other performances. And did you see our queen!"

Ninos brightened a little. "Our good queen! She saved me, and the production, and the very Odeum itself!" A slight exaggeration, as the Odeum was crown property and if Cleopatra so commanded it would be full of paying customers every day of the year.

"Has anyone heard from Herminia?" Apollodorus said, and squeezed Tetisheri's hand beneath the table. "There must be some explanation for her absence."

"I sent Stratos to her home when she didn't arrive in time for costume. She wasn't there. Her friend Calliope lives across the street from her, and she said she hadn't seen her all day."

Tetisheri's ears pricked up. "Calliope? Would this be Calliope, the well-known hetaira?"

Ninos nodded. He was only playing with his food and when Phoebe scolded him for treating her justly famous lamb stew with such a lack of enthusiasm he actually pushed the bowl away from him. "I have no appetite."

Phoebe opened her mouth. Tetisheri caught her eye. The cook subsided but they were going to hear about this later. "Well," she said, "she has to be somewhere, and certainly nothing less than a life-threatening emergency would keep her from the stage."

Absolutely the wrong thing to say. Ninos paled. "Are you saying she's dead? What if she's dead, gods above and below what will I do, what will we all do, this month is sold out, most of the money is gone in wages and set design and costumes, not to mention tickets and advertising, if you saw the printer's bill for those miserable stubs, they're mad the price they're charging for papyrus, if Herminia is dead there will be no tickets sold and if no tickets are sold there will be no bills paid and if there are no bills paid there will be no Odeum, it will end with my tenure as manager—oh." Now he looked terrified. "What will the queen say, what will she do, she will blame me, I know it, oh gods, how will this end, I am disgraced, I am dead, I—"

"Now, that is quite enough," Uncle Neb said. He said it loudly, so that the words boomed off the walls of the room and very likely the walls of the dining rooms in the next two homes as well. He smote the table for emphasis, making them all jump, and bent a very stern look indeed upon his friend. "You know very well how high you stand in our lady's favor. She proved it today beyond all doubt. She doesn't and didn't expect you to keep Herminia locked in a cage until it was time for you to produce her in Act I."

Tetisheri was impressed. Sometimes she forgot just how large a man her father's brother was.

Ninos muttered something. "I beg your pardon?" Uncle Neb said.

Ninos raised his head, a little flushed, but he met his friend's eyes straight on. "I said, queens always blame someone when they're angry, and it's usually the first person they see."

There followed a moment of silence. Ninos wasn't wrong and everyone around the table knew it. When he spoke again

Uncle Neb's voice was more gentle. "Cleopatra isn't Arsinoë, Ninos, nor is she Berenice."

The citizens of Alexandria and Egypt had been conditioned to fear royal authority during Cleopatra's sisters' reigns, which had tended to be capricious and cruel. Tetisheri thought of Melitta, a previous holder of the Eye of Isis during a different reign, and of how Matan the jeweler still mourned her brutal and unnecessary death.

Ninos gave a shuddering sigh. "No," he said. "No, she isn't, and of course you're right, Neb." He attempted a smile. "No doubt Herminia will reappear tomorrow morning full of apologies and explanations and eviscerate poor Valeria for daring to step into a role that Aristophanes would have written for her had she lived then, actors, I ask you, a more flighty, intemperate, unreliable, vain, superstitious, and unreasonable race of people never lived to blight the life of a poor producer who only wants to entertain a full house for a reasonable price, not the loftiest goal I agree, we're not discovering a cure for swamp fever here, are we, but what is the harm in making a few drachmas and sending people home with smiles on their faces, and what is it with every actor who comes to work for me insisting on dolmas from Edeva's cart before every performance?"

He noticed the bowl of stew he had pushed away and pulled it back to take a second look. It appeared to pass inspection and he took a spoonful. "Mmm, so good, Phoebe, I salute you, you are an artist of the stew pot, you're always cooking with spices I can't name, so mysteriously delicious—"

Phoebe's hackles were laid before Ninos had ended his sentence and the conversation became general again.

"What's this I hear, Nebenteru, that you are building a new boat?"

This time Tetisheri squeezed Apollodorus' hand in thanks.

Neb looked as if he might burst with pride. "Not one, Apollodorus, but three!"

Which Apollodorus knew perfectly well, but put on an expression of astonished admiration anyway. "Three! Three brand new cargo ships! Nu and Poseidon, you'll have your own fleet before you're done!"

Neb beamed, the pearl at the tip of his beard trembling with the anticipation of never again having to deny a cargo or a port, of the sheer volume of shipping space afforded by multiple holds, all flying the flag of Nebenteru's Luxury Goods. Nebenteru wasn't a greedy man; what he hated was denying a friend (and all his customers were friends) a commission because he didn't have room to carry it in the hold. Thanks to Caesar's legions the Middle Sea was mostly at peace for the first time in a long time, at least for the moment. Nebenteru was determined to seize that moment, vowing to move every bag of grain, every amphora of olive oil, every block of Syene granite, every priceless artifact allegedly raised from a dead pharaoh's tomb, and every bale of papyrus as fast as it could be carried from its origin to its intended port. Tetisheri, his partner in the business, didn't disagree. She also loved him very much.

"Your average trading ship, made in the Greek fashion, is,

as you know, on average sixty long," her uncle said. "As you know, my *Hapi* is a full seventy."

Apollodorus made an encouraging noise. Satisfied, Uncle Neb carried on. Tetisheri sat back and enjoyed the show, although a part of her brain worried at the problem set before her by the queen, and why. How did Cleopatra know Herminia? The Eye of Isis was tasked to resolve threats to the realm. An errant actor did not qualify.

"But these new ships? They will all be fully seventy feet in length, with hulls deep enough to carry six hundred libra!"

"Each?"

"Each! I can have as much freight in motion at one time as I have shipped in four years altogether." His brow darkened. "Or I did when bloody Pompeii and Caesar were not chasing each other all over the Middle Sea and burning down all my best ports."

"Indeed." Apollodorus had perfected the one-word reply, just enough intelligent interest to allay any fear that he might be bored. Tetisheri wondered what he was really thinking about, and had her answer when she felt his hand on her leg. By an inordinate effort of will she didn't leap from her chair, although she nearly did when his hand slid upward. She looked at him. He grinned at her and slid his hand a little higher and squeezed before removing it. "I'm sorry, Neb, but I've got to go, I've got an early morning." He stood up and looked at Tetisheri. "See me out?"

Neb watched them leave the room with an indulgent expression.

"There is no doubt in my mind that my entire household is laying bets on the progress of our relationship," Tetisheri said, stopping before the front door.

He slid his hands around her waist and pulled her close. His interest manifested itself as a long, hard length pressed against her belly. All by themselves her knees seemed to loosen, liquefy, dissolve. "You're going to have let me do something about that, sooner or later."

"Take me home with you tonight," she said without thinking, and blushed to the roots of her hair.

He laughed, sounding a little breathless. Imagine: Apollodorus. Breathless. And she had done that. "And so I would, my lovely, but I can imagine what our queen would have to say when she heard that instead of embarking on her commission we dallied a while in bed." He smiled at her. "And I do want to dally, Tetisheri. I don't want to be rushed when you and I come together, not for the first time, or any time thereafter."

She shivered involuntarily, and his eyes darkened. "At this point we'll need to plan a journey up the Nile, far out of her royal reach, if we want any privacy." He kissed her and as always when he did so she lost the ability to remain upright on her own. But he always caught her. This time he did more, sliding his hands down over her bottom and urging her legs apart so that hot, hard ridge of flesh pressed between them.

"Oh," she said, her eyes closing, her head falling back.

"Yes, oh," he said, and kissed her again.

And then he let her go and the door was open and he was halfway through it. "A river journey. A long one."

Half a step beyond it he turned to smile at her again. "Tetisheri?"

Dazed, she looked at him, unable to speak. She wanted to run to him. She wanted to wrestle him to the ground. She wanted to follow him home then and there. "What?"

"Lock the door," he said softly, and vanished into the night.

Fumbling, she managed to get the door closed. She reached up to push the top bolt into its bracket and stooped to do the same for the bottom one. Her hands weren't entirely steady on either bolt.

When she turned, her entire family—uncle, adopted sister, cooks, pages, maids, and cabria—were standing in the hallway watching. Simultaneously, they burst into applause louder and more sustained than had been heard at the Odeum at the conclusion of that afternoon's performance.

3

Four members of the Order of the Owl gathered in Tetisheri's office the following morning, tired but alert. Alternating between bites of honeyed bread and sips of Phoebe's strong breakfast tea, they reported on their activities of the night before.

"We didn't even have to knock on any doors," Babak said. "Everyone in Alexandria knows what happened at the Odeum yesterday and it felt like half of them had gathered in the streets around her house. Many remained long after nightfall."

Bast leapt from Tetisheri's desk to his lap in a graceful feline swoop, arranged herself in a black curl on his legs, and stuck her nose under her tail. A sound like a handsaw ripping through green cedar filled the room. Babak beamed and ran a careful hand down the black cat's spine. Bast's favor was always to be appreciated, lest it be withdrawn with prejudice.

"In the Promenade," Tetisheri said. "How sits her house in relation to Calliope's house?"

"Across the street and a little south."

Tetisheri raised her eyebrows. "Herminia has a house right in the Promenade? Acting pays better than I thought."

"It's a small house but very pretty," said Roshanak, who had a weakness for beauty.

"With a very nice garden all the way around," said Bradan, who spent part of his time off the job in Phoebe's herb garden where, the cook admitted, he was more of a help than a hindrance.

"Her household is small in number, and all freedwomen," said Narses, who could always be counted on to pay strict attention to the details. "A cook, a maid, and a steward, a woman named Eua."

"Nubian?"

He looked up, surprised. "Yes, or so she appeared. How did you know?"

"It's a Nubian name. You saw her?"

"She answered the door once," Babak said, "when a group of young men trampled over the garden to look in the windows. She chased them away, and after that we didn't see her again."

"Or anyone else of that house," Roshanak said.

"Are we certain Herminia isn't at home?"

Bradan said, "I went around the side and looked in all the windows, lady. The three women of her household were the only ones present."

Tetisheri nodded. "Well done. What is said of her by her neighbors? Her friends? Her hobbies? Her habits?"

Roshanak, Bradan, and Narses looked at Babak. "She doesn't go out socially a great deal, and she never hosts parties. Now and again she attends one of Calliope's gatherings, but not by any means all of them."

"Are she and Calliope close?"

"I don't know about close, but we heard of her attending no one else's at-home events." He nodded at Bradan.

"She has a studio at the back of her house, a small room that stands alone behind the kitchen. I managed a look inside one of the windows." He shrugged. "A couch, a table, a lyre, a tambour, a flute, a set of pipes. A wax tablet on a desk with a stack of papyrus with notes. She practices there most mornings when she is in residence, and is known to."

"Which means what, exactly?"

"She can be heard by the people living on either side of her and even from the street," Babak said. "People gather there every morning in hopes they will hear her."

"How annoying for the neighbors."

Narses shrugged. "From what we could tell they seemed to enjoy it. I overheard a story on the street that some Greek with more money than sense offered to buy one of the neighbors' houses at ten times its value."

"The neighbor said no, I take it?"

He shook his head. "From what I could tell, they all enjoy living near the Voice of Alexandria."

"'The Voice of Alexandria?'"

"It's what they call her."

This was news to Tetisheri and interesting in and of itself. Quite a responsibility, inhabiting the role of the Voice of Alexandria, the largest and most sophisticated city in the world, where reposed a Library containing all human knowledge, the best schools, the greatest architects, where running water was a given before the Romans ever thought of building aqueducts. Such a role would carry with it the expectation never to put a note or a foot wrong. Exhausting. Tetisheri wondered if that might lie at the heart of Herminia's disappearance. "Who was her current lover?" The four of them exchanged glances. "What?"

Babak finished his bread and honey and washed it down with the last of his tea. He set the cup aside. "I don't think she had any."

"Lovers?" She stared at him. "But that's nonsense. There has been gossip about her and every second man in Alexandria and most of the ones who have only visited her, including—" She broke off.

They nodded in unison, very solemn. They knew who she meant. "We can't say for sure, lady," Babak said, "but we talked about it last night. Every other conversation we, ah, overheard last evening was one man or another claiming she had graced his bed. Roshanak said that if Herminia had had as many lovers as was claimed, she would never have had time to appear on stage."

"That doesn't mean she's had none."

"No. But her neighbors hold her in respect and I would

even say affection. The people on her left as you look at her house from the street, the ones who turned down the offer on their house? I listened under their window to them talking with friends who were visiting. They're worried about her almost as if she were a daughter of their house."

Roshanak, more bluntly as was her wont, said, "None of them would have spoken of her like that if she'd tossed her skirts for every man who asked. These are all respectable—" sarcastic emphasis on the word, but then Roshanak had had too much experience of respectable Alexandrians "—citizens. There was no hint of scandalous behavior by Herminia in the neighborhood."

"On the streets, among the people who don't know her, it's a different story, of course," Babak said, rolling his eyes.

"But among her neighbors," Narses said with a finality that drew the line beneath their collective opinion, "she is known to be a hard worker and a pleasant neighbor." He glanced at Babak. "They don't even seem to blame her too much for the color of her skin."

Babak grinned, taking no offense, probably because he'd heard it all too many times before. "Her talent and her popularity does seem to have turned her into a black Greek."

"Ouch," Tetisheri said mildly.

They shrugged in unison this time. "You know it's true, lady."

She did, for reasons quite outside the purpose of this discussion. "Very well. A job well done, all of you."

"We earned a lot of tips, too," Babak said. "There were

many in the crowd who needed a messenger to tell their wives they'd be late for dinner."

"Easiest drachmas I ever made," Agape said, who had remained at home and on call the evening before.

Tetisheri laughed. One of the things she liked so much about her Owls was how scrupulously they came together at the end of the day to pool their earnings and divide them equally amongst themselves, so that the one Owl remaining on duty at the house would receive their fair share. "Well done, all. Now? I want you to do it again."

"Lady?"

"You observed one set of people gathered around her home yesterday. There will be different people there today. The same clothes you wore then, although you might change them around between you. We don't want our interest in this matter talked about, so be discreet, and do your best not to be recognized if there is anyone there from last night." She hesitated. "Did anyone you saw on stage yesterday visit her within the last week?"

"Perhaps especially Valeria?" Babak said with his grin.

Tetisheri laughed again. "Off you go then, but first? One of Uncle Neb's friends brought us half a bushel of kumquats from Punt that seem to have mellowed on their journey. Nebet is guarding them jealously as she plans to make a cake the likes of which, she says, none of us have ever tasted. Tell her I said you can have the leftovers to speed you on your way."

As cynical as a life on the streets had made them they were

still children and all children thought with their bellies. They stampeded for the kitchen.

She collected her stola, retrieved the Eye of Isis from its hidden compartment, and went to tell Uncle Neb she was going out.

"Hah," he said, looking up from his messy desk. "This business of Herminia, I take it? The queen asks?"

She threw up her hands. "There are no secrets in this house." His pearl trembled as he laughed. She kissed his cheek and departed.

The Odeum looked deserted, even forlorn. The angled rays of the morning sun drenched the street and the building with pale golden light that somehow seemed to leech the painted and inlaid columns of their color, flattening their illustrations and rendering them lifeless.

Rhode spoke Tetisheri's thoughts. "It looks like a ghost of itself in this light."

"It does at that," Tetisheri said, making sure the Eye was hidden beneath her tunic before descending to the street.

"How long will you be?"

"An hour, perhaps. Does anyone else need you this morning?"

"Nebenteru is visiting Demetrius' shipyard."

"What morning isn't he?" Tetisheri waved off Rhode's answer. "He'll probably be there for hours."

Rhode nodded. "He usually is."

"After you drop him there return here, please. I'll want to go on to the Promenade."

Rhode clicked her tongue at Astarte, who thought about it long enough to make sure everyone watching knew that moving forward was her own idea. The stocky little dun was fully alive to their change in circumstances, Tetisheri noticed. She held her head higher, she leaned more firmly into her harness, she moved more fluidly between the traces, her starts and stops were almost unnoticeable. No more living hand to mouth, day to day, never knowing if they would earn enough for Rhode to afford more than hay for her supper. No more nights spent stabled in old Panek's filthy tool shed. Rhode had always kept Astarte's coat brushed and her hooves shined but now they positively glowed with life and health.

Tetisheri watched as Astarte and the cabrio executed a neat three-point turn, Rhode standing tall and holding the reins at exactly the correct angle, looking every bit as proud as Astarte. It was good to see.

The main doors of the theater were barred but she had expected that and so passed around to the side, where a smaller door was unlocked. She entered the narrow but cavernous space that occupied the back of the proscenium to find assembled there the entire cast and what appeared to be most of the crew of yesterday's production of *Lysistrata*. There was barely room to walk between the stacks of wood-framed papyrus screens painted with scenes, shelves full of props, and racks of costumes from past productions. A space had been cleared in the middle of the room, around which the cast and crew had draped themselves over various bundles and bags and boxes. Myrrhine of the black eye was present, as was Koryphaios the limping policeman, and the illustrious Valeria, Herminia's understudy. By now "Illustrious Valeria" might well be her official title. It wasn't as prestigious as "the Voice of Alexandria" but it would do for a start. And of course Tetisheri had to wonder if that might be what lay behind Herminia's disappearance. It wasn't a terrible motive.

A man stood in the center of the circle, a sheaf of papyrus over his arm, that hand holding an ink pot. He had a stylus stuck behind both ears and was gesturing grandly with his free hand. All people associated with the stage talked with their hands; it was as much as your life was worth to stand too near any of them when they were trying to make a point. Tetisheri stopped short of the circle while remaining within earshot, and stood quietly, listening.

"Has anyone seen her or heard from her?"

A collective shaking of heads.

"Did she say anything to any of you about being unhappy with this production?"

No.

"Did she appear to be ill, or hurt the last time you saw her?"

No.

He sighed and scrubbed his ink-stained hand through an untidy mop of hair, dislodging both styli. He was tall and slender and long-fingered, with plain features of which the most prominent was a large, firm chin that demanded respect. "If Herminia remains among the missing, Valeria, you must prepare to go on again tonight."

The illustrious Valeria did her best not to look ecstatic at the thought but she wasn't that good an actor.

"Dula, you'll take over Valeria's role."

"What about Dula's role in the chorus?"

"We'll look for someone but for the next few nights we'll be one voice short." The stage manager—for this was who he must be—sighed. "I don't know how tonight's audience will react when we tell them the news. We won't have the queen present at every performance, ready to quell any incipient riots." He sighed again. "Very well. Let's get on with it." He consulted the sheaf of papyrus, the pages of which were covered with scribbles in black ink and festooned with smears rendering most of them illegible. "I took a few notes during the performance last night and—"

There was a chorus of boos and jeers.

His smile was a surprise, lighting his eyes with a charm not previously in evidence. "All right, all right, let's get to work. Claudia, you stepped in front of Doris when you entered last night. Now, I'm sure you didn't mean to—"

"Not much she didn't," someone said, probably Doris.

"—and I know we rehearsed that bit until we were all sick of it, but I'd like to run through it one more time—"

A chorus of oaths and groans ensued, but the company got to its feet and everyone trooped out through the columns and onto the stage proper. Tetisheri went down the right-side paraskenion and took a seat in the center of the front row. The same seat, she realized after she sat down, that Cleopatra had occupied the day before.

The cast broke down the scene line by line and repeated each one over and over again: where they stood, in which direction they faced, how loudly they spoke. From time to time Basil—the stage manager—sent a minion up the aisle to the farthest row and had the actor repeat his or her line to ensure that it could be heard in the cheap seats. The interior space had been so well designed that they always could be. Auletes had been a fool about many things but he knew how to build something that would ensure a performance of any kind be heard in the farthest corners of the theater.

After an hour of this they took a break. Tetisheri rose to her feet and approached Basil. "Excuse me."

He looked around. "Oh. I didn't see you there, forgive me. I'm sorry, the theater is closed for rehearsal."

"And I'm sorry for interrupting you, but I wondered if I might ask you a few questions."

"About what?" His expression hardened. "If you're looking for gossip about Herminia—"

"It is about Herminia I have come," she said, raising a hand, palm out, and was secretly surprised when he closed his mouth in reaction to the authority inherent in that simple gesture. In a lower voice she said, "I am tasked with finding Herminia and returning her safely to your stage." She gestured. It was catching.

He looked skeptical. "Tasked by whom?"

"There is no higher authority." Before he could inquire further she said, "You are the stage manager here, I believe?"

Her phrase "no higher authority" had worked its magic and he answered readily. "Of this production, yes. I split my time between here and the Pan Amphitheater."

"Has Ninos come in yet this morning?"

"He doesn't, generally, after we're in production. This time, though…" He brooded.

"You have no idea where Herminia is, or why she missed yesterday's performance?"

"I wish I did, lady…"

"Tetisheri, of House Nebenteru."

He looked confused for a moment and then his face smoothed out into a bland mask, although his bright eyes were curious. "Of course. No, lady, as I said, I don't know where she is. I would have gone to my grave swearing that she could have broken both legs getting here and still have hit all her marks. She's not unambitious, Herminia, and she is a professional. This is the first performance I have known her to miss, and I've worked with her off and on for—" he thought "—at least six years now."

"Were you with her in Rome?"

He shook his head. "Those were a series of private performances. She had no need of a stage manager."

"I didn't realize."

He made a face. "I wish she had needed me. She made a packet of money out of them."

"Did she." Tetisheri reflected for a moment. "Does she have any family?"

"Not to my knowledge. We meet chiefly at the theater, though. I've never been to her home. She's a very private person, Herminia." He saw her look. "I don't mean she's rude to her fans, not in the least, but she keeps her private life separate from work. Or she does as much as anyone of her status can. Sometimes it's impossible. People behave in such extraordinary ways."

"Oh?"

He grimaced. "There was an incident, just before she left for Rome. A man showed up at every single one of her performances."

"That can't be that unusual."

"No, but he would also appear at the stage door before a performance to hail her arrival and wait for her afterward to compliment her and fawn over her." He frowned.

"What?"

"I was leaving at the same time she was one evening. After one of our *Medea*s, I think. He stepped up out of the gloom like the ghost of Euripides and frightened her. For that matter he startled me, too. I thought—for just a moment, I thought she knew him."

"What made you think so?"

He hesitated. "The way she addressed him."

"Did she call him by name?"

"No, but she was angry and she showed it."

"She could have been angry with anyone in like circumstances."

"Yes, but she raised her voice. She is always excruciatingly polite to everyone. We all are, especially to repeat customers. I never saw her lose her composure that way before. She almost shouted at him. It felt almost… familiar."

"Has he been back since Herminia returned from Rome?"

His brow creased. "I think—a few times? But not as regularly, and never again at the stage door."

"Can you describe him?"

"Egyptian. Near her age, dark hair and eyes, medium height, medium build. Richly dressed in the latest fashion in the rarest fabrics, with enough gold neck chains and gold bracelets and gold and gemstone rings to sink a small ship to the bottom of the Middle Sea." His mouth twisted up on one side. "I may exaggerate."

She smiled. "Only for effect, Basil."

His smile was wry. "The theater is my life, after all. I thought at the time he would have made a good Paris." He saw her expression. "As in Paris in our production of *The Fall of Troy*. Herminia played Helen. Of course."

"Of course. He wasn't an actor himself, I don't suppose?"

"Oh gods no. Nowhere near it. No presence to speak of. One can always tell."

"Did anything else about his behavior give you cause for concern?"

He shook his head. "There have been others better born who were far worse behaved."

She said curiously, "Is this kind of thing common?"

"Lately, yes. I think at least some of this reaction comes from the fact that Ninos has been experimenting. Performances without masks. Women taking female roles. Musical numbers made from what once were orated soliloquies. It shocks some people, offends others, and…"

"Yes?"

He met her eyes. "That proximity, that revealing of the human face behind the mask." He shook his head. "It changes the relationship between the actor and the audience."

"How so?"

"It makes that relationship more immediate, more… more intimate, even if that intimacy is only imagined from the seats in the nosebleed section. That intimacy—it unleashes something in people. We've hired a guard to stand outside the stage door before, during, and after performances now, and I heard Ninos not long ago tell Herminia that she should consider hiring a personal guard."

"Did she?"

His expression was bleak. "If only she had."

She looked at him for a long moment. "You believe she was kidnapped."

"Short of death itself," he said soberly, "I cannot think of anything else that would have kept Herminia from this stage."

4

Tetisheri had Rhode drop her at the corner of Lochias so she could approach the neighborhood of the Promenade on foot. She'd been there the month before to interview a witness, but today she looked at the street with new eyes. The homes there tended to be of a similar size, well kept, each with a narrow strip of garden facing the street. The Promenade was a lovely park planted with flowering shrubs and shade trees, crisscrossed with footpaths flagged with polished granite. At every turn there was a marble bench and a small fountain made in the shape of a dryad holding a dish on her shoulder, from which trickled water into a pool at her delicate feet. Sometimes it was Artemis with her bow or Pan playing his pipes.

The park was open to all of Alexandria but the homes clustered so thickly around its edges that it was difficult for any but the owners to access. A result that was almost certainly by design.

It was easy to identify Herminia's house, as it was the

one with the crowd still gathered in front of it. She spotted Roshanak, who had acquired a wooden tray full of cups of lemonade and was selling them for an obol each; she caught sight of Tetisheri on the fringe of the crowd and made so bold as to give her a broad wink. Farther on she saw Babak hustle up to a portly Roman in tunic and toga. To this gentleman he reverently proffered a papyrus note rolled and tied with a red ribbon, accompanied by his very best bow. The citizen unrolled it, read it, and was evidently so pleased with its message that he tipped Babak a whole drachma before strutting off with the air of a man looking forward to arriving at his destination. Bradan had attached himself to a group of children playing dice across the street, which produced shouts of victory and groans of defeat from time to time. Agape was nearly an invisible presence tucked into the shadow of a pillar, hearing everything, saying nothing.

Tetisheri met Babak's eyes and gave her head a tiny jerk. A few minutes later he met her around the corner, out of sight. "I want to get into Herminia's house, and I don't want the crowd to see me doing so."

"Follow me, lady." He set out down the street at a brisk pace. Almost but not quite where Lochias intersected with the Canopic Way, he cut down a small, overgrown path between two houses where brambles scraped at her hair and clothing. He turned left on a path perpendicular to the first, leading back in the direction of Herminia's house. This path ran through the backyards of the houses on the west side of Lochias, often through everyone's kitchens, open-air affairs beneath a roof on four posts. There were no fences, and only a few low stucco walls easily traversed. Babak appeared to be on a first-name basis with everyone he saw, exchanging greetings and once fielding a fresh-baked caraway seed roll, fresh out of the oven, which he had to juggle as it cooled before he could eat it. He saw Tetisheri's expression and grinned at her. She grinned back. She couldn't help herself.

They came to Herminia's house, which Tetisheri recognized from the dainty pink wash of the exterior paint and from Narses' description of the small studio standing alone at the back of the yard, against another stuccoed wall with a wooden door that led into the park. The kitchen was unattended. Babak knocked at the door at the back of the house. There was no answer. He knocked again, more firmly this time.

It was yanked open and a woman with a fierce expression stood glaring, first down at Babak and then over his head at Tetisheri. "Will you people never cease from disturbing our lady's peace? How dare you come skulking around the back door in this fashion? Have you no shame? Be off with you!"

"Hold," Tetisheri said in a voice that had the woman halting involuntarily in her tracks.

Since there was obviously nothing else for it she reached for the chain that disappeared beneath her tunic and produced the Eye.

Even in her peripheral vision the Eye of Isis was an impressive sight, no less so at the moment because it was in the full light of day. Layers of nacre, turquoise, and lapis were worked together to form the badge of office of the queen of Egypt and Alexandria's private representative, one trusted with the power of the eye, the ear, and the hand of Isis Herself. It was seldom seen but invariably recognized, and universally among the subjects of Egypt and Alexandria was known to command instant obedience.

The woman's face went white and for a moment Tetisheri thought she might fall to her knees, but she stiffened her spine and rallied. "And a good thing, too, that the Lady of the Two Lands finally takes an interest in this matter!"

But the sting had gone from her tongue and she stood back to admit them into the house.

It was a compact space, elegantly but not particularly richly furnished. Tetisheri glimpsed a large bedroom, a spacious and well-appointed bath, and a cluster of smaller rooms comprising the servants' quarters, before they emerged into a sitting room which took up the entirety of the front of the house. The couches and chairs were comfortable rather than fashionable and the colors throughout were soothingly muted.

"Please." The servant indicated the seating. "Make yourself comfortable, lady."

"Thank you." Tetisheri chose a straight-backed wooden chair upholstered in zebra skin. She sat, spine straight, folded her hands, and bent a stern look upon the woman. "Your name is Eua, I believe."

"Why—why yes, lady, although I don't know how you know that." She sounded almost accusatory.

"It is my job to know these things that I may better serve our queen."

Babak goggled. He had never heard that tone from Tetisheri before. Eua flushed, probably more at the cold reproof in Tetisheri's voice than at her actual words. "Of course, lady." She became aware that she was wringing her hands and let them fall to her sides, although they knotted themselves in her tunic almost immediately.

Tetisheri allowed an austere smile to cross her face, albeit briefly. "Come, my good Eua, you have nothing to fear from me or our queen, so long as you tell me the truth." She caught the servant's eyes and held them. "All of the truth."

Tetisheri let the silence between them draw out until Eua dropped her eyes and began to fidget again. She leaned forward and said gently, "Where is your mistress, Eua?"

Eua plumped down onto a convenient stool and burst into tears.

That was all it took for the maidservant and the cook to rush to the defense of their fellow servitor, upbraiding Babak and Tetisheri for upsetting their dear Eua, who was a good and faithful servant to her mistress, as were they all, and the two of them defied anyone to say otherwise, and if anyone did they demanded that ingrate be dragged before them immediately. This went on for too long for Babak who said in an impressively loud voice, "That is enough! Cease this caterwauling immediately, you silly women!"

The three of them were startled out of their collective snivel and Babak used the momentary peace to take cook and maid by the elbow and escort them inexorably from the room. He nodded at Tetisheri over his shoulder, which she understood to mean—correctly, as it turned out—that he would interview them separately and report back to her. Quick-witted servants were the greatest gifts the gods could bestow, and Tetisheri made a mental note to make a special offering in gratitude to Bast at her earliest opportunity.

In the present, she used the scarf Eua wore around her head to mop up the woman's tears. Eua sniffled and gulped and stared at Tetisheri out of red, swollen eyes. Her grief and fear appeared genuine, so Tetisheri gentled her voice. "Where is your mistress, Eua?"

Tears threatened again but this time Eua managed to control herself. "Lady, I don't know, truly I don't. I only wish I did."

"When was the last time you saw her?"

"Yesterday morning."

"At what hour?"

"At Fourth Hour, or no, I'm sorry, at Ninth Hour as this dratted new calendar would have it."

"Where was she going?"

"To her stylist."

"Her what?"

"Her stylist. The artist who styles my lady's stage makeup. She—the stylist, has a shop in the Emporeum, on the west side, near the canal."

Tetisheri cocked her head. "Herminia did her own shopping?"

"In the case of the stylist for her stage makeup, she would allow no one else to do so." From Tetisheri's expression, Eua saw that more explanation was required. "Stage makeup is different from the ordinary paints and creams used by ladies of fashion. It is applied so that the artist's features can be clearly seen from the last row in the house. The eyes are lined and shadowed, the cheeks and lips brightly tinted. And it must remain in place for the duration of the play, resistant to perspiration and smearing. Because it is applied so thickly, and is made from so many different separate ingredients and tinctures, it can be injurious to the skin if improperly prepared. It can even be poisonous. If one wishes one's skin to survive the continued application of paints performance after performance, one purchases those of only the best quality. My lady Herminia insisted on personally selecting only the finest products, those created and mixed by an expert hand. There are many actors who have not taken such care, and when the masks came off it was the end of their careers."

"I see." The unexpected perils of the thespian profession. "And the name of this stylist?"

"Karis. Her shop is small but very fine, and her stock is only of the very best. And Set only knows her prices show it."

"Expensive?"

Eua shuddered. "Not that my lady Herminia can't afford it." Her face began to crumple again. "Where is she, lady? What has happened to her?" She began to cry again.

Tetisheri handed Eua her scarf for something to sob into. She let her gaze roam around the room, struck again by its emphasis on comfort. Herminia had achieved the pinnacle of her craft and adoration of the masses. With them must also have come fortune. This house, if one ignored its location in one of the pricier neighborhoods in Alexandria, looked as if it belonged to the wife of a shopkeeper who had done well by himself and his family but had hardly achieved the heights of, say, House Nebenteru. She smothered a grin, and then paused, her gaze arrested.

The usual altar of household gods was tucked into an alcove next to the door. Two gods, she saw. They were small figures and she got up to take a closer look. After a moment's study she recognized the god on the left, or rather goddess—a woman's figure draped in a peplos belted over a chiton, holding the mask of comedy in one hand and the mask of tragedy in the other. Her gown was painted in vibrant shades of orange and pink, with three thin bands of blue just above the hem. The goddess Thespia, the patron of Greek theater.

The figure on the right was instantly recognizable as that particular god had had a great deal to do with Tetisheri's last investigation. It was also the figure of a woman, but this one was Egyptian, not Greek. Seshat's dress was painted to resemble a leopard skin. She held a stylus in one hand and a palm leaf rib in the other, for the tallying of figures and the writing of letters, both of which looked to be made of gold. The green ribbon that bound her hair was some green gemstone Tetisheri didn't recognize and the spots on her leopard skin were inlaid with opals. Seshat, the goddess of scribes, and, possibly in some sect of which Tetisheri was unaware, a patron of the written arts, which could be supposed to include playwrights and could thereby at least indirectly be revered as the Egyptian goddess of the theater. She was exquisitely crafted, and in some indefinable way felt much older than the statue of Thespia. Tetisheri wondered what her friend Matan would make of it. No doubt he would say the hacks of Alexandria's arts and crafts industry were turning them out by the dozens, all the better to tempt credulous Roman tourists into quick sales.

To round out her lares and penates Herminia really ought to include a Roman god as well, just to cover all the realities of this modern day. Dionysus, perhaps. Although who would want that drunken sot around even in the form of an image was beyond Tetisheri's understanding. Roman gods had very little sense of dignity.

"Eua, does Herminia have any family?"

Eua shook her head, Tetisheri thought a little too quickly. "No, lady. It is why she is so ambitious. She knows she has only herself to make her way in the world."

"No family at all? No brothers, no sisters, no mother, no father?"

Eua folded her lips and shook her head again, looking down at her hands which were folded together very tightly in her lap.

Tetisheri let it go for the moment. "Lovers?"

Eua shifted uneasily. "Surely, that—"

"Eua," Tetisheri said, and the extreme patience in her voice was enough to stop Eua with the rest of her words unsaid. "You are a good servant to your mistress to respect her privacy so fiercely, and I know she will appreciate it when she returns. But to make that happen, I must know everything you know. It wouldn't be the first time a jealous lover was betrayed by his feelings into extreme behavior." She laughed suddenly. "The plays Herminia has appeared in during her career are almost all of them cases in point."

A faint smile crossed Eua's face. "That they are, lady." She took a deep breath and let it out slowly. "She has only one male friend, lady, that I have ever met, and that only once."

"When?"

"A month ago." Eua sighed. "I suppose you will speak with him?"

"I must."

Eua bowed her head. "His name is Heron. He is a younger son of the Nomarch of the White Walls, in Memphis."

"Is he a member of either of the royal courts?"

She shook her head. "He is a natural philosopher, a Fellow of the Great Library, and a teacher at the Mouseion, lady."

"And her friends?"

"Not many of those, lady."

"Even among the theater folk?"

Eua's brow creased. "There are too many rivalries and jealousies there to make any true friends, she says. She says also that she will have time to make friends when she retires."

"No friends at all?"

"Well." Eua hesitated. "I suppose one could call the lady Calliope a friend."

"Calliope the hetaira?"

"Yes. She lives nearby. She hosts many small gatherings in her home. My lady receives invitations to them all. Sometimes she attends, especially if there is to be a musical performance or a dramatic reading." She gave a faint sigh. "My lady was always on the watch for new material that could be adapted onto the stage."

"With her in the lead?"

Eua looked surprised at the question. "But how else, lady? She has to make a living."

And pay my wages, she could have added.

"Does she follow any particular god?"

"She wears an amulet of Seshat, and in the past she has sent sizable contributions to the Great Temple of Seshat in Memphis. But I don't know that she is regular in devotion to the Temple of Seshat here in Alexandria." She thought, and added reluctantly, "Or at all."

Tetisheri cast an involuntary look at the altar next to the door. "Is there anything else you can tell me about her, Eua? Have there been any arguments with cast or crew of past productions, or this production of *Lysistrata*? Any quarrels with her neighbors? Any family, no matter how long ago, reappearing and demanding a share of your mistress' fortune as blood guilt?"

Again something shifted behind Eua's eyes, but she shook

her head. "Nothing like that, lady. When she isn't on stage she lives a quiet, modest life."

And that well might be true, Tetisheri thought, getting up to leave.

But then where was Herminia?

5

They departed the way they had come, back through the kitchen and by the path that led between the Promenade itself and the row of homes along the street. This trip, Tetisheri had the leisure to take in the invogue aspirations of Herminia's neighbors, who had spared no expense in a competition to host the most vivid friezes in the most garish colors. One more sextaurius of carmine on any surface would have pushed the street into looking like the section of Hermes between the Heptastadion and Poseidon's Head. It was nicknamed Aphrodite's Walk for a reason. One hoped that in the interests of a good night's sleep the exterior adornments did not repeat themselves on the interiors. And there again, even in home decorating, Herminia remained an outlier. The more she learned of the woman, the more mysterious Herminia became.

Regaining Lochias, they paused some distance from the crowd still gathered outside Herminia's house. "What did you learn?"

Babak pulled a face. "I wager not much more than you did, lady. Both maid and cook swear Herminia lives a quiet, retired life. She has very few visitors, she doesn't host dinners or receptions. The cook seemed a little disappointed at this, as she would like more scope to show off her skills. Other than work, the lady only goes out occasionally to shop for those necessities she prefers to choose with her own eyes."

"Cosmetics."

"Yes."

"And the boyfriend?"

He raised an eyebrow. "According to Myrto, the maid, who had the privilege once of admitting him to the house, he is young and virile and oh so handsome." He clasped his hands next to his cheek and gave a soulful sigh. "'I wouldn't mind him kicking any of my lovers out of my bed, didn't I tell you so, Chloe?'" His imitation of a breathy adolescent female was so on the nose that Tetisheri laughed outright, and he grinned at her. "Chloe being the cook."

"So I gathered. Nothing else?" He shook his head. "Very well." She set off down the street, Babak tagging along at her side.

"Have you further instructions for us, lady?"

"Other than continuing your surveillance, no."

"This evening again?"

"Yes, but only two of you, and only until Herminia returns or is found. Take it in turns and, again, change your appearance if you feel yourselves coming under scrutiny from the people here."

"Where are you going?"

"To visit her neighbor, Calliope. From all I can tell she may be the only friend, if you can call it that, that Herminia had."

Babak brightened. "Calliope the hetaira?"

"Yes. She lives almost across the street from Herminia. According to Eua, Herminia has a standing invitation to Calliope's parties. As I'm sure you know, Calliope hosts a great many, and Herminia has actually been known to grace a few with her presence."

"Really." From the corner of her eye she could see Babak straighten up to his full height. "Lady, it is my duty to accompany you to this interview. There may be servants to speak to and you can't be in two places at once. Further, it is my understanding that the hetaira entertains many guests. You don't know who you will find behind her door. You should have someone with you for safety's sake. I'm sure Apollodorus would agree."

She gave him a sharp look. He returned one of such unassailable innocence that she was hard pressed not to laugh again. "I think I'm fairly safe before noon, Babak, even in Calliope's house, but certainly you may accompany me. Just watch your step with Cerberus."

His step faltered. "Cerberus?"

They crossed the street and proceeded down the other side until they reached a house twice as large as Herminia's. Even from the outside one had the feeling that considerable funds had been expended to ensure that it led the architectural and design fields in fashion, not just in this neighborhood but in the city itself. Having met the lady, Tetisheri was certain that none of said funds had been Calliope's own.

She knocked at the door and waited. When the door opened Babak nearly fell off the doorstep. Tetisheri caught the neck of his tunic and set him back on his feet. "The lady Tetisheri of House Nebenteru to see the lady Calliope."

The woman who answered the door, grim and grizzled and who bore an uncanny resemblance to the wolf god Wepwawet at his most unsociable, looked down upon the both of them with disfavor. "I will inquire if my mistress is at home."

The door closed again with a firmness that was not quite a slam. Babak looked up at Tetisheri with big eyes. "Who was that?"

"That was Phryne, the lady Calliope's housekeeper. And possibly her personal assassin. Scary, isn't she?"

"I'll say." Babak straightened his tunic, annoyed that he had been betrayed into showing fear in front of two women.

Phryne kept them waiting as long as she could without incurring reproof from her employer or insult to a guest, but only just. They entered the luxuriously appointed house and followed Phryne to the parlor that still looked like an overlarge display case for only the rarest and most beautiful—and most expensive—of items. The weight of wealth and history that crowded every corner of the room was almost stifling.

Tetisheri smiled sweetly at Phryne. "Perhaps you could find some tea in the kitchen for my page."

Phryne looked as if her head might explode instead and Tetisheri waited hopefully, but from behind her Calliope said, "Phryne, if you would, please? And refreshments for us here as well." She stepped around her servant.

Phryne marched off, grumbling, toward the back of the house, Babak trailing a safe distance behind.

The two women had met for the first time only a month before, in the course of Tetisheri's last investigation in her office as the Eye. Tetisheri was fairly well known by name in Alexandria but Calliope was notorious by name and by profession. The most infamous hetaira on two coasts, she had been tried before the Senate of Rome for impiety. Her patron, Cilnius Maecenas, a dear friend of Gaius Octavius, nephew to Julius Caesar himself, had, so the story went, put on a unique defense which rested on stripping Calliope of her clothing before the entire body of the Senate and defying them to condemn to death a female young enough to be their granddaughter, who, lacking the benefit of fortune or family, was only making her way in the world as best she could. An eyewitness told Nebenteru that the single tear tracing down Calliope's cheek at Maecenas' closing words had melted the hearts of the last of the holdouts. No one had been surprised when she was unanimously acquitted on the spot.

Tetisheri was conversant enough with the fussy conservatism of some of the Senate's older and more easily shocked members to believe that Calliope had been, if not blameless, certainly guilty only of selling her companionship for cash. The deities may have been called upon during these transactions but Tetisheri doubted with any religious fervor for or against.

Slim-hipped and slight-breasted, Calliope was no taller than Tetisheri herself, who had been expecting something more Junoesque at their first meeting. Her creamy skin and her large, thickly lashed hazel eyes were her best features, along with her hair, an indeterminate brown but thick and shiny, bound into a braid that reached her waist. Today she was dressed much as Tetisheri had found her on her last visit, in a simple chiton belted with a thin strip of knotted leather and plain sandals. She wore no jewelry. She gave a slight bow. "The lady Tetisheri come again to visit my house. I am honored."

Her voice was unexpectedly full and rich from so slight a vessel, no doubt an asset in seduction. Tetisheri wondered how Apollodorus heard her own voice when she spoke, and pulled herself together enough to return the bow. "The lady Calliope again welcomes me, displaying no hint of the disruption I must be causing her day. I am grateful."

The hetaira indicated a chair carved in the shape of a lion, its head rising up over the back of the chair, mouth open in a snarl. "Please, be at your ease, lady."

"A new acquisition?" She sat down, taking care to avoid the lion's fangs, and trying not to feel as if she had entered the belly of the beast.

Calliope subsided much more gracefully on a simple stool opposite. "A gift from a friend."

"How kind."

"I have many such friends."

"I am aware." Tetisheri's voice was dry as the sands of the Red Land, and Calliope unexpectedly grinned, showing off a dimple in her right cheek that her patrons must have found enchanting.

Phryne came in with a tray and set it on the table between them. "Will there be anything else, lady?"

"Nothing, thank you, Phryne."

Phryne whisked herself off. Calliope busied herself with pouring the tea. "It is still cool enough for tea, is it not?"

Tetisheri accepted the cup and drank with pleasure. It was a deep, rich blend that tasted of the lands far to the east. One could always be assured of only the best food and drink from Calliope's kitchen.

"A savory cake? They are one of my cook's specialties."

Sharp cheese and herbs, it melted in Tetisheri's mouth. "Delicious."

"Aren't they? Korinna's pride and joy." She drained her cup and set it down. "How may I help you this day, lady?"

Tetisheri sat back. "You will have heard of the disappearance of the lady Herminia."

"It is all anyone in Alexandria can talk about." She looked toward the street. "Especially in this neighborhood."

"As I saw. I am informed that you are a friend of the lady."

Calliope hesitated in a manner that reminded Tetisheri of Eua's similar response to that question. People wanted neither to name nor to claim friendship with Herminia. The actor inspired a protective instinct in all who knew her. "May I ask what your interest is in this matter, lady? Herminia is jealous of her privacy. I would not like to betray her trust in someone's pursuit of vulgar curiosity."

Tetisheri took no offense. "Such care does you credit. This should not go any farther, you understand?"

"Of course not."

Tetisheri looked toward the door and lowered her voice. "Our queen has requested that I look into the matter, and if I can to discover what happened to Herminia."

Calliope's eyes widened. "I see." She mulled this news over in silence for a moment. Few knew that Tetisheri was the new Eye of Isis but everyone was aware of the friendship between her and Cleopatra. House Nebenteru stood high in favor at Cleopatra's court, and had done so in Auletes' court as well. "Yes," she said slowly. "I suppose you could call us friends."

"How did you meet?"

"We both returned home from one of her performances at the same time. I introduced myself and complimented the production. It grew from there."

"Into what?"

A graceful shrug. "I included her on the guest list for my events, especially those that included a musician. And we met occasionally for tea."

"At her house or yours?"

The hetaira's brow creased, and Tetisheri wanted to say something about such expressions encouraging wrinkles, a liability to a woman of Calliope's profession, but restrained herself. "Always mine," Calliope said.

"Do you know her other friends?"

"I'm not sure she has any."

"Gentlemen friends?"

Calliope's eyes narrowed. "Why do you ask?"

"I have learned she had one particular male friend, a scholar at the Mouseion."

"Ah." The hetaira was silent for a moment. "She never introduced us, but she did speak recently of a friend in a manner that led me to believe that he was more than a friend." She sighed. "And if you know this much I will say that I saw a man going in her front door as I returned home one evening."

"Do you remember when that was, exactly?"

Calliope gave a faint smile. "It was as I was returning from Otho's reception last month. One could not mistake that day."

Tetisheri smiled as faintly. "One could not indeed. Would you know him if you saw him again?"

Calliope showed her empty palms. "It was dark." She frowned.

"What?"

"He was carrying something under his arm, something wrapped and tied. No idea what it was."

"Did she call him by name?"

"No. Or if she did I didn't hear her. And it was the only time I saw him. Or any man come to her home."

"He went inside with her?"

"He did, but I don't know how long he stayed."

"Did she mention him to you? Had they quarreled?"

She shook her head. "Herminia is a very private person, lady. She keeps her personal life completely separate from her public life." She looked again toward the street. "Until last night I would have said that few people in Alexandria had any idea where she lived."

"Any arguments with her neighbors?"

Calliope's smile was wry. "Isis above and below, no. There is much reflected glory in living so near to her. Not to mention the free concerts whenever she practices in her studio. No one would jeopardize that. And she herself never gave anyone offense that I heard of."

"Did she ever mention family, or where they lived?"

Calliope shrugged. "I did ask, once. She changed the subject."

Tetisheri frowned and allowed herself to speak the thought in her head. "If she wanted to make it difficult for someone to find her when she went missing, she has done a wonderful job of it. Can you think of anything else that might aid my search?"

"I wish I could, lady."

Tetisheri believed the hetaira to be sincere. She rose to her feet and shook out the skirt of her tunic. "Strictly to satisfy my own curiosity."

Calliope looked wary. "Of course."

"Is there no feeling of competition between the two of you?"

"I have no competition," said the most sought-after hetaira of her age.

Their eyes met. Simultaneously they burst out laughing.

Recovering first, Tetisheri said, "If you think of anything, lady, anything at all, any detail no matter how small, or learn anything new that might aid in my search, please send a message to my attention at House Nebenteru."

"Of course."

Tetisheri nodded at the wall. "You have a new bookshelf, I see."

Calliope stood up as well and they gazed at the wooden bookshelf together. "And some new books as well."

"Indeed."

Their eyes met in perfect understanding, Calliope's a little mocking. Tetisheri called for Babak and took her leave.

Outside she said, "Did you learn anything useful from the lady's servants?"

He looked disgusted. "Hardly. Cerberus was there every minute, and they're all terrified of her."

"Understandably."

He snorted. He was very brave out of her presence.

"Very well." Tetisheri fixed an absent gaze at the crowd in front of Herminia's house. It was thinning. "New orders. Keep your people on site until after dinner. Leave one on watch overnight. But I think we have learned all we can here."

"Which isn't much."

"Which is almost nothing." She contemplated her sandals, lost in thought. It was difficult not to compare the two women, both young, both professionals, both unmarried, both successful and well-to-do by any standard on any shore of the Middle Sea. *I have no competition.* Tetisheri did not doubt it. Neither did Herminia have any competition. Probably the only way the two women could be friends was that they had chosen entirely different paths to success. They put that success on display in different ways, too. Calliope filled her home with valuable items of rare beauty, validating her wealth and influence in culture and the arts and patrons wealthy enough to afford a presence in both. Herminia filled the Odeum and the Amphitheater with crowds. Whatever wealth she had accumulated was...

Her head came up and she looked across the street at Herminia's house.

"Lady?"

"I must return to Herminia's house."

They followed the same path in back of the residences and Eua answered the door at the first knock. This time her manner was much more resigned. "Yes, lady."

"Stand aside, please," Tetisheri said, and walked down the hallway to the front room and straight to the altar of the lares and penates of the household. She stood staring at the two statues.

It was as she remembered. The statue of Thespia with her two masks had been cast from some durable ceramic and was a businesslike example of the craft, an unmistakable but uninspired representation. The goddess looked like every other traditional statue of a Greek god large or small Tetisheri had ever seen, square of jaw, breasts an afterthought affixed to a male torso, muscular arms and legs. The only truly feminine characteristic was the wealth of finicky curls restrained by a fillet painted silver.

The statue of Seshat, on the other hand, was unmistakably female in curve of breast, waist and hip, and hands and arms looked amazingly proportionate to the head, torso, and legs. Tetisheri felt if she watched closely enough, she might be able to see the stylus moving on the palm leaf rib, tallying up the years.

"May I help you, lady?" There was a note of determined patience in Eua's voice, with perhaps an undercurrent of unease.

Tetisheri turned to survey the room, confirming her first impression. The other furnishings were sturdy, comfortable, and of good quality but they had been purchased to be used, not displayed. There was a tapestry covering most of one wall, a fine, colorful weave hung mostly to give the room a feeling of warmth and life, but it was a little faded. If it had been hanging in Calliope's parlor it would have had a price tag on it long before there was any danger of it aging in place.

She turned back to the alcove. No, in this room, the figure of Seshat was the one thing that stood out, the one thing that was like nothing else. "This figure of Seshat," she said. "How did your mistress come by it?"

"I—I don't know, lady."

Tetisheri turned to give the servant a stern look. "Come, Eua. This is an item you notice when it appears. How long has she had it?"

"I—I—a month, perhaps?"

"Was it a gift? Or did she purchase it herself?"

Eua's head came up and she said more firmly, "My lady is not in the habit of spending her hard-earned money on something so easily broken or stolen."

"So a gift, then." Tetisheri made up her mind. "Eua, I'm going to take this item into custody. I want to show it to someone who has extensive knowledge of such things. It may help me in my search for your lady. I will give you a proper receipt if you will bring me stylus, ink, and paper."

If anything Eua looked relieved. "In truth, lady, I will be glad to have it out of the house. It is the most valuable item in my lady's possession. I worry about it every time I go out the door."

Pen and paper appeared and the receipt was duly written and locked in a sandalwood box with the rest of the household's important papers. A length of sacking was brought and the Seshat figure carefully wrapped and tied and consigned to the care of Babak, who held it as if it were a live cobra.

Tetisheri paused in the doorway leading toward the kitchen, and looked at Eua. "If your mistress doesn't spend her money on expensive curiosities, it must be collecting somewhere. I pray not in this house?"

Eua was shocked and showed it. "All the gods forbid, no!

Ezra the Jew of House Sakal looks after her investments. Her plan is to one day buy a small farm in the country and live quietly."

"Ah. Where in the country?"

Eua replied readily. Either this information was not as closely held as everything else about the lady Herminia or Tetisheri had worn down her resistance. "Memphis, lady. As close to the river as possible, she always says."

Memphis again. Barely a day's journey from Alexandria by the Nile Canal.

And the home of the Temple and Sanctuary of Seshat.

6

"Where to now?" Rhode said.

Tetisheri thought about it as she and Babak climbed into the carriage. Clearly it was necessary to speak to this Karis person as soon as possible. The stylist might have been the last to have seen Herminia before her disappearance, and therefore might have some idea as to where she was now.

But the Emporeum was nearly all the way to the Gate of the Moon, whereas they were now much nearer the Gate of the Sun and the eastern edge of the city. She looked down at the bundle cradled in Babak's terrified arms. It would save travel time if she spoke with Matan first. "To the Jewish Quarter, if you please, Rhode."

Matan the jeweler's home was a square block of a building the size of a small warehouse, appropriate since most of its interior space was dedicated to his workshop. Located near the Canopic Way, it was not generally speaking open to visits from the public, but Tetisheri was a privileged person, and not just because she held the title of Eye of Isis. Although, by his expression, Nephilim could wish it were otherwise. Tetisheri knew enough not to take it personally. "Well met, Nephilim," she said cheerfully. "Is your master at home?"

Nephilim, roughly the size of one of the blocks used to face the Great Pyramids, glowered first at her and then at Babak. Babak had had enough of being intimidated by house guards this morning and glowered back. Nephilim snorted and without a word closed the door in their faces.

"Lady?"

"Don't worry, Babak, he'll be back shortly."

"He certainly is big."

"Just wait. He looks even bigger inside."

Babak did not look reassured.

The door opened again. "The master says you are welcome." He stepped back, holding the door open. They managed to squeeze through between him and the wall. He pointed at an open door. "Master, the lady Tetisheri and slave."

"I'm not a slave!"

"Whatever." Nephilim returned to his post, there to resume his accustomed facade of imminent threat. She wondered if Apollodorus could take him, and then returned her mind sternly to business.

"My dear Tetisheri!" The short, stocky man with the bright eyes and the cap of curls going gray was dressed in a canvas apron burned and stained to a point where its original color was indiscernible. His arms were roped with muscle and his hands were scarred and callused. He bustled around the overflowing tables crowding the room and caught her in a hug. "How wonderful to see you!" He let her go as she tried to catch her breath and looked down at Babak. "And who is this, hey?"

"This is Babak, my new page. One of five."

Matan's eyebrows went up. "Five?"

"They were a package deal."

Babak bowed as well as he was able, still cradling the precious bundle in his arms. "Master Matan." He looked around the room, at the many tables piled high with gemstones of every shape and size and at the walls festooned with strings of many more. "What do you do, sir?"

"What don't I do?" Matan replied with a sweep of his arm. "I manufacture dreams, young Babak, waking dreams for the connoisseurs of the world to wear on their persons and display in their homes and present as gifts to their loved ones and offer as bribes to their lords and masters."

Babak's brow puckered. "You make jewelry?"

Matan laughed. "Well, if you want to strip it of all its grace and poetry, yes, young Babak, that is what I do."

"Show him something you're working on, Matan."

Matan was delighted to do so, and led them on a tortuous route between the crowded worktables to where a gold bracelet was held in a vise between wadded cloths. "So as not to scratch the metal," Matan explained, "although I'll have to give it a final polish just to be sure before I send a message to the man who commissioned it that the final payment is due." He winked at them.

It was a slim round of gold that widened to a flat space at the top, which was in the process of being inlaid with a complicated pattern of tiny pieces of coral, turquoise, lapis, malachite, and some yellow stone Tetisheri didn't recognize. "Jasper," Matan said when she asked. "Your uncle found it somewhere on his travels and it's such a rare color in nature that I bought the lot."

The gold shone in the reflected light of the sun through the skylights in the roof above, and the gemstones glittered almost with a life of their own. "It's beautiful, Matan."

"It is, isn't it?" Matan regarded the bracelet with pride. "Although I doubt very much that I made it for the gentleman's wife, whatever he may have told me." He waggled his eyebrows at them and they laughed. "Now, Tetisheri, what is it I can do for you today?"

"I brought something for you to look at, Matan. I'd like you to tell me everything you can about it, what you know as well as what you think you know."

He looked at her, his brows coming together. "Well, this is all very cryptic. You have certainly piqued my curiosity." He motioned. "Produce this marvel."

Tetisheri looked around for a clear space. There wasn't one. Matan, seeing the difficulty, led them to a table with thin slabs of polished stones laid in a graduated row of the colors of the rainbow. He set these aside with due care—"A commission for a set of plates for one of the Nomarchs with more money than is good for him"—and stood back for Babak to lay his burden down in the middle of the cleared space.

Whereupon Babak did so, heaving an enormous sigh of relief and backing as far away as he could in that cramped space.

Matan's eyebrow went up. "Like that, is it, young Babak? Well, let us see what we have here." He undid the knots and unfolded the swaddling cloth with care. When the Seshat was at last revealed, Matan's eyes widened and he gave forth with a long, low, reverent whistle. "Tetisheri, Tetisheri, what have you brought me this day?" He set the statue upright with reverent hands and stood staring at it for a long moment, after which he took a step back, bumping into Babak before dropping down into a low bow. "My lady Seshat, goddess of scribes and stars," he said, and it was almost a chant, "keeper of years and numbers, patron of architects and builders and scribes, recorder of history so that the people of Egypt and Alexandria do not forget. Be you welcome to my house."

Tetisheri looked at her friend in surprise. She had never known him to be religious, and if he were he was Jewish, which, while that faith gathered prophets from many other faiths, was not so far as she knew inclusive of Egyptian gods. "Matan?"

He turned to her, his face full of awe. "Where did you get this work of art? My poor shop is honored by its very presence."

A chill coursed down her spine. "Is it so very valuable, Matan?"

"Valuable? Valuable!" He snorted. "As if one could put a price on such a work."

"Everything has a price, Matan."

He shook his head. "That is the trader in you speaking, Tetisheri. I tell you there is no pile of coin high enough that could match this artifact's worth."

"What precious material is it made of, then?"

He put on his patient face. "It isn't what it's made of that makes it so... so... all right, valuable, for lack of a better word. It is the art of its creator. The proportions are such that one expects to hear her draw breath. Look at the upraised arm holding the stylus, the delicate definition of the musculature. The tiny knuckles of the hand holding the palm rib, the individual fingernails. You can even see the nipples of her breasts through her dress, which, I point out in case you unobservant louts missed it, even though it is carved of alabaster, which is itself already a translucent stone, looks transparent and as real as the finest weave of the thinnest of linens. You could almost comb her hair." He stepped to one side and then the other. "Her eyes are inlaid with onyx and nacre. They are so well crafted they seem to follow one as one moves in her sight."

He stepped back again and looked at the statue for a long moment. "Where did this come from, Tetisheri?"

He made it sound like an accusation. She cleared her throat and tried not to sound as guilty as she suddenly felt. "It was on the altar of the lares and penates of the lady Herminia." When he looked blank she said, "The actor? She was to sing the part of Lysistrata at the Odeum yesterday afternoon?"

"Actor?"

She sighed. "You don't really live in this world, do you, Matan? Herminia is an actor and a singer. She was to sing Lysistrata in the new production at the Odeum, beginning yesterday. She never came to the theater, and no one has seen her since yesterday morning when she left her house in the Promenade." She gestured at the Seshat. "This was one of the statues on the altar next to her door."

"A lar? This work of art was relegated to a lar?" His voice was scaling up to a level to rival Herminia's and she tried not to cringe. "It should be in the Great Library, or in the Mouseion, teaching those who labor in the art the error of their ways! A lar! Isis and Horus, forgive these cretinous idiots who know not what they do."

Tetisheri tried to look appropriately apologetic for her lack of taste. "Matan, I must know as much as I can about it. It is the one thing in the lady's possession of this quality and rarity. It might be a clue as to her whereabouts." In a lower voice she said, "I am tasked by the queen herself to find the lady Herminia and return her to her life."

"The queen! Hah! I might have known. Has she seen this?" Tetisheri shook her head. "Good! Do not show it to her unless you wish its owner never to see it again. All art, no matter how old or great, is only money in the treasury for our good queen."

Babak's jaw dropped at this disrespectful diatribe, and he looked involuntarily over his shoulder, probably in search of the shurta who were surely coming to arrest them all for sedition. Tetisheri gave his shoulder a reassuring squeeze.

"Matan." His eyes returned to her. She smiled. "Please help me. I can see that this is a beautiful thing, but I have no idea where it came from, or who made it. Do you have the name of an artist, or artists, who do this kind of work?"

He closed his eyes briefly. "My very dear Tetisheri," he said with infinite patience. "There is no sculptor or jeweler or lapidary or goldsmith or silversmith living who even aspires to this level of our art. No, my dear, not even me." He sighed. "I'm very much afraid that the artist who made this is long lost to us."

Tetisheri caught her breath. "You mean—"

He met her eyes and said firmly, "I couldn't guess its age but from the style of the carving and the detail of the embellishment and the quality of the paint I would guess before Alexander ever stepped ashore and cast the grain that became the walls of this city."

"This came from a tomb, you mean." She hadn't meant to put it so bluntly.

There was silence in the workshop for a long moment.

"A discovery of this quality…"

Matan nodded. "Yes. It would definitely be news."

"And the fact that we haven't heard anything…"

"Means some unlucky idiots will be headless as soon as the queen gets her hands on them. And she will. She always does." He scowled at Seshat. "I did hear something…"

"What?"

He gave his head an irritated shake. "It is nothing more than a rumor, you understand. I first heard of it two or possibly three years ago, I can't remember exactly. A great and ancient find, in its entirety. Various dealers in antiquities were said to be moving pieces of great value, but only one at a time and only one dealer at a time. And then the rumor died away, and nothing more was heard until another rumor surfaced of another piece even more rare and valuable than the last one."

"They are supposed to report such discoveries."

Matan snorted. "So the queen can take her half with no effort on her part?"

Tetisheri kept her tone conciliatory. "Well, she is the queen, Matan." Matan had his own reasons for despising the Ptolemies, no matter how marginally enlightened the current one might be.

He sniffed. "As I said. It is only a rumor."

Tomb robbing was an ancient and ignoble profession in Egypt. The tombs of the ancient pharaohs, along with their nobles and priests and officers and administrators and leading craftsmen, had been subject to plundering at least since the door of Tuthmosis I's tomb had been barred behind its builders. It was a cottage industry handed down from generation to generation. Some of the most notorious families of tomb robbers shared house names with the likes of the Nomarch of the White Walls and the Nomarch of the Southern Shield, in whose demesnes were found respectively the Great Pyramids and the Valley of the Kings. These noble families of course publicly ignored the existence of their disreputable relatives but it was a matter of open speculation from Alexandria to Syene how they managed to maintain such a lush standard of living in comparison to the rest of their fellow nomarchs.

Roman legions marched on Egyptian grain, true enough, but the nomes were fairly similar in size and the incomes derived therefrom equally so. The farther up the Nile one traveled, the closer mineral-bearing outcroppings appeared, which added to those nomes' incomes, but only insofar as each nome had the population to work the mines. The nomarchs of Upper and Lower Nubia, which was roughly all of them south of Thebes, were constantly crying out for labor, and guilty of armed incursions into their neighbors' lands to take by force what had not occurred by nature. Settling such conflicts was a continual headache for the crown.

Such conflicts were non-existent in White Walls and Southern Shield. They had all the labor they needed and each year, come flood or drought, enough income to sustain their dependents.

It was impossible for this fact to have escaped Cleopatra's attention. Tetisheri looked at the statue of Seshat again and saw nothing but trouble coming. "Would you be willing to take custody of this goddess, Matan? I'm not particularly comfortable carrying it off again."

"I'm astonished you managed to carry it all the way to my house without being murdered for it out of hand," Matan said tartly, and then relented. "Of course I will, Tetisheri. If nothing else, it will give me an opportunity to study it, and perhaps discover some of its maker's secrets." His smile was more natural this time. "And Nephilim is an entire army in and of himself. You need have no fear of not finding it here upon your return."

Back in the cabrio again. "Where to now, lady?"

"To the Mouseion," Tetisheri said. It was on the way to the Emporeum.

Babak's stomach gave a protesting growl.

"But stop at the first decent food cart you see, Rhode."

"I should think so."

There was an endless row of food sellers in front of the stadium, where Tetisheri bought lamb kebabs and cups of fruit juice.

"And now so to the Mouseion, Rhode."

"To the temple of the overeducated and the chronically out of temper, lady, at once."

The Mouseion was the teaching arm of the Great Library, a comparatively nondescript building whose plain stucco cladding demonstrated its priorities: specifically, on embellishing the inside of the head as opposed to the outside of the building. As a child Tetisheri had studied here along with Cleopatra, Arsinoë, Theo, Philo, and Aristander. The building was filled with classrooms and workrooms and offices where scholars thought and taught and wrote and experimented. And argued, loudly, and sometimes violently, although Cleopatra Philopator had made it known that she preferred disagreements among the literati of Alexandria to be confined to the kind of civil disagreement that facilitated education, not evisceration. Fat lot of good that did. Scholars, as evidenced by Rhode's cheerful commentary, were an infamously choleric bunch.

Tetisheri motioned for Babak to join her. Rhode held up her hand. "I know, I know, find a place to park."

"We shouldn't be too long," Tetisheri said.

Rhode rolled her eyes and clucked to Astarte, whose snort sounded exactly like her driver's. They moved off and Tetisheri and Babak climbed to the doors at the top of the stairs.

There they were met by an attendant, a fussy man in his forties who had used his tunic as a penwiper once too often. "Heron, Heron," he said, fluttering through a list. "Ah yes. A guest lecturer in natural philosophy and engineering." He snorted. "One of our more notorious tinkerers. Await him here in this parlor, if you please." He showed them into a cramped room and bustled off.

No one offered them refreshment, but then Tetisheri hadn't expected any. Librarians always fed you. Teachers never did.

He returned in good time, Heron the scholar in tow, and left them with the merest bow, off to his far more busy and important life.

"Lady?" the scholar said. "I don't believe we have met."

"We haven't," Tetisheri said. "I am Tetisheri of House Nebenteru, merchant trader. You are Heron, son of the

Nomarch of the White Walls, and lecturer here at the Mouseion."

His brow creased but he sketched a bow. "It is pleased I am to meet you, lady. How may I help you?"

"My lord." He merited the honorific by his birth, and politeness was almost never wasted. However, Tetisheri had found that scholars existed more in their discipline than in the real world. Getting and keeping their attention was always a challenge, and blunt force the most effective means. "You are an intimate friend of the lady Herminia."

The moment of silence that followed hummed between them like the bass string of a lute. Tetisheri took the momentary silence to give him a critical survey, which she made no attempt to hide.

Heron, son of the Nomarch of the White Walls, lecturer at the Mouseion, fellow of the Great Library, stood a little over average height and moved with the controlled, graceful assurance of a client in good standing at the Five Soldiers. Odd, for a scholar, who as a group held physical fitness in far less esteem than they did the ability to hold one's own in a Socratic back-and-forth on Stoicism versus Epicureanism. His tunic was plain but made of a finely woven linen. His hair was dark brown, thick, and shiny, and gathered into a club at his nape. His eye were the same color, large, thickly lashed, his nose and chin strong, and his clear skin and white teeth showed the lifelong effect of a good diet. He was the obvious product of a privileged childhood, never having gone hungry or scrambled for the rent money a day in his life. The one jarring note was his hands, which were large-knuckled, callused, and scarred. The scars continued up his arms to his elbows. If one looked only at them he could have been an apprentice of Matan's.

He also looked oddly familiar, but she couldn't remember where or when they had met.

"I am," he said in answer to her question, surprising her. She had expected more attitude.

"You are aware she is missing."

"I am," he said again.

"When was the last time you saw her?"

He hesitated. "Sunday last."

"Eight days ago."

"Yes."

"And you haven't seen her since?"

"No." He sat down suddenly, leaning his elbows on his knees and clasping his hands, it seemed, so he could stare at them instead of looking at her.

On a sudden intuition she said, "Did you quarrel?"

He drew in a deep breath and expelled it on an explosive sigh. "Yes."

"What about?"

He raised his head, his mouth a hard line. "Pardon me, lady, but I fail to see how that is any of your concern."

Ah, there it was, the arrogance of the aristocrat on full display, a peacock spreading its tail like a shield between their elite world and everyone else. "I'm sorry," she said, "did

I not say? I have been tasked by the queen to find the lady Herminia and restore her to her legions of adoring fans, of which the queen herself is first and foremost."

Something clicked behind his eyes. "Oh. Ah. I see. You are that Tetisheri."

Tetisheri returned his stare without expression and waited. Outside the door footsteps approached and receded, and in the distance could be heard a dim version of the hum of activity rising up from the Canopic Way.

His hands loosened and he sat back. He looked into the distance at something she could not see. "Yes, we quarreled."

"What about?"

He hesitated, looking away from her. "I asked her to marry me."

"My congratulations."

"She turned me down."

Tetisheri worked to keep her face bland. "Why?"

"Why did I ask or why did she say no?" His smile was slight and entirely lacking in humor. "I asked for the usual reasons a man asks a woman to be his partner in life. She said no because, she said, she is at the peak of her career and a husband and children would be too distracting."

"So you parted?"

"Yes. She made that very clear."

"Were you angry?"

He leaned his head back and rubbed his eyes with the heels of his hands. "I was—disappointed."

Tetisheri thought it an odd word for him to choose, and he seemed to realize it at the same time she did. "And hurt. And yes, angry. We haven't spoken since."

"And you haven't seen her?"

He shook his head. "I was at the Odeum yesterday."

She looked again at the club of hair at the back of his neck and remembered where she had seen him before. In the priest Natasen's train, one of the young men seated in his company. To a man they had worn their hair in that same fashion. "I would have thought seeing her again so soon would only bring you pain."

He glanced at her and away again, but she caught the wariness in his eyes. "I'd heard her rehearse the part so many times, of course. I wanted to hear her sing it in performance. And then..."

Tetisheri thought of the studio in back of Herminia's house. There wouldn't have been enough room left over for Bast the cat, let alone a second person, while Herminia was rehearsing. "And then she didn't appear."

"No."

"Where do you live, my lord?"

"I have an apartment in my father's town house in the Royal Quarter."

"Is he currently in residence?'

He shook his head. "My father is always at home the first month of Peret, seeing to the planting."

"Was he aware of your wish to marry the lady Herminia?"

He gave a short laugh. "Oh yes, he was aware."

"Do I take it he was not in favor of it?"

He made a face, for the first time looking his age, which Tetisheri estimated at his early twenties. "He holds all the old conservative values very dear. He disapproves of women on the stage, and has a very low opinion of people in the theater as a whole." He stared again at that invisible place and a very faint smile crossed his face. "Vain, conceited, irresponsible, inconstant, immoral, careless with money, most of them mongrels of no family, with no useful connections, and incapable of walking past a mirror."

He sounded as if he was quoting, and he reminded Tetisheri of Ninos' several diatribes of the previous day. "That sounds oddly personal. Had he met the lady?"

"No." He stared at her. "I had never thought of it that way before. It is a fairly specific condemnation, isn't it?"

"So far as I can tell Herminia has no family and few friends. How did you meet?"

"At one of Calliope's receptions."

"When?"

"It was the one Caesar attended. It was quite the crush. I escaped into the Promenade, and found Herminia there before me."

"Are you familiar with the figure of Seshat that occupies the altar next to Herminia's front door?"

He stared at her. "I am."

"Do you know where Herminia came by it?"

He thought seriously about his answer before speaking. "I gave it to her."

"Where did you get it?"

A shadow crossed his face and when it had passed his features had done that thing that only aristocrats seemed able to manage. The scholar and the lover had disappeared and only the son of the Nomarch of the White Walls remained in the room. His eyebrows rose ever so slightly, his nose seemed to have lengthened, and his voice had cooled to a degree more appropriate to the highest elevations of Abyssinia. "What does this have to do with her disappearance, lady? I would think other avenues of inquiry could be pursued to better effect."

"It is the most valuable item she owns. It does rather stand out among her other possessions."

"I think she would say that her most valuable possession is her voice, lady."

"What do you think happened to her, my lord Heron?"

The rejected lover warred with the haughty aristocrat. "She would never have missed that performance willingly, lady, as no one knows better than I." Something in his demeanor gave her to understand that Herminia's rejection had wounded Heron's heart less than his pride. "After all, she had just refused marriage in favor of the stage."

There was a knock at the door, which opened without invitation, and Vitruvius stuck his head in. "Heron, how much longer are you going to be? The students are getting restless. And we don't have enough stylus or ink or paper for their notes. Oh, lady Tetisheri, I didn't know you were here. I beg your pardon." He saw Babak and smiled. "And Babak, too."

Babak achieved a creditable bow, very much on his official dignity. "Sir."

Vitruvius raised an eyebrow. "If I'm interrupting something official, I'll take myself off at once."

"Stay, Vitruvius." Tetisheri rose to her feet. "I'm done here. For the moment." She looked at Heron and back at Vitruvius. "Are the two of you working together?"

"Yes. We're inventing an aeolipile." Heron took his leave with a curt bow and walked into the hallway as Vitruvius stepped back out of his way.

Both eyebrows went up this time as Vitruvius looked from Tetisheri to Heron, who waited for his colleague with an expression of long-suffering patience that to Tetisheri looked less than genuine.

"Really," she said dryly. "How fascinating."

Vitruvius laughed. A Roman architect and engineer, he had come to Alexandria in Caesar's legions. After the war, he had stayed on to study at the Great Library and, evidently, work at the Mouseion. He had been yet another witness in her previous investigation. "Yes, yes, I remember, you're a self-professed mechanical illiterate. It's a machine to make power using steam."

"Make power to do what?"

"Anything and everything. Operate a saw for use in building, or a drill in the mines, or a mill in a place where there is no running water. Any tool that can be adapted to work without a human on the other end."

"It sounds a very useful sort of invention. I encourage you to get right to work on it."

"It's not all we do, of course," Vitruvius said. "Heron is a gifted surveyor, and is making great strides in discovering past works of Egyptian engineers long buried in the sands of the Red Land." He gave an emphatic nod. "We have much to learn from them."

Heron looked less than pleased at this compliment to his craft, and Tetisheri wondered why. Vitruvius smiled a farewell and joined his fellow scholar to hustle back to their classroom. As they turned the corner she heard Heron say, "And how do you know the lady Tetisheri, Vitruvius?"

"Oh, we met at a party once."

"Do you believe him?" Babak said as they descended the stairs.

"Heron? What do you think?" Tetisheri said, waving at Rhode, waiting just up the street.

"He didn't seem all that upset about Herminia's disappearance. Or her turning him down."

"No, he didn't, did he," Tetisheri said, pleased with his perspicacity. "His story will need to be verified in every particular, as much as we are able. As soon as you pull the

Owls off of Herminia's house, set them on his to gather as much information as they can."

"Yes, lady. You don't think he kidnapped her, do you? And him a lord and all?"

"Lords as a class suffer from a lifetime of getting anything they want whenever they want it. She refused him. Whether she broke his heart or not, there are few among the nobility who would take that kind of rejection without some kind of retaliation."

Rhode pulled up in front of them and Tetisheri climbed in. Babak scrambled up behind her. "He doesn't seem the type."

"No, he doesn't, but when dealing with the nobility remember always two things: that they are accustomed to having everything their own way, and that they will do almost anything to avoid the ridicule of their peers."

"They had been very careful, though, to keep their relationship quiet."

"They had, hadn't they? I wonder which of them wanted that more."

"Where to next, lady?" Rhode said.

"The Emporeum."

7

The Emporeum was a collection of hundreds of shops, stalls, carts, and markets gathered together beneath an enormous tiled roof built on plain stone columns. It filled in almost the entirety of the space between Hermes Street and the Canopic Way and the Heptastadion and the Nile Canal. Beneath its roof everything was for sale, from food to clothing to household goods to livestock to building supplies, although those last were found in larger quantities and varieties across the Canopic Way in Rhakotis, where most contractors and craftsmen lived and worked.

Here were bolts of silk from Sinae in every color and pattern imaginable, always with a tailor ready to cut and assemble the garment of your choice from the material purchased. Racks displayed ready-made chitons, pallas, stolas, tunics, togas, and cloaks in wool from Gaul and cotton from Nubia. Small booths enclosed by curtains hid the fitting of more intimate garments. Three generations of men sat in a semicircle of stools, making and repairing sandals and boots, across from a small shop on whose highly finished shelves were arranged rings and bracelets and necklaces and collars, every item lovingly made so as to enhance the charms of its wearer. Or so the seller would earnestly have you believe.

There was an antique dealer displaying everything from rusty gladii dating back to the Punic Wars, to ushabti, the little wooden servants made by the hundreds and placed in burial tombs to wait on their masters in the afterlife. Sellers swore every single one of the ushabti came direct into their hands from the tomb of Rameses II, which if true meant that Rameses II's tomb was the size of all three Great Pyramids combined.

There was a cart laden with pots and pans and cauldrons and kettles from Khorasan, made of the finest copper by the finest coppersmiths in the world. Next to it an immense wooden table was heaped with piles of spices, ground and whole, from salt and pepper to the more rare cinnamon and cloves. The exotic mixture of aromas rising up from that table was intoxicating. Next to the spice table was a craftswoman who specialized in spice containers, shakers, grinders, mortars, mixers, and elaborately decorated boxes made from various kinds of woods, all beautifully finished, all promising to enhance the value of what was contained within.

It was a feast for the senses, dazzling the eyes, delighting the nose, bewildering to the ear when one tried to disentangle the shouts of the vendors, all trying to attract the attention of shoppers to their wares, to their prices, and all trimming their dialects to be understood by the approaching customer be they Greek, Egyptian, Roman, Parthian, Judaean, Hispanian, Gallian, Alemanni, Rate, citizens of any one of a hundred other realms from as far away as Punt and beyond. Whoever they were, wherever they came from, they all came to Alexandria to look and marvel and buy what could not be found anywhere else along the shores of the Middle Sea.

And that was just the section of the Emporeum that faced the Way. Tetisheri was more familiar with the denizens of those shops facing Hermes Street but she was still well known enough here to respond with a wave and a smile to those who shouted out her name. The traffic was understandably dense, with many vehicles stopping to let down their occupants and much in the way of foot traffic. Rhode threaded a slow, careful path through the many hazards, pulling up just before the canal with a distinct air of triumph, as well she might have. "Find somewhere to wait where you can be seen from this corner," Tetisheri said.

Rhode nodded, and Tetisheri led Babak down the sidewalk separating the western end of the Emporeum from the Nile Canal. The canal side contained a broad verge of green grass and flowering plants and plane trees with benches at inviting intervals. On the right was a strip of food vendors with long queues obstructing progress. The first three people they asked had never heard of Karis or her shop. The fourth misdirected them to an apothecary specializing in love potions, who was keen to sell Tetisheri a tiny bottle of liquid he swore would vastly enhance her charms in her lover's eyes.

"She doesn't need any help," Babak said, and snickered when Tetisheri smacked his head.

They consulted a fifth person, a middle-aged woman, Persian by dress, selling an excellent small beer by the cup. They refreshed themselves and followed her directions unerringly into a narrow space between a pile of snowy-white sheepskins and an ironmonger's shop. This debouched into a narrow alley that ran behind the businesses facing the canal. It was, for the moment, deserted.

"Four doors down, she said, lady," Babak said, leading the way. He counted and paused in front of a small door and knocked. There was no answer. He looked at Tetisheri.

"Knock again."

Again, there was no response. Tetisheri stepped forward and tried the latch.

The door swung inward soundlessly. The smell would have overwhelmed even the table of spices they had passed earlier. Tetisheri put out a hand and pulled Babak behind her. "Wait here."

"Lady, what—"

"Wait here, Babak." She pulled her palla up over her nose and stepped inside.

It was a small, square space with shelves on every wall from floor to ceiling and a square counter in the center made of more shelves. The shelving interrupted itself only on the wall facing the Nile with a long, narrow, high window. There was at least one hand mirror on every shelf, where there was room. Boxes and jars and phials and brushes and pots and flasks crowded every horizontal space in tandem with small thin palettes of black stone carved into the shapes of fish and birds, used for grinding the galena from Syene into the black liner used to elongate the eyes of men and women both, of every level of society.

Everything was wrapped and tied in bright colors and labeled with strips of papyrus. Light streamed in through the window and it would have been a cheerful, welcoming space had it not been for the smashed glass and various powders and paints scattered across the floor.

And the body sprawled beneath the central counter.

Tetisheri stepped outside again, pulling the door closed behind her. Babak peered up at her. "Lady? Are you all right?"

She took a deep breath and let it out slowly. The awful nausea that had threatened receded. Enough, anyway, for her to speak. "Find Rhode. Have her take you to the Shurta with all possible speed. Ask for Aristander. Tell him there has been murder done in the Emporeum, and that his presence is required on the scene immediately."

He gaped at her, his small face white in the dimness of the alley.

"Babak," she said. "Do you understand your instructions?"

He pulled himself together. "To the Shurta. Tell Aristander there has been murder done. Bring him here."

She made herself smile at him, although she feared it was more of a grimace. "Good. Go. Now."

He took off at a run.

Less than half an hour passed before she heard the tramp of booted feet approaching. She had been sitting on a stool borrowed from the sheepskin vendor, with her back to the door of Karis' shop. She rose to her feet as Aristander and Dejen, led by Babak, rounded the corner into the dim little alley.

"Tetisheri," Aristander said. "I wish I could say well met."

"I wish you could, too." She smiled at Babak. "Well done. Go and wait with Rhode."

"But, lady—"

"Go and wait with Rhode, Babak."

His face fell. "Very well, lady."

She waited until he was around the corner before putting her hand on the latch. "You should put something over your nose. There is an open window but it's a small shop and the air is very close inside."

He grabbed the corner of his headdress and pulled it over his nose. She pushed the door open and stepped to one side as he entered, following him in.

He stood silently for a long moment. "She's been here a while."

"Since yesterday morning, I think."

"That would seem about right. Do you know who she is?"

"While I waited for you to arrive, I knocked on a few doors and asked who their neighbor was. Karis, they said. I asked them to describe her, and they did. It's Karis."

"You didn't bring anyone in here to look at her?"

"No."

He seemed to relax. "A break-in, do you think?"

Tetisheri breathed shallowly through her mouth. "Could we step out into the alley?"

"Of course." They left the shop, closing the door behind them. "How was it you came to find this body, Tetisheri?"

She leaned her head back against the wall and closed her eyes briefly. When she opened them again he was still standing there, waiting, the steady, expressionless gaze of the practicing police officer trained on her face. "You'll have heard of the disappearance of Herminia, the actor?"

"It's the only story being told in Alexandria at the moment."

"Our queen tasked me with finding her. Karis may have been the last person in the city to see her." Tetisheri recounted Herminia's morning's activities as described by her steward.

Aristander, a trim man in the neat kilt and headdress of the chief of the Shurta, listened without interruption. At the end he said, "And have you examined the scene?"

"I have."

"And you found?"

She sighed. "It looks as if her death might have been the result of a struggle."

"With whom?"

"I can think of two possibilities. One, someone tried to rob the store. But I know you saw her cash box on the shelf. I opened it. There is a significant amount of coin inside. Which leads me to my second possibility, that Herminia was here, was the target of a kidnapping attempt, and that Karis was injured either trying to fight them off or..." She shook her head. "It is possible she just got in the way."

"Hmm." Aristander looked at her. "The fault is not yours, Tetisheri. She was dead long before you began looking for Herminia."

"The queen asked me to begin my search yesterday afternoon."

"Karis was dead before yesterday afternoon." He folded his arms and frowned at his sandals. "The Emporeum does not, as a rule, suffer from break-ins or robberies."

"No." Her voice trembled a little and she took a moment to steady it before continuing. "Many of the merchants have pooled together to pay for their own guards."

"I see none here, however."

"No, but I have difficulty seeing a store that specializes in high-end cosmetics as a target worthy of the risk." She smiled faintly. "The Shurta under its current head being notably successful in the pursuit, apprehension, prosecution, and sentencing of evil-doers to the fullest extent of the law."

His smile was broader. "It's what she pays me for."

"True." They stood in silence for a moment, listening to the low-voiced conversation coming from his men, still gathered at the corner of the alley and the narrow walk to the street. Beyond them was heard the larger rumble of the marketplace entire. Beneath the tiled roof, the roofs of individual shops stair-stepped one to the other in different heights, styles, and materials. Almost none of them shared a common wall, as this would only have complicated matters if and when the time came to sell one's business.

Combined with the general hubbub of the Emporeum from daybreak on, this would have helped ensure that whatever happened here yesterday passed unnoticed by Karis' neighbors. "I tried to trace the items on the floor back to their original places on the shelves. I found nothing that looked as if it had come from somewhere else. However, I did notice that one of Karis' hands was closed around—this."

Aristander looked at what rested on her palm. "An amulet?"

"I believe so. You'll notice that part of the cord is still attached."

"Hmm," he said again. "It wasn't hers?"

Tetisheri shook her head. "She is still wearing hers. Aphrodite."

"As one would expect."

"Yes. And this one, you'll notice, is of Ptah."

He communed with the amulet for a moment. "You think it belonged to her attacker?"

"To one of them, at least."

His eyebrows went up. "You think there was more than one? Is there evidence to support that?"

"Only that I think it would take more than one person to subdue two others. From the state of the shop I think both of them fought."

"Well reasoned." He examined the amulet again. "Not of a high quality. You can hardly make out the ankh, or the beard for that matter."

"No, and made of plain stone, granite, I think, and unpolished. It looks like one of hundreds you can buy for an obol on any street corner in the city." She looked at him. "Do you mind if I keep custody of it?"

His smile was wry. "The Eye of Isis does not have to ask."

She straightened where she stood. "Nevertheless, Aristander, I do."

"And I appreciate the courtesy, Tetisheri. Keep it safe. It may be the only evidence we have." He waved his men forward. "In the meantime, I'll get on with moving the body, and finding and informing her family." He shook his head. "I hate this part of the job."

Tetisheri, having brought the news of the death of a loved one to the bereaved herself, took her leave with relief.

8

The queen was in audience. Charmion ushered Tetisheri into the back of one of the larger public rooms in the palace, where a single golden throne took pride of place on a pedestal reached by a short set of marble steps. On this throne sat the queen with the Double Crown of Egypt on her head and the crook and the flail crossed on her breast. Her gown was of some pleated gold material that gleamed in the sunlight slanting through the wall of west-facing window. She looked like a statue of herself, and a far cry from the relaxed informality of the woman attending the theater the day before.

On a vastly lesser pair of daises on either side of her throne were arrayed assorted courtiers in two curving lines of glittering regalia, nomarchs, nobles, priests, scribes, administrators, and various officers of her armies marched out in dress uniform who to a man looked as if they'd rather be at the point of Vercingetorix's sword. Fuscus, the High

Priest of Serapis, was present and making a production of looking as far down his nose as he could.

The object of the exercise had his back to Tetisheri so she couldn't see who it was. From his garishly striped robes and the overabundance of gold bracelets and chains she thought he might be from Cappadocia. He was speaking Isaurian through an interpreter who spoke Greek with a heavy Thracian accent. The strained expressions on everyone's faces indicated that they were getting about one word in ten. The queen herself wore her usual public expression: alert but untroubled, demonstrating that they had her attention and that what they had to say was important to her. Tetisheri rested her shoulders against the wall and settled in to enjoy the show. She could use a little light relief.

"—her Serene Highness, Dynamis, daughter of Pharnaces, King of Pontus, wife of Asander, King of Pontus, heir by blood and divine right to the throne of the Kingdom of Bosporus, and friend of Rome—"

He had that part off by heart.

"—offers her condolences to her sister in divinity, Cleopatra Philopator, Queen of Egypt and Alexandria, Seventh of her Name, Lady of the Two Lands, and heir by blood and divine right to the thrones of Upper and Lower Egypt, Cyprus—"

He had the last part of that by heart, too, but "condolences?" One hoped he had meant "congratulations."

"—on the birth of her son, Ptolemy XIV Caesar, Isis and Osiris made manifest on earth—"

Either the interpreter or his master's speechwriter had his Egyptian gods confused.

"—son of the great Gaius Julius Caesar—"

"—may he and you be blessed by all the gods that be with short life, bad health, and—"

An involuntary titter ran around the room. Cleopatra found its source with her eyes and with a look killed the titter dead in its tracks. Aurelius Cotta, the omnipresent Roman legate, had the honor of a stool on Cleopatra's right, the only other person allowed to be seated. He caught Tetisheri's eye and grinned openly. It might be the one thing she held most against him: that he had a sense of humor. He would be so much easier to hate if he had no redeeming qualities.

His presence in Alexandria along with three of Caesar's legions indicated Caesar's continuing interest in the mother of his only son. Or so said the romantics. Cynics would point out that the three legions were there to ensure that the bulk of Egypt's annual harvest made its way to Rome.

"—please accept these gifts from one mother to another, your sister in divinity and devoted enemy—"

Really, Tetisheri was beginning to wonder if this many mistakes in translation could be anything but a deliberate attempt at insult. At one point Pharnaces II had offered Julius Caesar his daughter's hand in marriage. Possibly Dynamis was indicating her resentment at being married off instead to the man who had killed her father after the Battle of Zela. Was that really only two months ago?

The ambassador threw up one arm, bracelets clanking,

and behind him the doors were flung open for a parade of slaves bearing gifts, including a tray of melons, one of which rolled off and fell to the floor with a spectacular and comprehensive splat; a collection of art worked in precious metals and studded with gemstones representing the Greek gods and whose mediocre craftsmanship would have had Matan shuddering in horror; piles of bleached fleeces; a single amphora of olive oil, another of wine, both of which, the ambassador assured them, were simply tokens of the total offering still secure in his ship's hold.

Saving the best for last, and superbly ignoring the slaves scurrying to clean up the mess the melon had made, the ambassador gestured again. One felt that there should have been trumpets, and indeed, the court appeared to stir from its communal somnambulism and look interested, or at least awake.

"—a gift for the young prince, that son of the great Gaius Julius Caesar, senator and dictator of Rome, conqueror of the known world, master of sea and sky and of the body of Egypt itself—"

The body of Egypt did not by the flicker of an eyelid betray recognition of the implied insult, but if Dynamis thought that an entire sea was enough to insulate her from retaliation she was much mistaken. Cleopatra never forgot.

The ambassador waved at someone beyond the door. Nothing happened. He waved again. Still nothing. A restless murmur rippled over the crowd, and the ambassador, fearing he was losing his audience, stamped forward and Tetisheri saw his face for the first time. Bearded and bloated by too much food and wine and not enough exercise. A fearsome scowl contracted his features and his thinning hair was brushed forward over his crown to end in wisps over his forehead. Really, Caesar had a great deal more than burned books to answer for.

There was a muted protest from outside, followed by a shouted command.

The interpreter, doing what he'd been hired to do, translated the phrase. "Get that fucking beast in here right now or I'll have all your heads on pikes by sunset!"

Another titter ran around the room. This time Cleopatra pretended not to notice. Her expression didn't change but Tetisheri knew her rather better than anyone else present and she thought it wouldn't be long before the Lady of the Two Lands found a way to express her displeasure at this farcical scene.

The ambassador reappeared with a fixed smile, took up his position, and waved a third time, relaunching into his speech.

"—a horse for the son of Caesar, a steed worthy of the scion of the man who brought the world to heel, a stallion Caesar's son may ride with pride into battle next to his alleged father—"

Surely he meant "esteemed."

A horse appeared in the doorway and, in spite of the gasps and low-voiced protests and a few abortive moves on the part of the queen's personal guard, proceeded right on into the room, the ambassador's retinue pulling back on either side as if rehearsed for the purpose. The horse was a fine specimen indeed, with well-developed muscles roiling beneath a pure white coat. No small amount of gold and silver had gone into the manufacture of halter, reins, and saddlecloth. His hooves had been polished, his forelock, mane and tail braided with gold and silver cord, and a wreath of white roses set in gold wire encircled his neck. His shoes struck the floor tiles with precision, breaking each and every one they fell on with a loud "Crack!" that echoed off the roof. This appeared to upset him as much as it did the ambassador, who screamed at the slave holding the horse's leading rein. The slave screamed back. The interpreter didn't bother to translate, which wasn't really necessary anyway.

The stallion that was to bear the royal heir, all four months of him, into combat danced in place, breaking still more tiles. He pulled at the leading rein. When the slave refused to let go, he lunged, and then reared, coming down with a crash. Bits of broken tile projectiled in every direction, causing many of the eminent present to leap out of the way in a manner unbefitting their dignity. There was more screaming and possibly some gnashing of teeth and tearing of hair by the ambassador. The horse dropped back to all four feet with a thud and more breakage, after which he demonstrated his opinion of the entire affair by voiding his bladder. The stream of urine was bright yellow and copious and its splatters ricocheted as far as the royal court, which proved the last straw. They vacated the premises at speed, managing to wait just long enough for their queen to precede them. Fuscus, Tetisheri was delighted to see, slipped in the urine, fell flat on his backside and slid across a few of the remaining unbroken floor tiles into the wall. He, gloriously, wasn't the only one.

The odor of the urine was acrid enough to make Tetisheri's eyes burn, if she hadn't already been laughing so hard they had filled with tears.

She was still mopping her cheeks when Charmion ushered her into the antechamber.

"Get this thing off me, Iras!"

"Patience, my queen, we don't want to tear it."

"I don't care if the damned thing falls into a thousand pieces. Take it out and let that horse stomp on it! He certainly made a good job of those tiles." Cleopatra shoved the hot, heavy braided wig from her head, which Iras caught just in time, and scrubbed her fingers through her hair so that it stood up in an untidy bush. She glared at Tetisheri. "Oh yes, laugh, do please, Tetisheri."

Which only set Tetisheri off again, to the point that she had to wrap her arms around her stomach for fear it might fall out onto the palace floor, which had already seen enough abuse for one day. "It was the horse, Majesty," she managed to say, choking over the words. "I was fine until the horse."

The royal glare transferred to Charmion and Iras, both red-faced and straining to maintain their own composure. She stripped off the collar and bracelets and stamped out of the gold dress, ignoring the rending and tearing sounds. She kicked the cloth-of-gold slippers across the room and snatched the plain linen tunic held out by Iras, yanking it over her head. "Be off, the two of you! And send food and drink to my private parlor. And bring me my son! My breasts are about to explode."

She slipped her feet into plain leather sandals and jerked her head at Tetisheri, who followed down different corridors and through several doors, the queen's personal guard a silent presence behind, servants and slaves abasing themselves before. They reached a small, simply appointed room off a balcony overlooking the Royal Harbor. Through the window the Pharos stood tall and proud against the deep blue of the Middle Sea. The harbor was filled with boats large and small, coming into and leaving port or riding at anchor. The shouts of ships' captains and stevedores came but only faintly to the ear. The isle of Antirrhodos squatted like a small but venomous lizard just offshore of Poseidon's Head, waiting to bite anyone who was unwise enough to come into reach. It was where Ptolemy XIV now lived and held court and conspired with his intimates to depose and murder his co-ruler, wife, and sister.

The woman who inhabited all three of those titles cast herself upon a couch facing the window. A nurse appeared with Caesarion, four months old now and squalling in a most unregal manner. Cleopatra pulled down the neck of her tunic and the baby latched on to her breast with a ferocity that made her jump. The nurse vanished, to be replaced by a servant bearing a tray of cheeses, fruits, and rolls, and a pitcher of pomegranate juice. The servant likewise escaped in a manner that demonstrated how fast word of the disastrous audience had circulated the palace.

Tetisheri poured juice and set the cup and a filled plate within the queen's reach. She served herself and sat down on the couch opposite, occupying herself with food and drink and the view.

The baby fussed and his mother sighed. "All right, all right, you bottomless pit, you." She shifted him to her other breast.

Time passed. Peace reigned, disturbed only by the sound of the baby suckling and the noises coming from outside the window. The repairs necessitated from damage suffered by the Pharos during the Alexandrian War had been completed and the last of the scaffolding enclosing the lighthouse's sides had vanished, along with the workmen who had populated it, leaving the harbor to the sounds of a healthy, working port. Longshoremen bellowed as they unloaded trade ships and chandlers bellowed back as they tried to load ships' stores onto those same boats. Cartwheels and donkey hooves clattered over the stone wharf, and seabirds soared and called and fought over scraps. Ra was in the descendent and the heat of midday was beginning to pass off. A breeze stirred the gauze curtains separating the parlor from the balcony.

A distinct snore could be heard, and Tetisheri looked around to see Caesarion fast asleep, eyes scrunched shut and milky mouth pursed. Cleopatra blinked lazily at Tetisheri, slowly becoming more alert. "Oh, gods. It wasn't a dream."

Tetisheri chuckled. "No, Pati, it wasn't. In fact, my money has it that the story has already flooded the city from the Sun to the Moon and is gaining in invention by the street. In the tavernas tonight people will be toasting the ambassador's horse that turned the house of Ptolemy into a stable yard. There will be songs sung about this day."

A reluctant answering grin spread across the queen's face. "I suppose it was funny."

"It was hilarious. We could have sold tickets."

"So much for the dignity of my court."

"It has none left."

"Well, and damn you, too, you little ray of sunshine." But the grin persisted. "Was it my imagination or is Dynamis a trifle peeved with me?"

"It is not your imagination."

"No." The queen stared out the window meditatively. "How is this answered, I wonder?"

"It is not answered at all," Tetisheri said promptly. Cleopatra raised an eyebrow. "It is ignored with lofty disdain. It is treated as beneath your notice, as indeed it would be beneath the notice of any ruler who realizes that other, younger, lesser realms must be excused their barbarity and incivility as faults out of which one hopes they will one day grow."

Cleopatra relaxed into a smile. "Oh very good, Tetisheri, very good indeed."

Tetisheri bowed her head in mock humility. "I live to serve, O most high."

Cleopatra rolled her eyes. The nurse retrieved the baby,

who kept snoring right through the transfer and out the door again. Cleopatra noticed the food and drink at her side. Another silence, broken this time by the sound of the queen feeding, although she was much daintier about it than her son.

"You are always hungry," Tetisheri said, watching her curiously.

"You would be, too," Cleopatra said with her mouth full, "if you had to spend all your time moving from meetings with administrators to audiences with idiot ambassadors to inquiries into malfeasance and peculation to reports on what Jubal is up to lately on our western border."

"And what is Jubal up to lately on our western border?"

"Oh, the usual. After Zela most of the remaining followers of Pompey fled to his court, and you know how suggestible he is. They only had to whisper in his ear that Caesar's strength has been leeched by the evil powers of that Egyptian witch and Jubal was ready to begin raising troops. I'm sure Caesar's long stay in Alexandria and the trip we made up the Nile was produced in evidence to support their theory."

"And was his waning strength why he stayed so long, and why he allowed himself a pleasure trip unlike any other in which he has been known to indulge?"

"He was tired! The man is fifty-three years old. He's been fighting in one war or another, foreign and civil, for the better part of thirty years. He wanted a rest, and what could be more restful than a trip up the Nile?"

"You sound…"

"Disgruntled?"

"I was going to say moody, but disgruntled will do." Tetisheri hesitated. "Are you... missing him?" Cleopatra gave her a speaking look. "No, of course. What a silly question. Forgive your humble servant, O most high."

This time they laughed together. The queen refreshed both their cups. "Now tell me. What news of Herminia?"

"I wish I had some to give you, Pati."

"Meaning?"

Tetisheri set her cup down and clasped her hands. "I have reason to believe she has been kidnapped."

Cleopatra's lips tightened. "Explain."

"Her habit was to purchase with her own hands makeup to be worn in performance that day."

One royal eyebrow went up. "I would have thought Herminia could afford to have someone else shop for her."

"My thought exactly, but this was for stage makeup. Her steward says Herminia prefers to select her own. Since the masks came off the kind and quality of cosmetics worn by the actors has apparently become very important. There is some balance between making one's features equally clear between seats near and far, and melting your skin from your bones, which I'm told inexpensive products are rumored to have done."

Cleopatra, whose eyes were still outlined in the kohl applied for the reception, nodded. "And no one wants to pay down the price of a ticket to watch their favorite actor covered in pustules. An artist of her caliber would pay strict attention to detail as a purely practical matter." She frowned. "So doing her own shopping is explained. Continue."

"She patronized a small shop in the Emporeum, owned and operated by a stylist named Karis. I believe Herminia went there yesterday morning in preparation for yesterday afternoon's performance. I went there today." She swallowed. "I found the body of a woman, identified as the stylist Karis. There had been some sort of struggle, during which she had been struck, after which she had fallen, hitting her head on the corner of a shelf on the way down. She was, I believe, unconscious, and therefore unable to tend to her wound or stop the bleeding or call for help. She bled to death on the floor of her shop."

"And Hermina?"

"Of her there is no sign. Karis' cash box was there, and there was still a significant amount of coin in it. So far as I could tell, having never visited her shop before, her merchandise was present in its entirety."

"So robbery was not the motive."

"The evidence does not support that theory, no. She had not been raped or interfered with in any way other than evidence on her face of the blow that had struck her down, and the wound to her head. The question remains, why was she attacked? If Herminia was present, and if the object was her abduction, Karis could have gone to her defense. Which resulted in the assault and her death, and Herminia was kidnapped anyway."

"Speculation."

"I agree, but..." Tetisheri sighed. "I've had the Owls in Herminia's neighborhood since yesterday, talking and listening to her neighbors and the people gathering in the street outside her house. I spoke to Basil, the stage manager at the Odeum. I spoke with Eua, her steward. I spoke to Calliope the hetaira, who as it happens lives across the street from Herminia and who so far as I can tell is the only person who approximates the description of friend, although neighbor or acquaintance is perhaps more accurate. I have spoken with Heron, son of the Nomarch of the White Walls."

Cleopatra stirred and Tetisheri looked at her, but the queen made a motion for her to continue.

"He is a fellow of the Great Library and a lecturer in engineering at the Mouseion, and is her current lover. Or was."

"And?"

"And they all know her, but they don't know anything about her. They don't know where she was born, or who her family is, or if any of them are still living. They don't know who her friends are—she doesn't in fact appear to have any friends. And they are all of them reticent in the extreme on the subject of Herminia. It was like pulling teeth to get them to say anything at all. Basil was easily the most forthcoming and even then it was only about her work." She paused, thinking. "He did have some interesting things to say about her fans, however."

"Such as?"

"Apparently they are so numerous and so rabid that the theater has had to hire guards for the stage door."

"Anyone in particular?"

Tetisheri nodded. "That was my thought as well. He did mention one Egyptian man who was very persistent. He described him as vulgar but wealthy, who seemed new to it, convinced of all the imagined privilege that brings, including having great artists at your beck and call." She sighed. "But when I questioned Basil further all he said was there were those who were far better born who behaved worse."

"Well, and we number among our acquaintance many such, Sheri. Did Herminia entertain this vulgarian?"

"Basil says not at all. Hence the guards on the stage door."

"Hence." Cleopatra stared unseeingly out the window. "She would never have missed a performance."

Tetisheri very carefully did not ask how Cleopatra came by that knowledge. "Basil and Heron said almost exactly the same thing: that Herminia was devoted to her work. Basil said she could have broken both legs and she still would have appeared." Tetisheri thought of Myrrhine with the black eye and the limping policeman and smiled involuntarily. "Working while hurt seems to be characteristic of the breed."

Cleopatra got to her feet and prowled around the room, ending eventually just inside the curtains between the room and the balcony. She hesitated for a long moment and then parted them to step outside. When it seemed that she would remain there, Tetisheri joined her.

The balustrade was supported by a column of slender white spindles. The marble railing was high enough and broad enough to lean on comfortably, and the two women did so, enjoying the sun-warmed marble against their skin and the panorama: from the city on the left to the Royal Harbor before them, to the Pharos on the right, to the endless blue of the Middle Sea beyond. The sun was sinking into the west and all the large structures stood out in deep relief, the Great Library, the Odeum, the Heptastadion crossing from the city proper to the Isle of Pharos, the three aqueducts. The founding of the city on just this spot three centuries before may have been Alexander the Great's most inspired achievement. The location could not be bettered—between the Middle Sea and Lake Mareotis, the one providing an international port for trade and the other a bottomless supply of fresh water. A place where the dry heat of the Red Land met the cool onshore breeze of the Middle Sea and melded the two into the most temperate and enjoyable of climates. "He knew what he was doing."

"What?" Cleopatra said, and Tetisheri realized she had said the words out loud.

"Alexander. He knew what he was doing when he founded the city in this place."

"He did indeed. But it isn't the most important part of the realm, Sheri. The most important part of the realm is the farms along the Nile and the people who work them. Their crops feed us, and the sale of their crops keep us solvent." She looked at Tetisheri, her gaze somber. "We are only safe so long as the Nile continues to flood and the farmers continue to plant."

And sometimes the Nile didn't flood, Tetisheri thought, and the farmers had rather rebel.

"It's very fragile, this country of ours," Cleopatra said, echoing Tetisheri's thoughts. "We are never more than one bad harvest away from insurrection, and then Rome will march in and make us in truth what we already are. A client state. A province." She nearly spat the last word. "Our autonomy, our ability to make our own decisions, gone." A soundless laugh. "The Ptolemies. We'll be gone, too."

There was nothing to say. Tetisheri knew it to be true.

Cleopatra straightened, clasping her hands at her waist. Tetisheri recognized the pose and straightened to meet it with one of her own. "If Herminia was indeed kidnapped, Sheri, why? And where is she now?"

"Everyone who claims to know her says she would rather have died than not appear on stage when expected. Her profession is so important to her that she refused an offer of marriage in its favor."

"From Heron?"

"Yes."

Cleopatra's lips pursed in a soundless whistle.

"Yes, I thought the same. A son of White Walls, no less. Everyone in her circle, as few as they may be in number, appears distressed." Although as Babak had rightly pointed out, Heron had appeared less so. She held that thought close for the moment. Cleopatra would not be willing to hear adverse speculation about a son of White Walls, and it was by no means her only suspicion concerning Heron. "Either she is dead by accident or by design, or she has been abducted."

Cleopatra looked grim. "I agree, there are few other conclusions to come to, based on what evidence you have found thus far." She saw something in Tetisheri's expression. "What?"

"There is one thing. Well, two. They may separately or together be clues as to her whereabouts, but equally they might not." She told Cleopatra of finding the little statue of Seshat among Herminia's lares and penates, and what Matan had said of it, and that Heron had given it to Herminia. "And Matan made reference to rumors about artifacts coming to market in Alexandria, representative of what might be found in a funerary hoard."

There was a brief pause. "Well, and it would not be the first time a member of the family of White Walls had produced an ancient and valuable item seemingly out of the air."

Tetisheri breathed a little easier. "Yes, but too often and they attract attention."

"As they now have attracted mine," Cleopatra said, her lips a thin line. "What was the second thing?"

Tetisheri produced the amulet.

"Not exemplary of the carver's art." Cleopatra handed it back. "There is something else, Sheri."

"What?"

"The Temple of Seshat is at Memphis. And Memphis is—"

"—within the demesne of the Nome of the White Walls. I had forgotten."

"You may find some answers in Memphis." Cleopatra turned and walked back into the parlor. Charmion was clearing away the remains of their meal. "Charmion, send to Markos. Tell him to recall his crew and provision the *Nut* for a journey of some few days. He will be carrying two of my personal representatives and he will obey their orders as if they were my own."

"Two representatives?" Tetisheri said as Charmion left.

"One of my subjects has been kidnapped and another murdered. I would not send you into what might be a dangerous situation without protection, Sheri. Of course Apollodorus will accompany you."

Tetisheri opened her mouth and found she could not close it again.

A smile crossed Cleopatra's face so fleetingly that Tetisheri thought for a moment she might have imagined it. "The *Nut* is moored at the West Dock in the Royal Harbor. You should have just enough time to return home, alert your family, and pack a bag." Cleopatra waved a dismissive hand. "Off with you."

Obediently, Tetisheri found her feet carrying her to the door. She paused. "Pati, why are you so concerned about Herminia's whereabouts? I had not known you were close."

Cleopatra's face looked carved from stone. "Find Herminia, my Eye."

Tetisheri bowed. "Majesty."

9

"At least this time we don't have to worry about pirates."

There was a smile in Apollodorus' voice. "We weren't worried much last time."

They were standing at the railing of the *Nut*, watching the wharf fall away. Markos shouted a command. The sail went up and filled immediately with the reliable day breeze. Their speed increased. Boats large and small skittered hastily out of the way as they saw the royal standard flying from the mast.

They made for the break between the seawalls that extended from the Isle of Pharos on the left and the jumble of white buildings on Lochias that made up the Royal Palace on the right. Once outside the port the hull began to rise and fall with the swell of the sea.

Markos shouted another order. The sail luffed and filled again and the rowers dropped their oars into the water and began to pull to the slow beat of the sailing master's drum.

"Captain Markos?"

He was a burly individual with deep-set eyes beneath a wild tangle of black hair graying at the temples, dressed in a serviceable tunic and sandals. "Just Markos, lady."

"How long will it take us to reach Memphis, Markos?"

He squinted at the sun, which was by now much closer to the western horizon. "We got a late start, lady, so we won't get far today. We'll stop overnight at Merimda and get underway again at daybreak. Barring local traffic and any new obstruction due to the last flood, we should be in Memphis by or before nightfall tomorrow."

She hesitated. "We don't wish to attract attention, Markos."

The wrinkles at the corners of his eyes deepened. "Our moorage is north of the city, lady, and we will be gone before the Lord of Merimda breaks his fast."

She smiled at him. "Thank you, Markos. Carry on."

He bowed his head briefly. "Lady."

They watched the Pharos pass in review on the left, followed by the long, low island it rested on. In less than an hour they were rounding its western end coming into Eunostos Harbor. Again the Royal Standard superseded all other traffic, not without a few dark looks. The customs agents at Kibotos waved them through. In short order they passed between the city walls and entered upon the calm waters of the Nile Canal. The sails came down and from then on they moved by oar alone.

It was a testament to classical engineering, this ditch in the desert connecting the modern capital of Alexandria with the ancient capital of Memphis. It spoke well of the forethought and determination of Alexander and Ptolemy I, too. They realized that the many-branched delta of the Nile, which temperamental river could and did change course with every annual inundation, was often bewildering to sailors. Since the lush banks of the Nile and the grain grown on them was what made Egypt the richest country in the world, reliable transportation of that valuable cargo was essential. It also helped that the Port of Kibotos was manned by eagle-eyed customs agents whose salary was paid by a percentage of the contraband goods they confiscated and reported. Cleopatra was well known for her direct dealings with anyone who tried to cheat her, and after a few were publicly crucified as object lessons, such attempts became less common. It was rumored that smugglers still plied the delta in force, however, and offshore the pirate problem never went away.

She sighed. "If only cheats and thieves spent as much time working at a legitimate job as they did stealing."

"Smugglers?" Apollodorus said, following her train of thought without difficulty. "I think many of them regard it as a sport. A challenge to see who is smarter, if you will."

"Yes, it's very sportsmanlike to end up hanging from a cross in front of the Gate of the Sun."

He chuckled and turned to lean against the rail. She followed suit. They were moving swiftly down the canal now. The *Nut* had a single, narrow hull built for speed, with five oarsmen a side and a single square sail that worked best with a following wind. The bow was decked to house the ship's stores. There was a cabin on the raised stern with rolls of matting for walls that could be raised and lowered by cords. A single broad couch filled the wall nearest the stern, and Tetisheri's heart skipped a beat when she saw it. She looked up to see Apollodorus watching her. He shook his head, and caught her hand in a brief squeeze. "This was not what I had in mind when I said I wanted to take you on a cruise."

She was both relieved and disappointed. "No?"

"No," he said firmly. "I have no wish to enjoy your company with twenty strangers listening in, ready to spread the tale of it across Alexandria on our return."

Her face felt hot. "Oh." She hoped she didn't look as disappointed as she sounded.

He laughed. "And there is the little matter of your mission for the queen."

"Oh," she said, recovering. "That."

"Yes. That. Which is what, by the way? All I got was a message ordering me to join you aboard the *Nut*." He smiled down at her. "Mind you, I was delighted. I'll take any time with you I can get. Given how the queen has an almost preternatural ability to ensure we are on opposite sides of the city at any given time."

"Given that," she said, sighing.

"Or the Middle Sea, for that matter." He led the way to the cabin, where they found a tray with dolma filled with a spicy bean mixture, sliced melon, and pitchers of beer and juice. Tetisheri's stomach growled. "She does us proud, our queen."

"On occasion."

The banks of the canal slipped past. Two boys in a rickety

rowboat paddled out to catch hold of the rail and hitch a ride to the next village. Farmers ankle deep in rich black loam stood to wave and immediately stooped again to planting next season's harvest. Women fetched water from wells for dinner, shouldering the full amphoras with ease. Aside from the cry of ducks and doves, the hiss of ten blades slicing into the water was the only sound that marred the serenity of their passage.

Tetisheri felt tension ebb with every league. "As to the mission," she said, licking the soft cheese from her fingers. "You'll remember Herminia not appearing at the Odeum yesterday as scheduled."

"I was there."

She smiled a little.

"And I remember the queen whispering to you."

She nodded. "Yes. She wants me to find Herminia. I spent all day today looking, and found what may or may not be a few clues." She shook her head. "A very few. It almost feels as if Herminia designed her life so that she could disappear at will."

He listened without comment as she related her day, the sun touching the western horizon by the time she was finished. His eyes sharpened when she came to the scene in the Emporeum. "Murdered?"

"Someone knew Herminia's habits well enough to know that she would be at that shop yesterday morning. They were waiting for her. It is my belief that Karis got in the way, either intentionally or by accident, and—" She swallowed.

He pulled her into his arms, warm and strong about her. "I understand now why our queen sent me with you."

Her voice was muffled against his tunic. "You could see that she had been struck very hard in the face, and the blood where she hit her head on the corner of the shelf where she fell. The blood on the floor, Apollodorus. It was everywhere, all over the floor, and it had already turned that horrible brown blood becomes when it dries."

He made a comforting noise that rumbled against her cheek. "Head wounds always bleed a lot."

She sighed and pulled back to look up at him. "A thing I have learned that I wish with all my heart I had not."

"Do you regret taking on the job?"

"I wasn't allowed much choice in the matter."

She made as if to move away and he took her shoulders in both hands, forcing her to meet his eyes. "If you wish to resign, only say the word, Tetisheri."

"I don't think even you have that kind of influence with the Lady of the Two Lands, Apollodorus."

"Nevertheless." He sounded implacable. "If it is what you wish, I will help you make it happen. If necessary I will resign my position and we will leave Alexandria."

She was really startled this time. "Leave Alexandria? Leave Uncle Neb? Keren, Phoebe, the Owls?" She shook her head. "No. I am bound to my life in Alexandria. And truly, Apollodorus, happy to be so."

"Yes, of course." He sounded ever so slightly weary now.

"She is very good at choosing people who have no choice themselves."

She said nothing. They both knew who he meant, and they both knew he was right. "Did you know that Khadiga lives still?"

"Yes."

She stared out over the river, where the golden path laid down by the setting sun was beginning to narrow. "She's a multiple murderer, and yet she is allowed to live because she might prove useful one day."

"And so she might." His warm hand raised her chin so their eyes could meet. "Cleopatra is pressed on all sides, Sheri. The Romans envy her wealth and fear her power and are suspicious of her relationship with Caesar, especially since she managed to give birth to Caesar's only son. She has done and continues to do everything she can to ingratiate herself with her Egyptian subjects, including manifesting herself as their goddess on earth and speaking their language fluently and opening the royal granaries in times of famine—she even prostituted herself to that aspiring Roman emperor for them! And still there are rumblings of discontent from here to Syene. In Nubia the local warlords are always fomenting insurrection and have now taken to corresponding secretly with Philo and, we suspect, Arsinoë as well. And every ruler around the Middle Sea has their hand out for whatever they can get: money, influence, trade, treaties. It is a precarious time in the history of the realm."

"You're defending her." She was surprised, not accusatory.

"I understand her. Or perhaps I mean, I understand her situation. And don't forget that very few Ptolemies die in bed. She lives with the threat of assassination every moment of her life."

"Well, now you're just making me feel guilty."

He laughed, and so did she. "I have no wish to leave my post, Apollodorus. I have a chance to make a difference, if she'll let me. It's enough for now."

"Good. I believe it is the right choice."

One of the hands cleared away the debris from the meal and lit a lamp hanging from a corner of the cabin. Presently they approached a moorage on the north side of the canal. Oars were shipped and lines were looped around pilings driven into the bank. In a clearing on shore was an open-sided wooden shelter sitting in front of a large fire pit. In moments kindling was lit and an evening meal assembled. The conversation was a pleasant background rumble of sound broken by occasional laughter. The stars coalesced into view from horizon to horizon and the *Nut*'s namesake foretold her appearance with a white glow to the east.

Tetisheri leaned back and let out a long sigh, letting her eyes close just for a moment. "It's been a long day." She looked at Apollodorus sitting across from her. "It's been a long month, in fact. Uncle Neb is building new boats and new trade routes and sending out messages and invitations to bid from Judea to Hispania and Britannia and even points north of that. I don't think he's missed a single port on coastal Europe. The correspondence alone has been a nightmare."

"He'll need to build even more boats if he keeps this up."

"I'm very much afraid that that is what he has in mind. I have been buried in paperwork. We need to hire a clerk."

"Possibly several."

She smiled without opening her eyes. "Probably more. And add an office onto the warehouse because at this rate we're not going to be able to continue to run the business out of the house. But he's so happy about it, Apollodorus. The war and everything to do with it made him miserable. He hates waste above all else. I truly believe he felt every drachma spent to arm and train a soldier as a personal affront and every casualty suffered as another lost customer."

"I remember. About as angry as I've ever seen Neb was when Theo and Arsinoë forced him into that arms shipment."

Tetisheri shuddered. "Not pretty." Like many large men of benevolent disposition, Nebenteru looked upon the world with a kindly eye and it took a great deal for him to lose his temper. In fact, Tetisheri had seen it happen twice in her lifetime: once after the aforementioned coerced arms shipment, and the second time when she had run to him from Hunefer's house. It had taken everything in her power to hold him back that night and she hoped her mother never returned to Alexandria because Tetisheri was certain Hagne would not survive her arrival there by a day. "It's one of the reasons we went to Punt, I think. He wanted to get us and the *Hapi* away for long enough to outlast the war."

She opened her eyes to see Apollodorus watching her with a smile in his own. He held out his hand. "Let's get you to bed."

Those words spoken in that deep, sure voice sent an agreeable shiver down her spine. "I wish—"

"So do I," he said. He rose to his feet and blew out the lamp.

She woke to the feel of the hull dipping beneath her as the crew boarded just before dawn. Mist rose up from the river to form ghostly shapes and it felt as if they were setting off into the Underworld.

Apollodorus had risen before her. Her hand followed the shape he had left behind in the bedclothes and she allowed herself to remember what it had been like to fall asleep next to him, the steady beat of his heart against her ear, the strength and surety of his arms around her.

Her childhood had not been marked by either trust or security and there had been neither affection nor respect in her marriage. She was secure in the love and respect of Uncle Neb and his household but that was different than this. How different she did not know. But she was ready to find out.

She rose and tidied the bed and herself and stepped out on deck. The oarsmen were only dimly seen, known mostly from the drip of the oars as they pulled free of the water. The banks of the river were invisible. There was a low-voiced call from the bow. Markos' voice replied and the man himself materialized from the gloom. "Good morning, lady."

"A foggy morning, Markos."

"It will burn off in half an hour or so." She saw the flash of his teeth. "By then we should be well past Merimda and we can break our fast."

She smiled back at him. "Well done, Markos."

He sketched another of his truncated bows. "By the queen's command, lady."

She retreated to the cabin and sat down out of the way. Ra drove his chariot up over the eastern horizon just as Nut disappeared into the west, ceding him duty for the day. As Markos had predicted, the mist evaporated beneath the god's power. She looked over her shoulder and saw the outskirts of Merimda dropping rapidly astern.

Apollodorus straightened from his place in the bow, where she realized he had been spotting for hazards to navigation. He turned and made his way aft, pausing now and then to clap a shoulder and exchange a greeting. He and Markos nodded at each other and then he dropped down next to her. She smiled up at him and he put an arm around her shoulders and dropped a kiss on her brow. "You know them."

"Who?"

"Markos and his crew."

"Well, and this wouldn't be the first time they have carried me on the queen's business."

"Ah."

Cheese and bread and fruit were brought, along with hot spiced tea. "I could get used to this."

"Wait to say that until we're on the way back from Memphis."

She was surprised by the sober note in his voice. "Is there something you haven't told me concerning this investigation?"

He shook his head. "It's just that I've been tasked before with missions that seemed minor in the beginning."

"I don't like surprises, Apollodorus."

"Nor do I, Tetisheri, and yet in honesty I am bound to declare that surprises occur all too often in service to our queen." With that he changed the subject in a marked manner. "You've been to Memphis, of course."

"A few times."

"How do you see this inquiry progressing there?"

She gnawed the inside of her lip. "It all seems so amorphous at this point. We have a missing person, who may have been abducted, although we have no direct evidence that this is so. We have a lover of the missing person, and a statue belonging to her received from him, and an amulet that may possibly belong to one of her abductors. Heron is definitely from Memphis. The statue is an image of the goddess whose main temple is there. The amulet is a personal amulet of a god who also has a temple in Memphis, but then what god doesn't? Eua, Herminia's steward, claims that her mistress plans to retire in Memphis.

"They are the tiniest of threads but there are no other options available than to tug on them and see if something unravels that will lead us to Herminia. And I still don't understand why Cleopatra is so invested in discovering her whereabouts." She looked at Apollodorus, whose expression remained suspiciously blank. "Everything Basil said was true, and most of what Ninos said, too. Actors can be notoriously erratic, but both men are united in believing that Herminia would never have missed a performance. Especially one that much anticipated and with that audience." They were both thinking of Cleopatra sitting front row center. "And according to Heron, she refused a very advantageous offer of marriage because of her devotion to the stage, which only makes their statements more credible."

"Her failure to appear on stage for that performance was an insult to our queen, as well."

She made a sound of disgust. "You always have to make everything about politics."

"Because everything always is about politics, Tetisheri, and you would be wise to remember that."

She looked at him, momentarily outlined against a lush growth of papyrus fronds that grew right down to the edge of the canal and at places into it. It was odd to see him in that context. He was so much a man of the city, someone who could walk into a hostile king's court with the absolute certainty he would walk out again unscathed, someone who could also walk into the queen's court and be confident of having her ear and her trust. "You weren't in the Roman army for very long."

"Where did that come from?" When she didn't answer,

only met his look with a grave stare, he shrugged. "No, only a little over two years. Long enough to see action at Bibracte, Vesontio, and Sambre, and a few more battles. Although I don't know that Vesontio could rightly be described as a battle."

"Why did you join?"

He raised an eyebrow. "It seemed best to acquire some experience under arms, lest people speculate as to how we otherwise might have come by our undoubtedly superior fighting skills."

"Ah." As she well knew, Apollodorus and his four partners had a past that would not bear close examination, in particular close Roman examination. They were now the owners and proprietors of the Five Soldiers, the largest and most prosperous of Alexandria's gymnasiums. Lordlings and gentry alike vied for memberships there, and no elevation of fees seemed to discourage them. "You came to the right place for a life after the army."

"Well. I admit we didn't expect Caesar and his wars to follow us here, but the man does get around. We were looking for somewhere we could live in relative peace—" she laughed "—yes, I know, and I did say relative. He might do his best to burn it down, however accidentally, but at least he won't sack the place, as it feeds and funds too many of his legions. The five of us agreed when we arrived in Alexandria that we had found a place where we could thrive and where we could live well and relatively unmolested." He smiled. "And it's never boring, Alexandria. Half a million people, loving

and quarreling and teaching and learning and buying and
selling."

"And then you met Auletes."

He made a face. "Rather say Auletes met us."

"Head on."

"For better or worse." His smile was rueful. "Being his
chosen heir's personal guard was not in my plans, but he was
impossible to refuse."

"Did he loan you the money to build the Five Soldiers?"

"He insisted."

Royal favor in a city like Alexandria was not to be
despised. Or in this case, declined. "By way of placing you
under obligation."

"Of course. It's what they do."

"Who?"

"People in power. Especially royals, who have all the
resources at their disposal. Distributing them is how they get
what they want."

Of course it was true. Because Tetisheri might be the
only woman in Alexandria and Egypt who didn't have her
hand out didn't mean she wasn't perfectly well aware that
Cleopatra was buying as much local favor as she could.
Contracts to carry grain and papyrus to market to selected
merchants. Offering posts in her nascent Queen's Army
equally to citizens of every race and ethnicity. Ensuring that
the sergeants in charge of training said army were each and
every one veterans of Rome's legions, offering preference to
those of the Tenth, Julius Caesar's most trusted. Exclusive

contracts for mining gold in Upper Egypt and cutting granite in Syene. Letters of passage again to selected traders between Syene and Berenike, which in turn caused the goods of Punt and other eastern lands to pass to and through Egypt to avid buyers around the Middle Sea and on into Europe.

"She's a better juggler than any you will find along the Canopic Way of a Saturday afternoon."

"She has to be," Apollodorus said.

"How can this investigation benefit her reign?"

"Maybe it isn't her reign that will benefit."

"What, then?"

His smile was one part rueful to one part tender. "You aren't her only friend, Sheri."

They were interrupted by the arrival of lunch: lamb and vegetable kebabs with nutty brown bread and a pitcher of beer. Tetisheri bought some time by filling their cups. "I think I would like to begin my inquiries at the Temple of Seshat," she said, answering his original question. "That statue, Apollodorus. It is very beautiful and according to Matan very valuable, and very, very, very old." She frowned. "Cleopatra said it wouldn't be the first time an old, valuable artifact was magically produced by a scion of the Nomarch of the White Walls."

"It wouldn't even be the thousandth time if half the stories are true."

"Very well, then. Let's ask the High Priestess what she knows. Maybe we'll get lucky and the statue was stolen right off her altar."

"Maybe."

He wasn't convinced and neither was she, but they had to start somewhere. "While I'm wasting the High Priestess' time, would you feel comfortable insinuating yourself into such tavernas whose clientele seem particularly gossipy?"

He grinned. "I might be able to do that, just. How would you like me to proceed?"

She cocked her head, considering. "You're newly come from Alexandria, where the talk of the town is Herminia's disappearance. It will be the first they've heard of it. You probably won't have to buy a single drink. Follow wherever it goes from there."

"Understood. Do we move ashore or stay on the boat?"

She looked around for the captain. "Markos?"

They had been drifting as the oarsmen changed sides after a brief rest, and when that was accomplished he threaded his way through the crew with nods and smiles and thumps on shoulders. He had the gift of leadership, she saw. Of course it helped that the oarsmen in this crew were freedmen all and there wasn't a whip in sight. The only discipline provided came from Markos' charisma and the sailing master's beat on the drum. They were probably paid well, too.

"Markos, is there a moorage near Memphis that will keep us out of sight of the city?"

"And of the Nomarch?" He chuckled. "Of course, lady."

"And could you find a small boat to ferry us back and forth?"

"There is a boatman I have used before."

"Excellent. We will overnight on board, then."

He nodded. "Any idea how long we'll be staying?"

"I don't know. Several days. Possibly longer."

Markos nodded and moved off to consult with his sailing master.

To Apollodorus she said, "We'll go in the morning."

He held up a hand. "I'll go in tonight. Better we are not seen arriving together."

"Who knows?" He smiled. "If I get lucky, I'll find someone who started drinking early and who knows everything about everyone in Memphis."

The Temple of Seshat was set back from the riverbank but still accessible by means of a narrow canal in the shape of a half circle which began and ended in the river. Wide steps led up to a broad terrace fronting a hypostyle built on slender, marble-faced columns beneath lintels and a roof of granite. Columns, lintels, and roof remained free of carvings and paintings, boasting only a high polish. A line of clerestory windows just beneath the eaves allowed the rays of the sun, no matter where it was in the sky, to illuminate the marble-flagged interior with a reverential glow that somehow managed also to be cheerful. Seshat was the goddess who kept the record of the years and of the harvests and of the reigns of the pharaohs. It was a position of dignity and gravity and necessity in the Egyptian pantheon that she had not previously associated with joy, but Tetisheri found her steps growing inexplicably lighter as she ascended the staircase.

There was a fountain in the center of the room with a figure of Seshat in the center, stylus and palm rib in hand. She stooped to wet her fingers and touch them to her breast, lips, and forehead.

It was only an hour past dawn and she was the first person to approach the novice who guarded the door to the inner sanctum. "I would speak with the High Priestess of the temple," she said. "I am Tetisheri of House Nebenteru, newly come from Alexandria."

The novice, who might have been all of ten years old, bestowed a kindly smile upon the supplicant. "One may always speak to the goddess oneself, without an intermediary. Seshat knows all, sees all, loves all, and hears all."

Tetisheri bowed her head gravely. "It is not the goddess with whom I wish to converse. I follow another." She touched her breast, drawing the novice's attention to the amulet of Bast that rested against her plain white tunic. "I am known to the High Priestess. Be so good as to carry my name to her."

"As you wish. Be pleased to wait here for a moment only."

As Tetisheri waited a group of scribes entered the hypostyle and surrounded the fountain to make their obeisance. Their youth proclaimed them new to their trade and they were likely here to make their first offering to their divine patron. They were very solemn as they paid their respects and assembled in an orderly group some distance from Tetisheri, waiting their turn to enter into the holy precincts and be blessed.

A touch on her elbow made her turn. "Be pleased to follow me, lady."

She was led through the altar room, which featured another, and this time very tall, statue of Seshat in her star headdress and leopard skin, but still holding the stylus and palm rib. A group of priestesses had their foreheads pressed to the floor, although several had had the forethought to bring mats to cushion their hands and knees. Behind the statue a series of twisting passages led eventually to a large wooden door bound in brass. The novice knocked once, softly.

The voice that replied was low but perfectly clear. "You may enter."

The novice opened the door. "The lady Tetisheri of House Nebenteru has come to call, mistress."

"I thank you, Agathe."

The novice effaced herself and closed the door behind her.

The room opened out onto a garden featuring a riot of white roses in bloom, and their sweet scent suffused the air inside and out. A lattice formed an awning and dispersed the morning sun into placid patterns. Another, smaller room opened to the right, through which Tetisheri glimpsed a bed.

The High Priestess sat behind a broad table covered with tablets and papyri and styli and pots of ink and various official documents festooned with seals, some of which Tetisheri saw were royal.

"Well?" the High Priestess said. She sounded severe but Tetisheri could hear the humor that ran through her voice like a rich vein of the most precious ore. "And what excuse could you possibly have for interrupting my most holiness without so much as appointment?"

Tetisheri grinned. "Forgive my presumption, High Priestess."

The High Priestess stood and came around the desk, holding out her arms. "Tetisheri."

"Euphrasia." They embraced. "You still smell of cinnamon and apples."

The High Priestess threw back her head and laughed. "I see nothing has changed, including your tendency to think of your stomach first! Have you broken your fast?"

"I have not."

"Take your ease in my garden while I send for tea and something to eat."

Tetisheri passed through into the garden. Beneath the awning were two couches with a small table between them.

After a few moments the High Priestess joined her. She was a short, plump woman with thick dark hair and large, widely spaced dark eyes that tilted upwards at the corners, which tilt was accentuated by a tail of kohl trending toward her temple. She looked always to be on the verge of laughter because she always was. She plumped down on the couch opposite Tetisheri and regarded her with what looked very much like satisfaction. "It is so good to see you."

"That's not what you said the last time you saw me."

Euphrasia laughed. She gave herself wholly to it and the sound rollicked upward very probably to Ra himself, who only shone down all the brighter on one of his most favored subjects. "No," she said, still laughing, "as I recall that was the very day I caught you and Cleopatra removing the ladder you had placed against the eave of the observatory so as to inveigle Theo and Philo into climbing up there in the first place."

"They stole our paints!"

Euphrasia laughed again, rocking backward and forward, her arms wrapped around her middle.

Tetisheri was forced to laugh, too. "What am I, seven years old again?"

Euphrasia mopped her eyes with the tail end of her stola and beamed. "It is indeed so good to see you again, Tetisheri. It has been far too long."

"And you, Euphrasia. You appear to be flourishing. I know it wasn't what you wanted at the time. And it was so very sudden. We never got the chance to say goodbye."

"Auletes was most insistent, and who denies a king?" Euphrasia said lightly. "And it has turned out for the best. Seshat has been kind in the novices she sends me, and the properties owned by the temple are in the charge of men and women of ability and probity. Well. Most of them."

"Only most?"

Euphrasia smiled.

"I see. So no real flies in your ointment, then. Enviable."

Euphrasia sighed. "I only wish that were true."

"What, then?"

The older woman made a face. "The current High Priest of Ptah is becoming…" She frowned. "Troublesome."

"Natasen?"

"You've heard of him, then?"

"No, he was pointed out to me in Alexandria two days ago. I'd never heard of him before then."

"It would pain him to hear you say so." Euphrasia rolled her eyes. "Yet another scion of the Nomarch of the White Walls."

"One of the sons?" Tetisheri said, thinking of Heron.

"No, one of the cousins."

Tetisheri's eyebrows went up. "The disreputable cousins?"

"Unfortunately. And he has taken the Temple of Seshat and her servants in dislike. Or he purports to."

"Publicly?"

"Oh yes, otherwise what is the point? One must have an enemy. He speaks on it before the altar, at length and oh so eloquently. Such fire, such conviction! He says…" Euphrasia held up her hands and began to tick items off on her fingers. "He says we have become slack in our teachings, corrupt in our practice, and that the goddess has turned her back on us."

"And how would he know that?"

"He doesn't have to know it, Tetisheri, he only has to say it, over and over again. If people hear it enough it becomes the truth by repetition. No smoke without fire."

"He says that out loud?"

"Oh my, yes, before the altar and at receptions and dinner parties, in private interviews with any noble major or minor who has the misfortune to wander into his presence."

Euphrasia grimaced. "He has even said it within my hearing at events where we were both in attendance."

"He insults you to your face?"

"Not quite. Not yet."

Tetisheri's brow creased. "I don't understand. What does he want?"

"I expect he wants to bring the Temple of Seshat beneath his own authority."

"Ah." Tetisheri sat back. "He wants the tithe."

"Exactly. He is currently expanding the Temple of Ptah by some ungodly amount and he has to pay for it somehow."

"How long has this been going on?"

"A little over a year, now."

Something in the tone of her voice put Tetisheri on the alert. "Has he—Euphrasia, has he approached you for funding?"

The High Priestess' smile was thin. "Of course he has, Tetisheri. Small amounts only, at first, for a single bell, say, or a small chapel."

"And when you refused?"

"Why, then I would hear rumors of strange sexual practices in my own sanctuary."

"But that's blackmail, Euphrasia!"

"Indeed it is, Tetisheri."

"Refute it! Give your own speeches, host your own receptions and dinners!"

"Oh, I've done better than that."

"Meaning?"

"The Temple of Seshat is sponsoring a ten-day Festival of Seshat—beginning tomorrow, as it happens. You got here just in time." The High Priestess waved an airy hand. "Everyone is invited. There will be athletic competitions featuring Olympic athletes, no less. There will be games of chance and skill. Scribes, artists, illustrators, potters, weavers, jewelers, and more will be selling their wares. There will of course be food vendors, a great many selling a great deal of what I'm certain will be very bad wine, and musical performances and a different play every night." Euphrasia smiled a satisfied smile. "And every day begins with a blessing from the Temple, after which each person who attends will receive—" She got up and went inside, returning immediately with something in her hand. "One of these."

It was an amulet of Seshat, like Herminia's statue carved from alabaster. It was the length of Tetisheri's thumb. Palm rib and stylus were black, the star headdress a deep green, and the leopard skin yellow with black spots. She held it up. It trapped the rays of the sun inside it to positively glow. It reminded her of the inside of the temple itself, and she thought enough of Euphrasia's intelligence to think that was very probably deliberate. "Pricy. How many of these did you have made?"

"Enough for every citizen of Memphis and all our visitors, too."

Tetisheri lowered her hand. "Just how long have you been planning this Festival of Seshat, Euphrasia?"

"Oh, a little over a year."

"Immediately after the High Priest asked for his first bribe, and was refused?"

"Almost to the day. No, no, keep it. We have sufficient for our needs."

Tetisheri leaned back and started to laugh. "Oh well done, Euphrasia, well done indeed." She had a thought and sobered. "Have you hired guards?"

"We have. Some will be in uniform, some in their everyday best, and all have been strictly instructed to stop any trouble before it starts." She sighed. "And you will have noticed that we have opened the hypostyle to the public, and not just for holy days. It's a way of giving our devotees—"

"Ownership?"

"Of creating a constituency, at least, and of manifestly demonstrating there is no evil done within these walls. People can now see that for themselves."

"The High Priest of Ptah must be beside himself."

"Especially since he has closed off access to the Temple of Ptah to anyone but priests and acolytes. Well, and he has only himself to blame. Another sweet roll? More tea?" Almost magically a novice materialized with a fresh pot before vanishing again. "Well, and Tetisheri, you have heard all my news. What of yours?"

"Uncle Neb is building more boats. His plan is to take over trade in the Middle Sea before anyone else does."

"I see he has not changed, then."

"No." Tetisheri took a deep breath and let it out slowly. "I was married."

"I had not heard." Euphrasia sipped her tea. "You speak of it in the past tense."

Tetisheri could feel her lips drawing into a snarl and attempted to school her expression to match her tone, which she hoped was bland in the extreme. "I do."

"I see. Hagne's hand was in this, I have no doubt?"

Tetisheri did her best not to shudder at the mention of her mother's name. "Yes."

"And he was a son of some great house, I expect?"

"Yes."

"Hagne was ever ambitious."

"But it ended, and afterward Uncle Neb made me his partner and heir in the business. We have prospered. We journeyed together to Punt."

"Did you! What an adventure!"

"It was, and a profitable one."

"How could it be otherwise. And Hagne?"

"I don't know, and I don't want to know." Perhaps that came out with a little more force than she had intended.

"Mmmm." Euphrasia's eyes regarded her over the rim of her cup. "Not that I'm not happy to see you, Tetisheri, but why are you here?"

Tetisheri set down her cup very carefully. "I don't know how fast the news travels down the Nile Canal to Memphis."

The High Priestess went still. "Very fast."

"Then you may have heard of the mysterious disappearance of the actress and singer, Herminia."

Euphrasia set her own cup down even more carefully and

folded her hands in her lap, it seemed, expressly so she could examine them with all of her attention. "That story had reached us, yes."

Tetisheri had wondered about the correspondence she had seen on Euphrasia's work table with the royal seal affixed to it. "I have been asked to attempt to ascertain her whereabouts and to return her to her adoring public."

If possible Euphrasia became even more still, looking for all the world like a plump doe on the wrong end of a drawn bow. "Asked by whom?" she said, her voice subdued.

"Cleopatra."

There was a brief silence, which Euphrasia broke with a sigh. She loosened her hands and reached again for her tea. "Yes, of course. Who else would she send on this errand but her oldest and dearest friend? But what brought you to Memphis, specifically?"

"Herminia's most recent lover was Heron, son of White Walls, fellow of the Great Library and resident lecturer at the Mouseion."

Euphrasia frowned. "Heron. Yes, I remember, Timon's second oldest son, I think, and therefore allowed to follow his own way."

"Yes."

"And he says?"

"He doesn't know where she is. He seems to think she'd rather die than miss a performance, because he knows for a fact she'd rather stay single and be on the stage than give it up to marry him."

Euphrasia looked up at that. "She refused him?"

"He says she did."

A smile tugged at the corners of the High Priestess' mouth.

"I spoke to the stage manager at the Odeum and, like Heron, he thinks she's kidnapped—or dead—because it's the only reason he can think of that she'd miss a performance. Her household, too, was united in thinking some misfortune has befallen their mistress because they can imagine nothing else keeping her from performing that afternoon. And then..." If she told this story enough times, perhaps the day would come when she didn't feel sick doing so. Keeping her voice as colorless as possible, she related the scene at the Emporeum, and the tenuous conclusions derived therefrom.

There was a short silence. "But what a horrible thing for you to have seen, Tetisheri."

"Yes."

Something in the single word must have told Euphrasia that sympathy would be unwelcome. The High Priestess leaned forward to set her cup on the table. "None of this, however, tells me what in all this brings you to Memphis, and to me."

Tetisheri frowned at her tea. "Herminia lives modestly, but she had one possession that is worth more than everything else she owns, including her home. A statue of Seshat, very old. I consulted Matan—you'll remember Matan—and he is convinced that it is the product of one of the ancient tombs. Very probably an unreported find, which news of course delighted our queen no end." She looked up.

Euphrasia drank tea, not meeting Tetisheri's eyes.

"Do you know Herminia, Euphrasia?"

The High Priestess paused for a long moment, appearing to choose her words carefully. "As well as I know any of my novices."

"Herminia was a novice here?"

"Not exactly. She came here as a baby. It happens when a child is unwanted or orphaned or the family is unable to care for them."

"Yes, I know. The Temple of Bast does something similar."

"We women must stick together, goddess and mortal." This said with the ghost of a smile.

"No notion of who Herminia's family is, or was?"

The High Priestess gave her head a firm shake. "Herminia grew up here, among us. She received the usual instruction. When the time came to make her vows she declined, as is every novice's right. By then she had found her voice and none of us could have stopped her seeing how far it would carry her in the world. None of us would have if we could."

"You've not seen her since she left?"

"She does visit now and then." The High Priestess smiled. "And she has never forgotten us. She is a fast friend of the Temple of Seshat. We have cause to be very grateful to her, indeed, even if she weren't already in our hearts." She leaned forward to place her hand on Tetisheri's. "I don't know if she is here in Memphis, Tetisheri, but you may call upon me for anything you need in your search to find her.

"In this city or out of it."

10

Compared to Alexandria, Memphis was a small city whose primary income derived from the many temples devoted to the gods and goddesses of the pharaonic past. It had three distinct neighborhoods. First and foremost, of course, were the temples, which occupied the riverfront. Every one, large and small, had its own dock so its followers would not have their feet and presumably souls tainted by having to land at some other god's dock. There was always a stretch of farmland between one temple and the next, Tetisheri suspected less to separate the influence of one god over another's following than to raise more food and pay more taxes on it. It made for an elongated community.

Behind the temples came the mansions where the business of the temples took place, where overseers reported on annual crop yields and resulting tithes and inquired as to the projected rise of the Nile that year. Behind them was the usual jumble of housing where the artisans, craftsmen and women, servants, and slaves lived. Also known as the people who did all the work.

Scattered throughout were neighborhood markets where the real life of the city carried forward as it did everywhere else, but it was the temples one saw first in this ancient capital of the pharaohs. Even though the city, and for that matter the deities themselves, had been falling into a steady, inexorable decline since the first Ptolemy over three hundred years before, it was still a testament to the magnificent abilities of the builders of the old dynasties. It was an homage as well as to the unending supply of slave labor captured in battles from Nubia to Parthia, but then Tetisheri could be on occasion a cynic of the deepest dye and therefore not as fervent in her adoration of her forebears as others she could name.

She was looking at a perfect example of that now.

The hypostyle of the Temple of Ptah had columns twice the height and girth of the columns of the Temple of Seshat. These columns were formed into the figures of pharaohs from Menes to Thutmose III, Hatshepsut being notably absent. To a man they looked mighty and majestic and very, very masculine, down to the distinct bulge in their pleated kilts, just in case there was any doubt. The building itself was aggressively square and solid, faced with an uncompromising gray granite. The pylon was tall and thick and painted with scenes of battles and captured enemies and unending lines of tribute in the form of food, slaves, and the usual precious metals and precious stones. Even now there were novices on scaffolding renewing the colors, lest an approaching supplicant not be blinded by them from first setting foot on shore.

The courtyard was open to the sky and surrounded by more columns decorated with paintings of pharaohs making offerings to all the gods and goddesses, but primarily Ptah. Ptah himself looked everywhere as if he had been drawn or even stamped from a template, mummified except for his arms and head, skin green, bald and bearded, holding the scepter symbolizing power, life, and stability. Upon closer examination, he appeared ever so slightly taller than every other pharaoh or god with whom he was represented. If one let one's imagination roam freely, one could detect a certain resemblance about the nose and chin that might remind one of the family members of White Walls.

Tetisheri, not a religious person, was nevertheless quite sure that this was strictly against the rules.

The temple itself, what she could see of it through the massive open doors at the back of the courtyard (there was of course no sight of the sanctuary or the sacred lake permitted to the common citizen), was dark and forbidding, with an altar and a statue of Ptah that even in gloomy outline looked massive.

Tetisheri thought of Euphrasia throwing open every part of the Temple of Seshat to all comers and smiled to herself. Euphrasia had never been easy to outmaneuver as the head of the palace school, either. Someone should have warned Natasen. That no one had spoke for itself.

The temple itself had few devotees present. Their lack of presence was wholly overshadowed by a great bustle of activity at the back, where a construction project displayed an ambition to double the size of the temple. It reminded her of too many areas in Alexandria, currently in the throes of repairing and rebuilding after the war.

"Lady?"

Tetisheri turned to behold a novice of Ptah, shaved bald, wearing a plain white shift and the amulet of his god. He proffered a tray full of more amulets. His smile was ingratiating. "Would you care to show your devotion to the divine Ptah?"

His other hand held a bowl with a few coins in it, and Tetisheri saw that she was expected to underwrite her fidelity. More as a way to keep the boy in conversation, she said, "Of course," and dropped a coin in his bowl, accepting one of the amulets in return. She pretended to admire it. "What a magnificent temple this is, and how lucky you are to serve in it."

He was thinner than a boy his age ought to be. His eyes had a hollow look to them and he was pale, as if he did not often get outdoors. "Thank you, lady. It is a great honor to serve as a brother of the Great God." This said without enthusiasm.

"How long have you been here?"

"Only a year, lady."

"Your parents must be very proud when they visit you in such a magnificent place."

He looked faintly shocked. "Oh no, lady. They don't visit. They are not allowed. When one pledges oneself unto the Great Temple, one forswears all other allegiances."

Great Temple, as if no other temple could be called Great. She kept her voice gentle. "Even family?"

He nodded. She saw the remnants of old bruising where his tunic shifted with the motion. "Do they live far from here?"

"A village some days up the river from here, lady. My family looks to the Nomarch of the Falcon."

"You will never see your family again?"

He looked at the tray he held. "Never, lady."

"Are there any sisters of Ptah?"

He seemed relieved at the change of subject. "Oh no, lady. The worship of Ptah is exclusive to men."

She affected to look sad at this news. "Well, I don't know—I'm sorry, what was your name again?"

"We leave our names behind when we enter the Temple, lady."

She gave him her very best smile. "But that wouldn't apply just between friends, surely? My name is Agnes."

He flushed a little and gave a nervous look around. "Well, just between friends then, lady, my name was Tabe."

"Brother!"

Tabe started and looked guilty. Tetisheri raised her head to see a priest bearing down upon them, disapproval writ large upon his countenance. "Be off about your duties, sir."

The boy cringed, muttered an apology, and scurried off.

Tetisheri, trying to look as meek and mild as was humanly possible for a modern-day woman of Alexandria, said in her softest voice, "The young acolyte was only selling me one of your amulets, brother."

He eyed it and her with suspicion. "We do not sell amulets here, sister," he said severely. "They are a gift of the Temple. If you wish to contribute to its upkeep and maintenance, of course that is entirely your choice."

"My mistake," Tetisheri said, hanging her head and hoping she looked properly chastised. "Is there no way for such a one as my humble self to serve?"

He unbent a fraction. "All are welcome within the embrace of Ptah, the god of power and life and stability, wherever and whoever and whatever—" he gave Tetisheri a dismissive glance "—form one takes in this world."

"As you say, brother."

"The blessings of the great god Ptah be upon you," he said, not sounding in the least as if he meant it.

She watched him march off, no doubt on the trail of other miscreants. A novice master for certain and, if she guessed correctly, one with a heavy arm for acolytes who strayed from the straight and narrow. She pitied young Tabe.

She looked down at the amulet she held in her hand. It was crudely made and only by an exercise of imagination could it be identified as Ptah. She reached in her purse for the amulet of Seshat given to her by Euphrasia. By comparison to the Ptah amulet, it was a veritable work of art.

She exchanged the amulet of Seshat for the one she had

recovered at the scene of Karis' death, and held it next to the amulet of Ptah she had received from the hands of Tabe.

They were nearly identical.

She spent the rest of the day drifting about the city. It was a glorious place, no doubt, albeit with an unmistakable patina of decay and decline. Barring the Temples of Seshat and Ptah, the other temples and public buildings looked ill-kempt and unloved. Friezes were crumbling, mosaics missing tiles, broken steps and columns made of stone and marble were braced with wood. The repairs had perhaps initially been meant to be temporary but they had been there long enough now to turn gray with age. She searched out the Temple of Bast, a small, graceful square of stone and marble at the north end of the city, and even it was shabby. She entered to make obeisance and found an unattended offering basket before the statue of the goddess, containing a few copper coins. She waited, but neither priestess nor novice appeared.

The population was not unaware of the city's decline. Over the course of the afternoon she watched no fewer than three families with all their possessions embark from the public dock en route to Alexandria.

She stayed away from the cafes and tavernas so as not to cross paths and purposes with Apollodorus, and moved instead into the markets, listening to the gossip between vendors and servants. The slaves were more reticent, understandably so, but on occasion they were careless enough to let slip some tidbit of information she could use to inform the mental picture she was drawing. She bargained for citrus in the garden market, where all the talk was of the coming festival, which included some snickering at how neatly the High Priestess of Seshat had circumvented the High Priest of Ptah's ambitions to take the lead in all things religious. Some spoke in his defense, pointing to the employment he was giving dozens of craftsmen in the remodeling of his temple. "He has increased the tax base of the city ten percent with that one project alone," said one shopkeeper with a prosperous waistline. "Alexandria gets all the public projects—and the public money—these days. Natasen brought one home."

There were many empty storefronts, the doors locked and barred and the signs removed, but she found a shop that catered to scribes where she purchased a sheaf of papyri and half a dozen styli, while exchanging the latest Alexandrian gossip with the proprietor. He was pleased to hear that she had come to Memphis to attend the Festival of Seshat. "The old king knew what he was about when he elevated the High Priestess to that office," he said. "She understands the balance between commerce and religion, and how one cannot exist without the other. And besides, anything that hinders the ambition of that jumped-up jackass in the Temple of Ptah is good news for all of us."

They were momentarily alone in his shop. "'Jumped-up jackass?'" Tetisheri said with an inviting smile.

"I could have said worse, lady, much worse." He glowered. "My sister's son was essentially kidnapped into service in that temple. Her only son! And now she can't see him or talk to him. He even had to give up his own name, can you imagine?" He snorted. "The only thing Natasen has to recommend him is that he is some distant relation of the House of White Walls, which, given the reputation of that branch of the family, is no recommendation at all. How did he come by the wealth he brought to the Temple of Ptah?" He snorted again. "We all know the answer to that."

"We do?"

"He was nothing more than a lowly scribe in his younger days, lady! Many's the time he came bowing and scraping into this very shop, pleading poverty and trying to talk me down in price for every scrap of papyrus and every pot of ink. And then, suddenly, pfft! He appears in the position of High Priest, with a brand new name. He would not have been able to manage that if he hadn't been backed by serious funding, and there is no possible way Timon would have given him the money, not in this life or the next."

Tetisheri wrinkled her brow. "But if Timon didn't—"

"Ah, lady, we all know which side of the family Natasen comes from, now don't we?" He winked at her.

"You say he reappeared with a new name?"

He snorted again and rolled his eyes. "Yes, with characteristic humility he chose to rename himself after a legendary king of Kush."

Tetisheri made an encouraging noise but another customer entered the shop at that moment and turned the proprietor's attention away.

She wandered into the neighborhood housing the building trade and found a garrulous woodworker whose workshop was empty of other customers and who was delighted at the prospect of selling her a clothes press decorated with hieroglyphics, engraved and painted in the old style. "Here for the festival, lady?" he said, beaming at her. "It promises to be quite the crush. I hope you already have lodgings? If not, my good wife's brother-in-law's son has an apartment at the back of his house, quite clean with a very reasonable rent, although you do have to share the necessary with the family—"

She would have to fill the imaginary clothes press with imaginary garments, of course, so Tetisheri found the market where the tailors and weavers plied their trades. A brilliant spill of silk attracted her attention and she threaded her way through the display outside into a cool, dim interior. The proprietor, a tall, thin woman in her thirties with perfectly coiffed hair and a brisk manner, was acceding deferentially to the requirements of a wealthy matron of a noble rank low enough that she had to keep reminding everyone of it. She was buying a trousseau for her daughter, a lovely girl with large, wondering eyes and smooth golden skin, at present dressed only in a thin linen shift as various garments were pulled over her head and pulled off again. It reminded Tetisheri of her household choosing her dress for the play.

"No, not that one, it makes her look fat," the mother said, tapping her chin with a bejeweled forefinger. "My husband would not see his favorite child gowned in such a way as it would emphasize all of her detriments and enhance none of her attributes."

The girl, who was slender as a lotus reed, blushed faintly and cast a sheepish look at the proprietor, who ignored her, and why not? She wasn't paying the bill.

"That pale peach, yes, that's a possibility. Hold it up to her face—yes, very nice. Can you have it made up by the wedding? A week and a day." An eyebrow went up. "Well, as I'm sure my husband would say, there are other dressmakers—yes, I thought so."

She was gracious in victory and paid half the cost up front, promising the remainder on delivery, and swept out of the shop very much in the manner she imagined one might were she wearing a royal cobra on her brow.

Once she and her entourage were safely out of earshot, the proprietor blew out a breath and gave Tetisheri an unexpected grin. "I was just about to sit down for a few moments and enjoy a cup of tea. Would you care to join me?"

"How very kind," Tetisheri just had time to say before she was whisked behind a hanging carpet to where two comfortable chairs were placed between piles of fabric in every weave, texture, and hue, a few of which Tetisheri thought she recognized as having traveled west in the hold of the *Hapi*. There was a small footstool, upon which the other woman immediately placed her feet. Her head fell back and she let out a long, luxurious groan. A maid appeared with a tray of tea and savory rolls.

"Thank you, Ciara, I can manage from here." She poured tea and handed Tetisheri a cup. "My name is Thaïs." She settled back in her chair, cradling a cup in her hands. "Now what, pray tell, may I do for the lady Tetisheri of House Nebenteru, master trader?"

Tetisheri blinked. "How—"

Thaïs laughed, choking a little over her tea. "In truth it is no mystery, lady. I was privileged to attend a reception at House Nebenteru in—May, was it? I suppose we will soon become accustomed to this new calendar of Caesar's but for the moment it is a pestilence upon my profession. I never know when I'm supposed to have delivered what dress to whom for which event." She regarded Tetisheri over the rim of her cup, eyes bright with merriment.

Tetisheri swallowed her surprise. "I am sorry I didn't recognize you, Thaïs, and it is pleased I am to meet you again."

The dressmaker waved a hand. "It is nothing. You were much occupied."

Tetisheri thought of the events surrounding that reception and what came after and was hard put not to say, "You have no idea." Instead she gave the dressmaker a polite and, she hoped, noncommittal smile and sipped her tea.

"What brings you to Memphis, lady? I probably cannot hope for another shipment of silks from Sinae this soon."

"I'm afraid not."

"But in the not too distant future, perhaps?"

Tetisheri replied with a noncommittal murmur and said, "As to what brings me to Memphis, why, what else but the festival?"

Thaïs brightened. "And has word of the festival spread as far as Alexandria, then? How wonderful!" She leaned forward confidentially. "This festival of the High Priestess' making was sorely needed, and here you are, proof positive that it is working!"

"Why sorely needed?"

Thaïs looked grave. "Memphis has been growing more and more moribund. I was born here, lady, and I have lived here all my life, but lately even I have begun to think of moving to Alexandria. When the throne moved there three centuries ago it was the beginning of a long decline in trade, only exacerbated by the building of the Nile Canal. The communities downriver of Memphis have disappeared, and Pellusium itself has become only a place to land and embark armies. If Memphis were a league north, we would be barely a memory. All our goods now come through the Port of Alexandria by way of the canal."

"You mean there is no longer any reason to come to Memphis."

"I'm afraid not, not unless one is of a religious turn of mind, and fewer and fewer are these days." Thaïs nibbled at a roll. "And while I applaud the High Priestess for the idea of the festival, I fear that it is a temporary measure only. An annual festival will bring in the tourists, yes, but only for a set period, and then they will leave again. There is nothing to keep them here."

"The building trade is doing well, however."

"Ah yes, the High Priest of Ptah and the effort to build a monument to his own ego and vanity." Thaïs waved a dismissive hand. "A short-term project. Once it is done, where do the architects, the builders, the craftsmen go?" She pointed to the northwest. "I'll tell you where. Alexandria."

"And you?"

Thaïs looked troubled. "This is my home, but… tell me, lady, do the gods Seshat and Ptah hold such sway in Alexandria?"

Tetisheri considered her answer carefully. "I would say no," she said. "Isis is much in favor at the moment—"

Thaïs snorted.

"—but truthfully, I would say that the Temple of Serapis has grown in popularity and following of late. Particularly by Romans. Not so much Alexandrians, or not at least until the Lady of the Two Lands began identifying him as Osiris, husband of Isis and father of Horus. Then of course—"

"Of course," Thaïs said dryly. "Is it true she has commanded that no depictions of any god shall appear with animal heads?"

Tetisheri shook her head. "That might have been her father, or even Lathyros." And Philo, she thought, remembering the last time she had been in the queen's brother's court, over-embellished as it was in the Greek pantheon, all of them represented in human form. "But yes, she is enforcing it."

"The Egyptians won't like it."

"She'll worry about that when they march on the city. In the meantime, the High Priest of Serapis has an honored place in her court." Tetisheri thought of the venerable Fuscus slipping and sliding through a puddle of horse urine not long since and repressed a grin.

"The question is, what has any of this to do with Herminia and her disappearance?"

She and Apollodorus were back on the *Nut*, comparing the intelligence they had gathered during their respective day in Memphis over dinner. In the sky above, the ship's namesake rose on high to silver the waters of River Nile while washing the stars away. The water lapped gently at the hull, and on shore the crew was sitting around a fire, eating and talking in low voices, their faces reflecting the flicker of the flames.

"If anything at all," Apollodorus said. "I didn't hear a whisper of her the entire day."

"Nor did I, other than what Euphrasia said about her being given to the Temple of Seshat as a baby."

"I don't remember Euphrasia. Remind me."

"She was the superintendent of the Royal School. She was gone before Auletes hired you." Tetisheri frowned. "Just before, I'd say. It was very sudden. One day she was there, overseeing classes and exercise and meals, and the next—"

She shrugged. "They didn't tell us where she had gone, either. I only found out later."

"You sound suspicious."

"Any sensible person was always suspicious of Auletes."

He laughed, the sound deep and rich and somehow enhanced by the deepening dark of the night. "I make my apologies."

"As you should." She couldn't hang on to her temper, though, and relaxed into a laugh. "The old man bore watching, always."

"He chose the right heir."

He chose the right mother for her, she thought.

Apollodorus crunched a chicken bone between his teeth and sucked out the marrow before tossing the pieces over the side. There was a sudden splash as something else with teeth took advantage of his leavings. "Do we return home tomorrow?"

She set down her plate and wiped her fingers, thinking. "Not yet. I have an ambition to see this festival, a day of it at least. I have a feeling—"

"What?"

She gave a frustrated shake of her head. "I don't know. There is something brewing, something beneath the surface of all this posturing and show."

"Do you think Natasen will do something to disrupt the festivities?"

"I'm sure he will try. I'm equally certain that Euphrasia has planned for it. No, there's something I heard today, or saw, but…" She shook her head. "Let me sleep on it."

He took her hand and kissed it. "Far be it from me to cut short a trip when I have all your attention to myself."

She couldn't stop the smile from spreading across her face. "Well. Not all of it."

"I'll take what I can get." He leaned down and kissed her lightly on the lips. "Let us see, then, what the morning brings."

The morning brought the arrival of Ptolemy XIV Philopator, arriving in style on his royal barge. With him was an entourage of minor lords and ladies, all of them Greeks, half a dozen Roman hangers-on, a company of dancers, an entire orchestra of flutes, sistrums, and drums, his military guard that Apollodorus had long stigmatized as pretty but inept, and slaves in a proportion to the rest of the party of two to one. The gods forbid any of Philo's guests had to don their own cloak.

Apollodorus raised an eyebrow. "Is there anyone left on Antirrhodos?"

Tetisheri shook her head, speechless.

A small boat with a trumpeter standing in the bow preceded the royal barge. He took his job seriously.

"Gods," Apollodorus said, "my ears."

At a signal from Tetisheri, Markos and his crew had vanished into the trees and she and Apollodorus remained in the shadow of the screens. If Philo, or more likely some more aware member of his party, recognized the *Nut* she wanted no one on board available to answer a hail.

Philo occupied the gilt throne in the rear of the ship, attended by slaves with fans made from entire tails of peacocks. Thin, petulant, unintelligent, ill-informed, vicious, amoral, and wholly in the sway of his even more corrupt councilors, in the three-hundred-year-old homicidal tradition of his family his sole ambition was to depose and murder his royal sister/wife/co-ruler. Cleopatra returned his lack of regard in full measure. They occupied the double throne only at the insistence of Julius Caesar, who had been determined to return Alexandria and Egypt to the status quo after the war so as not to interrupt the flow of grain to the Roman legions, so necessary to his future plans of a throne in the City of the Seven Hills.

What happened to Egypt, Alexandria, and the Ptolemy siblings after that was anyone's guess.

Philo was dressed and lavishly adorned in silver and gold. Not a casual visit, then. Apollodorus was amused. "Narcissus come down from Olympus. Was this what you were waiting for?"

Tetisheri drew back as Philo passed by, letting the screen drop back in place. "I don't think so," she said. "Did you see?"

"Linos? Standing behind the peacock fans? He looked like he was trying not to sneeze."

"No," she said. "Aurelius Cotta is among Philo's guests."

11

The public dock was crowded with boats landing festival-goers, but Markos' boatman was adept and managed to wriggle in between a nobleman's pleasure cruiser and a dinghy holding two entrepreneurial women who were determined to make the Festival of Seshat pay dividends that Euphrasia had not envisioned. They appeared to be enjoying some success.

"You have to respect the initiative," Apollodorus said, handing Tetisheri to shore.

Tetisheri found a vendor selling souvenirs and bought a gauze scarf dyed with the figure of Seshat. She wrapped it around her head and shoulders, shadowing her face. There was nothing to do to hide Apollodorus; he was too large and too recognizable, so they didn't try. No one was paying them much attention anyway.

Philo and company were disembarking at the dock of the Temple of Ptah and the process had gathered its own crowd, one prepared to cheer every foot that stepped ashore from the royal barge. Tetisheri took a quick headcount. "The High Priest must have turned out all the acolytes in the entire temple."

"If I'm not mistaken, the High Priest himself is here to greet the king."

A man standing next to him snorted. "Oh my, yes, His High Holiness never misses an opportunity to bask in reflected glory."

A priest and two novices standing nearby turned as one to glare at this impiety. The offender lifted his lip at them.

"Is the Nomarch here as well?"

The man snorted again. "Trust Timon not to attend any event where the High Priest is determined to grab all the attention."

Tetisheri elbowed forward so she could see.

Natasen occupied the exact geographical center of the very large dock, looking very different from the man Tetisheri had seen at the Odeum three days before. His tunic was made of the sheerest linen with the green kilt beneath showing through and he wore a green skullcap on his newly shaved head. He was holding the blue-and-gold staff of power, life, and stability.

"At least he didn't dye himself green," the man standing next to them said. The priests and novices glared again, but really Tetisheri could see his point. Natasen had got himself up to look every bit the Great God Ptah live and in person, and she was fairly certain that the only people allowed by custom and by law to dress as gods were the living gods who currently occupied the thrones of Egypt.

What would Philo think of all this? Hard to say. She would await events.

Which happened apace. The orchestra landed first, evidently to provide a musical accompaniment to the royal progress, which seemed like a good idea until one of the sistrum players tripped on the gunwale and fell overboard. Fortunately he was fished out before the current crushed him between hull and piling. He'd even managed to hang on to his instrument and took his place, dripping, in line and on the beat.

"I admire competence in any endeavor," Apollodorus said, trying not to laugh out loud. Their new friend had no such inhibitions and was roaring along with the rest of the crowd.

Mishap seemed to breed mishap, as one of the dancers essayed a leap from deck to dock. The crack of breaking bone made everyone wince. Several of the younger nobles had evidently been drinking since departing Alexandria and debarked singing a vulgar testament to the charms of the ladies who walked the docks of Alexandria of an evening. The best that could be said for it was that it rhymed. Half a dozen boys with bowls of coins ran down the gangway and began to hurl the coins by the fistful into the crowd without warning. "Ouch!" "Watch out!" "Do they have to throw them so hard?" "Shut up and grab that one! Next to your own right foot, idiot!"

Royal dignity really wasn't having its best week.

There was a brief pause in the proceedings as the High Priest and the crowd waited for the appearance of the king. Beads of sweat ran down Natasen's cheek. It could have been the increasing heat of the day creeping up on him. Or, Tetisheri thought, something else.

Something else was not long in making its appearance. Linos appeared at the head of the gangway and signaled the orchestra, which complied with an enthusiastic if off-key fanfare. Philo appeared, a slight figure glittering in silver and gold in the rays of the rising sun. His collar was magnificent, strands of gold, carnelian, and coral beads stretching from shoulder to shoulder, and his bracelets were so wide his arms seemed made of gold.

At that moment, almost as if it had been planned, the crowd parted to admit the entrance of a palanquin that looked carved from ivory, although it couldn't have been given there were only six men carrying it. It was attended by eight female novices in white, ankle-length linen tunics, wearing the amulets of Seshat on their breasts. They carried no instruments, and they didn't dance.

Natasen perforce stepped aside, otherwise he would have been trampled, and the palanquin swept over the carpet rolled out for the king's arrival and set itself down. Two of the novices stepped forward and extended their hands, and Euphrasia, the High Priestess of the Temple of Seshat in Memphis, rose from her chair and stepped lightly to the carpet. She bowed to Ptolemy XIV Philopator, and in a deep, sonorous voice that rolled over the crowd and across the river to the regatta of boats full of people waiting to disembark themselves, said, "The Temple of the Goddess Seshat bids you most welcome, Ptolemy Philopator, O Most High King of Alexandria and Egypt, Lord of the Two Lands, ruler of Upper and Lower Egypt."

He stared at her, still on the barge. One could only describe the expression on the royal countenance as nonplussed.

Linos, his chief counselor, looked enraged, and offered his arm to his lord and master. "The High Priest of Ptah awaits, O King." His voice, too, was loud enough to be heard by all.

Philo looked from Euphrasia to Linos and hesitated for only a moment. He laid one hand upon Linos' arm. "Then we must not keep the High Priest waiting." The treble voice broke on the words but they were as audible to everyone listening as had been Euphrasia's words.

Surely not, Tetisheri thought.

But yes, Philo and Linos strode down the gangway in lockstep, sweeping past the High Priestess of Seshat in grand style, but only because she had taken a graceful sidestep while managing to maintain her obeisance.

It was a direct and public snub to the most powerful High Priestess in all of Egypt, on the opening day of a festival held in honor of her goddess. The entire city of Memphis seemed to suck in its breath. The man standing next to Apollodorus had his mouth in a thin line and general displeasure was being voiced in a low mutter that rose from the crowd.

Natasen looked as if he'd just bitten into a lemon but

he performed his office as best he could, greeting the king with a long speech of welcome that had everyone shifting impatiently on their feet, and stepped back to allow Philo to lead the way into the Temple of Ptah for the glory and mysteries of the ceremonial blessings in store.

But the first impression was always the one that stuck, and the memory of the day and very probably the entire festival would be colored by this one moment.

Euphrasia regained the vertical before the royal backside disappeared, and a voice cried out from the crowd, "All hail the High Priestess of Seshat, the kind and gracious Euphrasia of Memphis!"

"Glory to Seshat!"

"Glory to the Temple!"

"Glory to the High Priestess!"

"She probably only had to pay the first one," Apollodorus said.

"Maybe not even him," Tetisheri said.

Euphrasia waited for the tumult to die down before bestowing on the assembled public a kindly and beneficent smile. "Welcome this first day of the Festival of Seshat, Our Lady of the Days! Eat, drink, and be merry this day and indeed all the days of our festival!"

She was swarmed with citizens holding up their children to be blessed. Boys as well as girls, Tetisheri noted. The sympathies of the crowd were solidly with Euphrasia. To a man, woman, and child they appeared determined to atone for the royal snub they had witnessed and would no doubt recount with embellishments over the entire ten days of the festival and beyond.

"Oh, well done," Apollodorus said under his breath.

Tetisheri couldn't stop the smile from spreading across her face. "Never, ever underestimate Euphrasia's ability to confound her enemies."

"No, indeed." They turned to see Aurelius Cotta, legate of Rome and Caesar's cousin, who bore the mark of defending him in battle as an angry scar across his face. One never doubted where his loyalties were. "A woman to be reckoned with. I look forward to meeting her." He hitched his toga and gave a slight bow. "Apollodorus, well met. I saw you from the barge. On the *Nut*, wasn't it? And while she is so enveloped in that shawl as to be unrecognizable, I must assume this is the lady Tetisheri of House Nebenteru, because who else would be on your arm?"

They retired to the nearest cafe, whose proprietor summarily ousted other customers to seat them at the largest table. Cotta's personal guard, Fulvio, took a nearby table and affected to be deaf. A tray of tea was brought, along with a heaping tray of sweet and savory delicacies which the three of them pretended to nibble so as not to offend the feelings of the proprietor.

"And what brings the two of you to Memphis?" Cotta

said. "Good tea." He raised his cup in tribute to their host, who nearly expired from delight.

Euphrasia was continuing her outreach among the citizens of Memphis, the population of which seemed to be accreting around her. It was almost as if she were waiting for something, Tetisheri thought, and realized she had spoken the words out loud.

"Like what?" Cotta said.

"Like that," Apollodorus said.

Cotta turned to look, and froze in place with his cup in midair. His dropped jaw and bulging eyes were all that Tetisheri could have wished for.

Philo's barge, the *Osiris*, was the height of luxury, a slim, streamlined, single-hulled pleasure craft some one hundred feet long, with ten oarsmen a side. There was a high, carved stern, a square, striped sail, and a figurehead at the bow carved in the shape of, appropriately, Osiris, crook, flail, double crown and all. It would turn heads in any marina.

The barge now approaching the dock would have turned every head in Athens or Rome, if Rome had had a waterfront. The twin-hulled, two-story *Thalamegos* made Philo's barge look like a dinghy. It was four hundred feet long, fifty feet wide, and seventy feet high. It had been built by the fourth Ptolemy a hundred years before and had recently seen service in Caesar's sightseeing trip up the Nile.

The *Thalamegos* had twenty oarsmen a side and they pulled with one will, moving with efficiency and rapidity to the extent that they seemed to be flying a little above the surface of the water. They showed every appearance of running right over the *Osiris* if it didn't manage to get out of the way first. The crew of the *Osiris* was alive to the danger and was at present scrambling to undock. The *Thalamegos'* sail master knew his business and the oars were shipped, the sail down, and the lines out and fastened before the *Osiris* had cleared the end of the way. The prow of the larger ship almost clipped the stern of the smaller, but not quite, and Tetisheri was sure that that, too, was deliberate.

And of course, in the stern of the *Thalamegos*, on a far larger and much more ornate throne, sat Cleopatra.

What could only be described as a shriek began at the dock and rippled out all over the city. There was a concerted rush of citizenry to the waterfront as the word spread, which would have warmed the cockles of Natasen's heart, if only everyone hadn't rushed out of the Temple of Ptah at the news, too.

Apollodorus leaned down to whisper in Tetisheri's ear. "Did you know she was coming?"

She shook her head. "But she did."

Apollodorus followed her gaze to where Euphrasia, attended on either side by white wings of demure novices, stood waiting on the carpet for the gangway to be lowered.

Aurelius Cotta got his mouth closed and set his tea down very carefully. "I don't think His Majesty was aware that the queen was attending the Festival of Seshat."

Tetisheri and Apollodorus exchanged a glance. "I believe

you may be right," Apollodorus said with a gravity that nearly upset Tetisheri's already precarious composure.

Cleopatra rose and moved forward to stand at the top of the gangway. In direct contrast to her brother, she was dressed much as she had been at the theater: simply, in white linen with a plain gold circlet on her brow. The only evidence of her rank was the amulet at her breast, that of Isis and Horus, mother and child.

Speaking of which, she looked over her shoulder and beckoned. Iras appeared with Caesarion in her arms, who took a dive for his mother as soon as he saw her. Cleopatra caught him deftly, laughing, and the still-growing crowd laughed along delightedly at this evidence of their commonality.

"Did you see him, the little rascal?"

"Our queen will have her hands full with that one!"

"I remember when my boy was just about that age!"

Someone started a ragged cheer that gathered in strength and force, only abating when Cleopatra shifted her son to one arm and raised her other hand, palm out, suing for silence and making the gesture somehow less of a command and more of a plea from one mother to every mother and father here assembled. "Thank you all so much for your warm welcome, my good people! It warms my heart to hear how you hold us in yours." She beamed around the crowd with indiscriminate affection, and dropped her voice to a confidential level, though not so low that every word couldn't be perfectly heard—and repeated—afterward. "But I have only just arrived, and while I hope to introduce as many of you as possible to your future king—" Caesarion, displaying a diplomatic acumen well beyond his years, took this moment to burp, loudly, and the crowd laughed again, even more delightedly "—first we must pay our respects to the High Priestess of the Temple of Seshat."

This went over very well indeed. Euphrasia and all eight of her novices promptly bowed as Cleopatra and Caesarion descended the gangway. Euphrasia raised her head to bask in the royal smile, whereupon her queen extended her free hand to help the High Priestess to stand up again, a signal mark of high honor. "It is so good to see you again, Euphrasia. Thank you so much for the invitation to your festival." She looked around and said merrily, "It looks very well attended! We are a little tardy. Are you quite sure the city has enough room left over for our poor selves?"

Another wild cheer and multiple shouted assurances. Euphrasia waited for a break in the din and said with a broad smile, "We'll try to make room for you, Majesty."

The queen chuckled, the baby gurgled, and the crowd laughed along.

The queen waited for a diminution in the uproar. Really, Ninos could take lessons in stagecraft from Cleopatra. "But first, Euphrasia, I ask the blessing of the Goddess for myself, my son, and for all the good people of Egypt."

"Most joyously do I give it, Majesty." Euphrasia placed her hands on their heads and raised her face to the sky. "Seshat, scribe of the arts and sciences, the counter and keeper of days, mother, sister, and handmaiden to her rulers, I beg your blessing on Cleopatra Philopator, Seventh of Her Name, and Ptolemy Caesarion, First of His Name, on this festival day, as witnessed by the good people of the city of Memphis."

And in one of those strokes of fortune that Cleopatra seemed prone to at many key points in her life, at that moment the sun shifted in the heavens to cast down a ray of sunshine directly on the three of them so that they literally glowed as with some inner divine light.

After which Euphrasia saw the two into her palanquin— for the first time Tetisheri noticed there was a second seat facing the first—and they progressed slowly down the quay in the direction of the Temple of Seshat. It took them right in front of the Temple of Ptah, where stood Natasen and Philo, looking equally infuriated.

Four men, each bearing only a gladius at their hip, disembarked from the *Thalamegos* and fell into place equidistantly around the palanquin. "Apollodorus, is that—"

Apollodorus pressed her arm in warning. "They are on call, as I am," he said in a voice meant only for her ears.

Isidorus, Castus, Crixus, and Dubnorix, Apollodorus' partners in the Five Soldiers, passed in review before them, alert to any threat from the crowd that might menace their queen and her heir. Although Is did wink at Tetisheri.

Cleopatra and Euphrasia continued serenely upon their way. The citizens of Memphis fell in behind, ready to follow wherever they led.

12

"Report."

It was evening and they had been summoned to the Temple of Seshat to attend on the queen. They sat in the private garden where Tetisheri had first met with Euphrasia. Dinner, a series of small servings of various delicious delicacies from around the Middle Sea. A choice of sweet wine, chilled fruit juice, or small beer. Euphrasia, Tetisheri noted, was comfortable enough with Cleopatra that she didn't feel the need to drive her cooks to any extraordinary efforts.

Afterward, Euphrasia claimed some small errand and left the three of them, Tetisheri, Apollodorus, and Cleopatra, sitting in her garden. The queen had spent the morning in the temple making offerings and sending up prayers and the afternoon in progress around the city, pausing long enough at every park, square, market, and temple to exchange greetings with the citizens of Memphis. Timon, Nomarch of the White Walls, still damp from washing the dirt of his fields from his person, appeared in great haste to make his bow. The excitement at the queen's appearance remained high throughout the day, especially since she had come to Memphis with a very small retinue that taxed the hospitality only of the inhabitants of the Temple of Seshat, and at that not very much.

Unlike Philo. The last Tetisheri had seen of Linos was him in confabulation with a group of the city fathers. "Accommodations in the city have been booked for months in advance—" "If only you'd let us know sooner—" "I don't know how we are going to feed so many unexpected mouths—"

Serve him right, Tetisheri thought now, biting at first tentatively and then more enthusiastically into a Gallian speciality consisting of sautéed duck liver on a thick slice of toasted bread rubbed with garlic.

Apollodorus recounted their findings thus far. "What we agree we both find most odd is the appearance on the scene of Natasen. So far as I can discover, he was one of the many indigent relatives born to the wrong side of the White Walls blanket. He was certainly unknown to the ranks of the priests of Ptah until some two years ago. He was named High Priest by acclamation at their last conclave. Immediately thereafter, construction on the new addition to the Temple began."

"He brought money with him," Cleopatra said.

Apollodorus nodded. "That is the obvious conclusion."

Tetisheri recounted the conversation with the man in the stationery store. "And Euphrasia tells me that the demonizing of the Temple of Seshat began the first time she turned him down for a loan."

"He's recruiting."

"And what better way to discredit the Temple of Seshat in the eyes of patrons, parents, and potential acolytes."

They sat in silence for a few moments, eating, drinking, and thinking.

Tetisheri wiped her fingers and fixed her queen with a beady eye. "Majesty, we were sent here in hopes of finding news of our lost thespian. We have found neither her nor news of her, and I cannot help but notice that all our talk thus far has been of dueling temples. Has our mission changed?"

Cleopatra rose to her feet and took a turn about the little garden, stopping to sniff at a rose or two. The sky above her looked like a length of silk dyed with lapis, with a lavish interweaving of bits of silver that glittered with the movement of the heavens. Nut was rising in the east. Across the river the triangular hulks of the Great Pyramids loomed against the remnants of the light left behind by the sunset. The Egyptian engineers of the past had built to last.

And those tombs, too, had been robbed almost as soon as the final stone had been laid in place.

Cleopatra turned abruptly. "I suspect that the two investigations are one and the same."

Tetisheri and Apollodorus looked at each other and back at the queen. "How so, Majesty?"

She sat down again and gave them a faint smile. "I don't know. It is a feeling only, I admit." She settled back more comfortably on the couch. "And I admit equally that Philo appearing to be hand in glove with Natasen leads me to be even more suspicious, and that doesn't come from a feeling, that comes from experience."

As the poisonous little brat was at the heart or at least on the periphery of nearly every adverse event since Caesar had named him his sister's co-ruler, Tetisheri was inclined to agree. However. "A feeling is not proof."

"No, or I wouldn't need the two of you." A crease appeared between the royal brows. "I went to see the statue of Seshat."

"The one Heron gave Herminia?"

"Yes. We are agreed, Matan and I, that it must be from a very old tomb, and recently found, too, or it would be known to him."

"Did you speak to Heron, Majesty, to inquire as to its provenance?"

Cleopatra seemed to ponder her answer. "No," she said slowly. "Not yet."

"Because he is the son of White Walls, one of our richest, most powerful, and most influential nomarchs?"

Cleopatra gave Tetisheri an expressionless look. Tetisheri, unintimidated, raised an eyebrow.

Apollodorus grinned in an inappropriately unservile manner. "If the kinglet is involved, we will find it out, Majesty. For the moment, we have various lines of inquiry to follow. I suspect it would greatly increase our understanding if we found out how much Natasen brought with him to the Temple of Ptah."

"And where he got it from in the first place," Tetisheri said.

All three of them turned as one to look at the now almost indiscernible bulks of the three pyramids.

"We know where it came from," Cleopatra said softly.

Her companions did not disagree.

Their boatman was waiting at the temple moorage. In silence they climbed in and in silence made the journey back to the *Nut*.

"Bed?"

Tetisheri shook her head. "I'm not sleepy."

"Nor am I." He rummaged around and found a small amphora which proved to be small beer. He poured it into two cups and pulled the chairs forward to the edge of the sleeping platform, where they took their seats. The moon, higher now, lit both pyramids and river to the extent that their outlines took on wavering shapes in the water.

"What do you know about tomb robbing, Apollodorus?"

"I know what everyone knows, that most of the tombs of old from the lowliest merchant to the wealthiest pharaoh were broken into before the prayers for the dead ended. You can see the evidence everywhere in the Royal Palace and in the homes of the wealthy all around the Middle Sea."

"Natasen must have found one intact."

"Perhaps. Or perhaps the kinglet is financing this nonsense

as a way of sticking yet another pin into his sister's behind just to see how high he can make her jump."

They sat in silence for a moment. Then Tetisheri said, "Heron is a son of the Nomarch of the White Walls."

"Yes."

"And he gave Herminia a statue of Seshat that, according to Matan, is very old and beyond price."

"He thinks so." She saw where he was going with this. "But Heron is a legitimate son of the house, where Natasen is merely a son of a branch of the family the legitimate house does everything in its power to isolate and ignore. It's difficult to imagine Natasen, a son disdained and dismissed all of his life, gifting Heron, a son of White Walls himself, with so priceless an artifact. The jealousy and resentment must be overwhelming. Although—" She hesitated.

"What?"

"Heron was seated with the rest of Natasen's priests at the Odeum on Sunday."

"Huh." Apollodorus was silent for a moment. "So you don't think Heron would rob tombs?"

"He doesn't have to. He comes from a family wealthy enough to subsidize his life and work in Alexandria. He's the second son, so he's not on the hook to inherit."

"You said he offered for Herminia. Perhaps he needs the extra money to support a wife."

She frowned into the darkness, thinking of what Heron had said of his father's opinion of the acting profession. "Perhaps. But look, if Natasen robbed a tomb to finance his way into a position of power at the Temple of Ptah, and is now trying to consolidate that power by increasing the size of both the temple and its followers by fair means or foul, why on earth would he give away something so valuable as that statue?"

"Well."

"What?"

"It is a statue of Seshat, after all. If it had been a statue of Ptah, the story might be different."

"Good point. But still, why wouldn't he sell it and put it where the money would do him the most good?"

"If Heron helped him rob it, the statue could have been part of Heron's share."

"I talked to Pati about that. Heron's discipline is engineering."

"Ah. I see. Which discipline includes surveying, which would be useful in locating old ruins."

"Yes. But why would Heron go along with it?"

"For the fun of it?"

She stared at him. He shrugged. "Engineers are smart people." He nodded at the pyramids. "Proof positive. Maybe he is one of those who likes to prove to himself just how clever he is."

She smiled a little. "Like smugglers."

"And pirates."

They sat in silence for a few moments. "Have you ever seen them close up?"

He glanced at the pyramids. "A few times. You?"

"No. Only from the river. I was with—

Apollodorus' hand gripped her arm. She became aware that the boat had dipped beneath them, as if someone had stepped on board. She drew in a breath to call out to Markos, for surely that's who it must be, but Apollodorus' hand tightened in warning and she stilled.

The next thing she knew he was on his feet and he had picked her up in his arms and tossed her over the side.

Too shocked to scream, she hit the water with a mighty splash. The water closed over her head. She recovered and kicked for the surface. When she emerged, gulping for air, she heard the thud of flesh on flesh and the clang of blade on blade. She sucked air into her lungs and shouted at the top of her voice, "Markos! Markos! MARKOS!"

The watch must have dozed off because it took several more tries before the crew's camp began to stir. She struck out strongly for the bank and was just hauling herself out of the water when someone managed to kindle torches from the embers of the crew's fire pit and lead a charge toward the *Nut*.

Her palla had been lost in the river. She wrung out her hair and tunic as best she could, checked to see that the Eye of Isis was still secure round her neck, and met them at the landing. As the light from the torches reached the deck of the boat, it revealed one motionless body lying across a hatch cover and a bloodied Apollodorus holding two assailants at bay. One of them held a kilij and the other a mambele with a viciously sharp backward spike. As she watched,

Apollodorus sucked in his stomach just in time to avoid a vivisection by the mambele. He brought his gladius down with brutal force. It met the bronze of the mambele with a loud "Clang!" that jarred it from its owner's hands, just in time to parry a downward swing of the curved blade of the kilij, long enough for Apollodorus to open up the gut of the man with the mambele.

"What are you waiting for!" Tetisheri shoved Markos forward a step. "Go help him!"

Her shout broke the spell that had seemed to hold the rescue party frozen in place. They swarmed over the side with a roar. The man with the kilij cast a wild glance at them and began backing toward the river side of the boat.

"Take him alive, Markos!" Apollodorus' shout was loud but calm. "I want at least one of them alive!"

But his opponent dropped his weapon and dived over the side. Everyone rushed to the railing to see only a spreading circle of ripples.

Apollodorus took a long, deep breath and let it out slowly. In the flickering light of the torches it was obvious that there was much he wanted to say, none of it complimentary.

Markos kissed the amulet of Sobek he wore round his neck. "May he be food for the crocodiles."

The man with the gut wound was dead. The first man down was also dead, having bled out from a deep cut from belt to shoulder. "Move the bodies on shore. Search them thoroughly. Look for any clue that might tell us who sent them."

The fire in the pit was rekindled. The flames leapt high and illuminated the two bodies laid out nearby. The kilij and the mambele were set to one side along with the weapon of the first fallen man, which was a standard legionnaire spatha, the traditional weapon of the Roman cavalry. The weapons looked well cared for but bore no personal markings that might have been traced back to an individual or an organization. Like a court, for example.

Or a temple.

Markos grimaced. "Representative of the cross-cultural character of cutthroats for hire but not much else."

"The man who went over the side was wearing patterned leggings." Tetisheri picked up the kilij. "Persian, do you think?"

"Most likely." Apollodorus stooped for the helmet one of the men had been wearing. "Close fitting, with earflaps."

"A Greek helmet doesn't make him Greek," Markos said.

Apollodorus glanced at Tetisheri. "Nor a Persian sword and dress a Persian."

The crew stripped the bodies down to the skin. One was pale and fair and looked as if he had come from the northernmost reaches of Europe. The other was definitely Numidian, black-skinned and long-limbed. Pockets and purses were turned out. Neither carried any clue to their identities but both purses were heavy with coin. Markos held one up. "Denarius."

"All of them?"

Markos sorted through the shining pile. He looked up and

nodded, his expression sober. "A few other coins mixed in, but mostly, yes."

"Older coins?"

Markos nodded. "What anyone carries with them for pocket change."

Blood trickled from a slash on Apollodorus' forehead and he swiped at it impatiently. "Anything else?"

"No."

"No amulets, even?"

"No."

"How many denarii?"

"A hundred each."

"Give me one of the denarii and share the rest out among your crew."

Markos dropped the coin into Apollodorus' outstretched hand and gathered up the rest. He rose to his feet. "You are generous, sir, and I thank you." He raised his voice. "Who had the watch?"

"Cleitus, sir."

"Cleitus, you receive no portion."

Crestfallen but resigned, the young man hung his head. "Yes, sir."

"Back to camp, everyone."

Apollodorus waited until the men were out of earshot. "Markos?"

"Sir?"

"Don't be too hard on him." Apollodorus nudged one of the corpses with his toe. "These were professionals."

"Well, and so are we professionals, sir."

"Professional sailors, I grant you, Markos."

"Whose jobs regularly require them to stand watch, sir. Preferably while awake." Markos departed.

Tetisheri became aware of her hair still dripping down her back. She gathered it up into a single length and wrung it out again. "Who wants to kill us?"

"Who doesn't?"

"Roman coin."

"Which proves nothing." He swiped again angrily at the blood trickling down his face.

"Sit down and let me clean that for you."

"It's fine."

"Sit. Down."

He complied, grumbling.

Markos had left one of the torches behind and by its guttering light she found water and a clean cloth and dressed the cut. It was shallow and had stopped bleeding by the time she was done but she bound his brow with a clean pad anyway.

"Will I still be beautiful enough to love in the morning?"

She set water and cloth aside and looked at him in the light of the torch, hands on her waist. "What the hell was that?"

"What?"

"You know very well what!" She heard her voice begin to rise and controlled herself with an effort, not wanting to further alarm the crew on shore. "You threw me over the side!"

"You were in my way."

"What!"

He was suddenly on his feet, face thrust into hers. "You. Were. In. My. Way. We were in the dark and under attack in very close quarters. You weren't armed and I know you can swim."

"I could have—"

He kissed her. He tasted of blood and sweat and rage. His arms were so tight around her that she couldn't breathe. With a faint sense of shock she realized her arms were around his neck and she was kissing him as fiercely as he was her. His hands moved roughly over her, leaving her skin singing in their wake. Somehow the top of her dress was down around her waist and his mouth was on her breast, biting and sucking, while his hands cupped her hips and ground her against him. He was fully aroused and apparently determined to make her aware of that fact.

He pulled back and gulped for air. "If this isn't what you want say no now."

His voice was rough with an edgy need she had never heard before. In answer her hand slid up his neck to pull his mouth back down to hers.

He growled deep in his throat and picked her up to wrap her legs around his waist. They were moving and she dimly understood that they were now in the little house in the stern and he was blundering around trying to get the screens down.

"Leave them," someone said, and she barely recognized the distant words as her own. "It's dark. No one will see."

He didn't need telling twice and the next thing she knew she was flat on her back on the bed she had shared with this same man, who for these past two nights might as well have been her brother. There was nothing brotherly about him now. Her still-damp tunic was pulled down her hips and tossed over his shoulder to hit something with a sodden splat. His mouth returned to her breast and encountered the Eye and with a muttered imprecation that was yanked over her head and there was a clatter when it landed somewhere else.

His hands, his lips were everywhere, and she gave an involuntary murmur of discomfort when the linen of his tunic chafed the delicate skin between her thighs. He muttered something impatient and for an agonizing moment was gone from her. When he returned he was all smooth, hard skin and warm, sure hands. It was the most natural thing in the world for her legs to wrap around him again and when he thrust inside her it was as if they were both coming home.

"Oh!"

He stilled. In a voice she barely recognized, he said, "Are you all right?"

"No, it's just—"

"What?"

Her hips moved involuntarily, taking him impossibly deeper inside her. He groaned and let his forehead rest on hers.

"Can't I move?"

He heard the uncertainty in her voice and with a shaken

laugh he said, "You can do anything you want. I just don't know how long I'm going to be able to last."

In the darkness her hands found his head and she slid her hands into his hair. "Show me," she whispered against his lips. "Show me everything."

13

Warm lips feathered her skin and she shivered, swimming up from a deep, luxurious darkness. A voice, deep, low, insistent. "Wake up, Sheri."

She stretched, aware of various aches and pains and equally aware of a sense of well-being that seemed to ripple up from an inexhaustible well deep inside. Her eyes fluttered open. The sky was just beginning to lighten, enough so she could see Apollodorus up on one elbow, smiling down at her. He looked sleepy and rumpled and very, very smug.

She couldn't stop the laugh that tumbled out. "You look very pleased with yourself this morning, sir."

"No less than you do, lady." He brushed the hair out of her eyes and leaned down to kiss her. She made an anticipatory sound and he drew back. "Behave. I can hear the crew stirring onshore and unless you want to brighten the rest of their day by appearing before them in the altogether—"

She raised her head and saw that sometime in the night he had lowered the screens. "No danger of that."

"Yes, although we have our own work, too." He kissed her again. "But first, let me show you something I found the evening we arrived."

They dressed quickly and spent a few panic-stricken moments searching for the Eye, which was discovered under an oarsman's thwart quite halfway down the length of the boat. "Thank all the gods it didn't go over the side," Tetisheri said. She found the extra palla she had packed and tossed it around her shoulders. He rearranged its folds, stealing a kiss as he did so. She smiled up at him.

"What?"

Still smiling, she drew a finger down the side of his face. "Thank you."

"I think that's my line."

"We'll share, then."

"We'll share." He kissed her again and took her hand. "Come with me."

He paused to speak briefly to the sentry. The bodies of last night's assailants had disappeared. He led her to a thick stand of lotus in full flower which hid a small boat and two oars.

It was a magical time of day, or perhaps it was just this day at this time. The stars faded out one by one as Ra neared the horizon. Birds were calling in muted tones. The oars left tiny eddies on the surface of the river. A farmer early to his labors raised his head from weeding his grain as they passed and only smiled. Neither spoke, both perhaps fearing to break the spell.

As they approached the outskirts of the city Apollodorus put them ashore at a small, unattended landing. He led

Tetisheri up the gangway and across the dirt street to a square building that stood astride a small stream. Smoke came from the chimney of an attached building.

Apollodorus tried the door. It opened and they stepped inside. An old man in an abbreviated tunic scurried forward. "I'm sorry, sir, we're not open yet—" His eyes flicked toward Tetisheri and away again.

Coins changed hands. "And if you could lock the door and make sure we are left undisturbed for an hour, the same again."

"Of course, sir." The attendant melted away.

Apollodorus turned to see Tetisheri regarding him with a smile. "What?"

"Your staff work is amazing." She kissed him.

They left their clothing in the apodyterium—they were alone in the baths so no need to bribe the attendant to watch their belongings—and went naked into the tepidarium. It was too early for the water in the deep, rectangular pool to be hot but it was warm enough. They swam lazily for a while and then Apollodorus came for her with a gleam in his eye that she had no trouble recognizing. Now she knew what to expect and there was no apprehension, only anticipation. This morning he was determined to take his time and watched her with intent eyes as he brought her to pleasure with his hands and his mouth before he lifted her over the edge of the pool and settled between her legs. "All right?" he said, his voice barely a murmur.

"You asked me that last night."

"I was not quite in control of myself last night. I was afraid I'd hurt you."

She flexed her hips, searching for him. "Never. You have never hurt me, Apollodorus, and you never will. Now stop talking."

A smothered laugh, and then he came into her with a rush, all that love and pride and strength seated deep inside her as if he were at long last home.

They emerged from the baths to find the other four partners in the Five Soldiers waiting. Tetisheri, damp and laughing, straightened and took an involuntary step to one side. Apollodorus promptly pulled her back beneath his arm. "Good morning, gentlemen," he said, his tone a clear warning in and of itself.

Crixus winced a little and shook his head at Castus when he opened his mouth to say something. Dubnorix, on the other hand, grinned at them openly. "We were beginning to wonder if you'd drowned."

Isidorus nodded vigorously. "We tried to get inside to check on your welfare, but the door was locked. Why ever would the door to a public bath be locked?"

"That puzzled me, too," Castus said in spite of another meaningful look from Crixus. "Especially when we heard all those sounds."

Crixus gave in to temptation. "Those were odd. Almost as if a wild animal had gotten inside."

"We feared you were at risk," Is said solemnly.

"We are overjoyed to find that you weren't," Dub said.

Tetisheri could feel her face burning.

Apollodorus sounded bored. "Don't you people have a queen to guard?"

"She's gone back to Alexandria. She left early this morning while you were, ah, otherwise occupied."

Tetisheri's head came up and Apollodorus sounded less bored. "She left you behind?"

Is nodded. "Our orders are to assist you in your current investigation and then to travel back with you aboard the *Nut*."

Tetisheri looked at Apollodorus. "You sent someone to tell her of last night's attack."

"I did."

"She sent for us this morning and told us where you were moored and Markos told us where you were." Is waggled his eyebrows with a salacious grin that made him look even more like the goat god Pan than he did already.

"More manpower will definitely help," Apollodorus said, raising an eyebrow at Tetisheri. "Especially for what you have in mind."

She nodded. "Shall we go tonight then?"

"No reason to delay. Only lets the bad guys get another step ahead of us."

Crixus brightened. "Oooh, there are bad guys? Will there be swordplay?"

"There was last night. We've got a boat to take us back to the *Nut*. You?"

"Yes, yes, of course we have a boat. Lead on."

"Will there be food? I missed my breakfast. Our queen has no care for an empty belly."

"Get in the boat, Crixus."

The four of them inspected the bodies of the would-be assassins, which Markos' crew had concealed in a thicket of salt cedar. "I know this one from somewhere," Is said, nudging the Numidian's leg.

"He looks familiar to me, too," Dub said, his usual weary sophisticate facade displaced by the professional armsman.

"I thought so, too," Apollodorus said, surprising Tetisheri.

"You didn't say so last night."

His mouth quirked up at one corner. "I had other things on my mind last night." Before they could all start teasing her again he said to the others, "But I can't place him."

"Did he serve with us?" Castus said.

"In Spain? I don't think so. I would have remembered the mambele."

"We all would have," Dubnorix said with feeling. "Perhaps he was at the ludus in Sicily?"

"No." Is was definite. "I remember everyone we took on there and he wasn't one of them."

"In Alexandria, then. A student at the gymnasium."

Everyone shook their heads.

"A third man got away."

"Got away? You must be slowing down in your old age, Apollodorus."

A smile pulled at one side of Apollodorus' mouth. "Anytime you want to test that theory, Dub."

Dub grinned. "Zeus and all his women, no, I thank you. I like all my body parts right where they are." He sobered. "Who sent them?"

Apollodorus looked at Tetisheri, who shrugged. "Someone in the city must have noticed we were asking questions."

Is nudged the Numidian with his toe again. "And didn't like it. A lot."

Apollodorus absently raised a hand to touch the wound on his forehead. He looked down at Tetisheri again. "Natasen?"

"Philo?"

"Cotta?" he said. "Or someone else?"

"And why?" she said. "What does someone think we're getting too close to?"

"Herminia, perhaps?"

"Perhaps," she said, frowning. "Or perhaps word has reached the thieves who found the hoard that the statue of Seshat came from that the statue has been found, and they are willing to kill to keep it secret."

Is perked up. "Hoard?"

"Markos, could you please bring something to break our fast?"

"At once, lady."

Apollodorus led them aboard the *Nut* and they disposed themselves around the deck in front of the little house. Is glanced inside at the rumpled bed and the various articles of clothing tossed here and there and nudged Dub. There might have been a few subdued snickers, which Tetisheri ignored with such shreds of dignity as remained to her.

Apollodorus let the screens down without comment. The only grownup in the bunch.

"Tell the tale, Tetisheri."

By the time food and drink had been delivered everyone present was in possession of all the facts at her disposal.

"And then last night you were attacked by sellswords," Castus said.

"Yes." Tetisheri glanced involuntarily where the blood had stained the deck. Markos had had it scrubbed clean in their absence by Cleitus, who had failed them in his duty as sentry. She had a feeling that Cleitus would be performing most of the dirty work on board the *Nut* for the foreseeable future.

It was much easier to focus on Cleitus, alive and in disgrace, than on the roll call of the dead so far in this inquiry. Which was now three, beginning with Karis.

Dub touched her shoulder lightly. His smile was kind, but then Dub and indeed all five men knew more than she ever would about being haunted by their dead. "So you must be on the right track."

"Yes, but what is that track?" Apollodorus said. "And what does Herminia's disappearance have to do with any of it?"

"The queen seems certain that everything is somehow connected to the friction between the temples."

Is leaned back, thinking. "Herminia disappears. No one, not even her lover, or even more importantly her stage manager, knows where she is or what happened to her. Her lover gives her a gift connected to Seshat that Matan is sure is the product of the robbing of a very old tomb, which naturally led you to Memphis, the home of the Temple of Seshat as well as the center of the tomb-robbing industry. You discover that Natasen appeared two years ago with a full treasury in hand, which we think buys his way into his office, and begins recruiting and rebuilding.

"The High Priestess of Seshat perceives this to be an assault on her own institution, which perception has some merit to anyone with even half a working brain. She works to undermine his activities with the creation of a festival and the attendance of the queen, which certainly trumps Natasen's king."

At that moment Philo's boat appeared out of the morning mist as if they had summoned it, rowers laboring under the application of a whip liberally applied by the sailmaster. It whisked by without pausing, but Tetisheri saw Aurelius Cotta standing at the rail and was certain she felt his eyes upon her.

"You two show up asking nosy questions of all and sundry and are almost immediately attacked." Is nodded at where the bodies lay. "They were well fed and their weapons expensive and well cared for. They weren't amateurs."

"Which means they weren't cheap," Castus said.

"Which eliminates those who couldn't afford them," Crixus said.

"The problem is that all the big players we've encountered could afford them," Tetisheri said glumly. "Natasen seems to have money to burn, however he got it. We all know of Philo as someone determined to throw good money after bad."

"Cotta," Apollodorus said.

Apollodorus was only too ready to blame Rome for every evil deed committed in the known world. "Too much of a stretch. Besides, you know Caesar told him to stay out of internal affairs, and he mostly does."

"He practically interrogated us over what we were doing here yesterday morning."

"He is a prying little busybody, I'll give him that, but he's here to guard Rome's interests. For the life of me I can't see how a missing singer..." Her voice trailed off.

"What?" Is said. "A missing singer what?"

"Let me think for a moment." She stood up, catching her balance on Apollodorus' shoulder when the *Nut* rocked a little beneath her feet. He felt warm and hard beneath her fingers and her hand might have lingered. He met her eyes and the affection and knowledge she saw there made her forget for a moment what she was doing. A marked clearing of throats reminded her and she dropped her hand and threaded her way out of the circle without meeting anyone's eyes.

She walked to the bow of the *Nut* and stared out at the river. The boat was moored with the bow pointing south. The post-inundation current was mild and the hull of the *Nut* left only the smallest riffle in the water as it traveled downstream.

Two boys balanced themselves on the edges of a punt prefatory to throwing out a net. It fell in a perfect circle with barely a splash. The boys waited for a few moments, watching the ripples spreading across the surface of the water as the net sank. At some unseen signal they both began hauling on a line threaded through each edge of the net to draw it into a purse. It surfaced at the side of the punt, containing a wriggling mass of perch and tilapia and catfish, scales flashing in the morning sun. An exultant laugh and a spate of chatter carried clearly across to Tetisheri.

She didn't hear it. One could say she didn't even see the boys, although she was staring right at them with knit brows.

Herminia, disappeared.

Karis, murdered.

The amulet of Ptah inadvertently left behind.

Heron, more resentful than heartbroken that Herminia had turned him down. Who had given Herminia a gift beyond price. Or said he had.

Natasen, a member of the branch of a family whose income would never bear close examination. A man who put ambition above all, but what was it he wanted? To be the most powerful of all the high priests and priestesses? In a country that was rapidly leaving the old gods behind?

Euphrasia. Who put on a good show, an excellent show, really, but it was obvious that she was under a great deal of strain. More, Tetisheri thought, than could be explained away by her temple coming under increasing competition from a faded god.

Auletes. Had he not been born to the House of Ptolemy, he would have fit right in with Ninos' musicians on stage at the Odeum. Not a very wise man, Auletes, but one with a lively sense of self-preservation.

Cleopatra, his daughter, and inarguably his favorite child. *Find Herminia, my Eye.*

The two young fishermen were on their way to market when she stirred at last. She turned and walked swiftly back to the stern of the boat, where the Five Soldiers were conversing in low tones. They looked up when they saw her coming and fell silent.

"I believe the queen was right. In fact, it is all connected. The missing actor. The scholar's wooing. The rare statue. Natasen and his mysterious fortune."

She looked around the circle of men, these fast friends of hers, the most reliable, most stalwart, most capable men on the Middle Sea. The most trusted of Cleopatra of House Ptolemy, and of Tetisheri of House Nebenteru.

The queen knew, too, she realized.

"Knew what, too?" Apollodorus said.

She met his eyes. "I know what happened to Herminia. I

know why she was kidnapped, and I believe she is here, in Memphis."

Crixus rose to his feet, his hand on the hilt of his gladius. "Then let's go get her. I heard the lass sing once in concert. Never mind the queen's orders, I'd rescue her on the strength of that performance alone."

She shook her head. "They won't harm her." A grim smile which none of them understood. "They won't dare. No." She raised a hand to still Crixus' protest. "We'll get her, but we must do something else first." She clasped her hands together. "You won't like it. I don't like it. But we must have proof before we can make any accusation."

She looked at them. "We'll need ropes."

Castus shrugged and grabbed one of the mooring lines wrapped around a cleat. "Plenty to hand right here."

"Too heavy. It has to be strong enough to support our weight individually, but light enough for us to carry easily."

"In what length?"

She thought back to those days in the classroom and the interminable lectures on ancient burial practices. "Fifty feet. To be sure." She shook her head. "And in the end we may not need it."

"Better to have it and not need it than need it and not have it."

His voice steadied her and she gave Apollodorus a small smile. "I don't know how far we'll have to carry them. Can you go into town and—discreetly, mind you—find something appropriate? Two lengths, to be sure."

"What else?" Apollodorus said.

"Torches, and some small lamps, with extra oil. Flint and tinder. Flasks for water. A shovel, one for each of us. And packs for each of us, as light in weight as is possible."

"Shovels. Torches. Packs." Dubnorix glanced at Apollodorus. "Were you so energetic you scrambled the girl's brains last night?"

Apollodorus reached out a casual hand and shoved Dub over the side.

"And," Tetisheri said, looking down at her sandals, "I'm going to need some boots. And a sturdier tunic."

Dubnorix appeared on the riverbank and squelched up the gangway, sluicing water from his face with both hands and flicking the residue at Apollodorus. "I'm happy to offer my services there," he said cheerfully. "Because you and I know, my dear Tetisheri, that of all these louts I have by far the best taste in clothes."

Tetisheri laughed. "I'll manage, Dub, thanks all the same."

Crixus looked at Is. "Castus and I will be on the rope. There's bound to be a decent chandler somewhere on the waterfront."

"Torches and flint," Is said. "Lamps and oil."

"Don't forget the flasks," Tetisheri said, meeting his eyes. "It will be very thirsty work."

Is stared at her, and then looked over her shoulder at the outlines of the Great Pyramids looming up from the western horizon. "Oh merciful Jupiter, girl. Say it isn't so."

"Say what isn't so?"

Is broke off his gaze and slapped Castus on the back, propelling him to the gangway. "Come along, gentlemen. We have work to do."

"Everyone meet back here when your tasks are completed," Tetisheri said, raising her voice. "I'll leave orders for a good, solid supper. We're going to need it. We won't leave until well after dark."

"Of course we won't," Is said without turning around. "Because stumbling around in the dark is mostly what we do even in broad daylight." He grabbed Dubnorix by the arm and pulled him away along with the other two.

"We're really going to do this, Tetisheri?"

"We are."

"Do you have any idea where to start looking?"

She turned to look up at him. "An idea? Yes. Am I sure we can find it? No. But if we do, Apollodorus, if we do find it, we find everything."

"Including Herminia?"

"Indirectly, yes."

"Well." He sighed. "At least that will make her happy."

He wasn't referring to Herminia. Tetisheri bared her teeth in a grin that was more like a snarl. "Won't it, just. And maybe this one time the guilty might actually be punished."

He looked grave. "Be careful what you wish for, Tetisheri."

"What do you mean?"

He shook his head. "What are we doing while everyone else is out shopping?"

"Clothes and boots for me first."

"And then?"

"And then perhaps a little discreet surveillance."

14

Making her purchases was quickly done, along with another palla for Tetisheri and a cloak for Apollodorus. Enveloped in these admittedly minimal disguises, they made for the Temple of Ptah, Tetisheri one step in the rear as befit a traditional wife and Apollodorus ignoring her presence as befit a traditional husband.

They mounted the terrace at a leisurely pace, and were immediately intercepted by an eager young acolyte who was made happy by an exchange of coin for one of the cheap amulets in his basket, and left largely to themselves thereafter. The temple was but lightly attended, even as the happy hubbub of the Festival of Seshat went on in the streets outside. They were of course not allowed any farther than the hypostyle, but Apollodorus spent long moments in front of the door leading into the temple, all outward awe at the great statue of Ptah he could barely see from there.

After an amount of time they estimated to be sufficient to demonstrate unquestioning adoration they drifted outside, looking up to gawk at the great frieze that ran under the roofline. It depicted a vast procession of pharaohs, from Menes to Ptolemy XII, attended always by Ptah and his scepter. There was scaffolding, at present unoccupied, beneath the next square of stucco to Auletes' right, where by rights the figures of Cleopatra and Philo should be. The stucco square looked new and hung slightly askew, as if it had been changed out recently and hastily. "Who was up there, do you think?" Tetisheri said in a low voice.

"Berenice, Arsinoë, Theo," Apollodorus said, equally low-voiced. "Any, or all sequentially. I would expect the High Priest of Ptah, whoever he is at any time, makes a point of steering by the prevailing political winds."

"I wonder if the queen saw that while she was here."

"If she didn't see it you can be sure someone told her about it."

They continued to stroll down the side of the temple, pausing to point and exclaim at this or that architectural feature along the way, until they rounded the corner and beheld the addition to the temple currently under construction.

The new foundation was massive, looking fully equal in size to the existing temple. Two courses of granite blocks, which were of a size commensurate with the ones used to construct the monoliths across the river (and indeed might well have been harvested from there) were already in place and a third had been completed halfway. The ends of the two long walls abutted the back of the existing temple.

Inside the stone courses the footings for a double row

of columns were rising, and outside the walls a scene of concentrated energy took place in an unceasing cacophony of cutting, shaping, and polishing. Harried foremen hopped like fleas from project to project, accompanied by the full-voiced and unimaginative oaths that seemed required in any current construction taking place within the borders of Egypt and Alexandria. Sweating slaves with hammers and chisels cringed beneath both a freely applied lash and the heat of the sun as Ra drove his chariot ever higher into the sky.

They weren't the only people who had come to look upon this great endeavor. It was a crowd swelled by festival-goers, and there was something of a holiday air among the spectators. Hawkers of souvenirs and food vendors circulated, goods displayed on shoulder-held trays and in display cases on neck straps. They seemed to be doing an excellent business. The irony would not be lost upon Euphrasia.

"Sheri. Look."

Natasen stood deep in consultation with a tall, thin man clutching an armful of elongated scrolls to his dusty tunic. "The High Priest himself. That must be his builder." The second man had scant hair and a pained expression that indicated chronic intestinal issues. Either that or Natasen was telling him something he didn't want to hear, which was what any builder could expect in conversation with the commissioner of a project of this size. Even at this distance they could see that Natasen was talking right over everything the man was trying to say in reply.

As Tetisheri and Apollodorus watched, the two men were

interrupted by a third: large, armed, and sporting a bruised face with eyes so swollen it was a wonder he could see out of them. The wielder of the kilij.

"Ah yes," Apollodorus said in a satisfied tone. "That looks like my work."

The third man tapped the High Priest's shoulder. Natasen looked around angrily but the expression faded when he saw who it was. The man whispered in the High Priest's ear. Natasen listened intently, his expression darkening, and without taking leave of his builder set off for the back entrance to the temple, a much smaller and plainer set of double doors than graced the western portal. Before entering, Natasen paused momentarily to raise a hand and sketch a vague blessing in the direction of the onlookers, who responded with an equally vague cheer, which couldn't have pleased him. In fairness, most of them probably didn't know who he was. Which would have galled him even more, had he been able to imagine that could possibly be the case.

At that last thought she pulled herself up. She'd seen the man twice, and now three times, in her life. Most of her opinion of him was colored by what she had heard from Euphrasia, who was not herself entirely to be relied upon in this matter, as well as, admittedly, the performance she had seen yesterday in front of the temple, and gossip in the marketplace. Holding someone in contempt could lead one into underestimating their intelligence and their abilities, and she wasn't ready to do either. Not yet.

They returned to the massive frontage of the temple, so tall and so splendid, reflecting palely in the waters of the Nile. They entered again into the hypostyle and revisited all their favorite paintings on wall and column.

"What are we looking for?" Apollodorus said.

"Not what, who," Tetisheri said. "This is about the same time I saw him when I—Yes, and here he comes."

Tabe, the acolyte who had greeted her upon her first visit, approached them. He looked pale and strained, and he limped as he walked. "Sir, lady, welcome to the temple." His words sounded more mechanical than fervent.

"Tabe, well met this day." Tetisheri said, pushing back her cowl enough to show the boy her face.

If he had been pale before, now he went white at her words. He swallowed convulsively and looked around to see if anyone was watching. Thanks to the few people present their conversation was relatively private, but the boy was trembling enough to make the hem of his tunic shake. "L-l-lady, I—"

"Surely you remember me," she said with a reproachful smile it took a good deal of self control to maintain. "You welcomed me to the temple only a day ago, and we agreed we were friends." She parted the edges of the palla so he could see the amulet he had given her.

His face cleared a little. Surely no one could punish him for talking to her when the evidence of his devotion to duty was right there on her breast. "Of course I remember," he said, not very truthfully, "but lady, I'm sure I told you, we don't use our own names here."

"Remember, Tabe," she said, dropping her voice to a conspiratorial whisper, "names only among friends. I am Agnes, remember, and look!" She indicated Apollodorus as if he were a divine manifestation of a god himself. "I have brought my husband, Polycarp, with me today. He is eager to hear what you have to say, and wonders if he might have an amulet of his very own."

She touched his shoulder, a light touch only. He flinched away as if she had hit him. The rage building beneath her breastbone threatened to explode through it, and only Apollodorus' warning grip on her arm stopped it. "You're hurt, Tabe," she said as gently as she could.

His eyes darted to the left and right. "No, no, no, lady, I'm fine."

"You can barely stand upright. Has someone abused you? The master who dragged you away that morning?"

His eyes filled with sudden tears. He did his best to blink them away. "They all do, lady. It is part of our life here."

"Do you want to leave this place, Tabe?"

Apollodorus cleared his throat in a marked manner. She ignored him. "If you want to leave, you can. We will help you."

"I just want to go home." His voice trembled and despite his best efforts the tears spilled down his cheeks.

"Then home you shall go," Tetisheri said. She relieved him of his tray and set it down next to the wall. "Come with us."

"They won't let me go."

"It's not up to them."

Apollodorus whipped off his cloak and draped it around the boy's thin shoulders, hiding his acolyte's tunic. The cloak was so long it dragged on the floor behind him. Tetisheri took his hand in hers and Apollodorus took up station on his other side. Together the three of them walked slowly toward the great doors. They were almost there when another acolyte trod on the hem of Apollodorus' cloak, halting Tabe and nearly pulling him over backwards. It left his head and one shoulder bare.

Casting a look over her shoulder Tetisheri saw priests and acolytes converging on them, and wished for the first time that the Great Temple were crowded with the devout. She put an arm around the boy's waist and urged him forward. As she and Tabe crossed through the doorway Apollodorus turned and stopped on the threshold, one hand resting casually on his gladius. His other pulled his cloak free of Tabe's shoulder. He wrapped it around his arm in a practiced movement that would have looked familiar to anyone who had ever seen service in the legions. Or the inside of an arena.

"No," he said.

It would be unkind to say that their pursuers skidded to a halt, but they did stop. Those few inside the hypostyle saw something worth their attention was happening and turned to look and whisper among themselves.

Tetisheri stopped halfway down the stairs. Tabe was tucked against her and she draped her palla over his head, letting him hide there in the safety of the dark. He burrowed in, trembling.

She would get him away from this place if she died for it.

"Gentlemen," Apollodorus said. His voice was pitched for their ears only. "You are attracting attention. Shall we inform our audience of exactly what is going on here? I'm fine with that if you are."

"Return our property!"

"Property? Then we should call your acolytes by their true name. Slaves."

"All are here by their own assent and of their own accord." An older man thrust out from the crowd, the master who had harried Tabe back to his duty during her first visit to the temple. Tabe moaned at the sound of his voice.

"I am delighted to hear it. Then by his own assent and accord one of your number is leaving." Apollodorus' voice hardened. "Stand down, gentlemen. Let's not make a scene."

The priest looked around and indeed found himself the cynosure of many pairs of eyes. His fists clenched, but he jerked his head and the boys and men in the white robes began melting back inside. He himself stood glaring at Apollodorus for a long moment, just to show he wasn't intimidated by the big man with the gladius, before he, too, fell back.

Apollodorus turned and without hurrying made his way down the stairs of the temple. Tetisheri urged Tabe into step between them and they walked down the quay together.

"Polycarp?" Apollodorus said. "Really?"

Markos had a rudimentary kit of medical supplies that contained arnica and willow bark. Tetisheri dosed Tabe with the latter and applied the arnica topically to the bruises revealed when she stripped him down. He protested only half-heartedly, partly, she thought, because one and possibly two of his ribs might be broken or at least cracked. His body was one continuous, massive bruise.

"Did you received this beating because you spoke to me?" she said.

Apollodorus gave her a sharp look.

"They've been beating me since I got there," the boy said. "They beat all of us all the time."

"Why?"

"To frighten the demons out of us so that we may serve Ptah with pure hearts."

His response had the sound of rote teaching. She wrapped his ribs with a length of gauze and pulled it in tight. He gasped. "I'm sorry. You need the support to heal properly."

His smile was wavering but sincere. "I've felt worse, lady."

Apollodorus fetched a cup of thick soup from the crew's fireside. The boy only sipped at it, displaying nothing like a ten-year-old's usually voracious appetite. Tetisheri suspected it hurt his chest to swallow.

"Where is your village, Tabe?" Tetisheri said.

He shook his head, weariness making him look far older

than his years. "I know I said I wanted to go home, lady, and it's true, but I can't go back there."

"Why not?"

"I have too many brothers and sisters. My father can't feed us all. That was why when the priest of Ptah came through, looking for acolytes—" He dropped his eyes.

"It seemed such a good chance to provide for one of his sons."

"Yes." Tabe's voice was very small.

"Well, and so it would seem to any responsible parent." She tucked the medicines and the gauze back into the wooden box in which they were stored. "You told me yesterday it was only boys the priests of Ptah recruit?"

Apollodorus looked up at the carefully casual note in her voice, but the boy didn't notice. "No. That's what they tell us to say, but they take girls, too, sometimes. They took a girl from my village. But I never saw her again after they brought us to Memphis. They say…" He reddened and ducked his head.

"What do they say, Tabe?"

"The older boys, the ones almost through their novitiate." His head was still bent and his voice had sunk to a shamed whisper. "The priests tell them that they will be rewarded when they take their final vows."

"With one of the girls."

He cringed at her tone. "I never saw it myself, lady. But the older boys talk of nothing else and we can't help overhearing. We sleep in the same dormitory."

"I see." Tetisheri was silent for a moment. "Do you know where the girls are lodged?"

"Apart from us, lady, is all I know. But it can't be far. We see them when they come back, the new priests. They are always back before curfew."

"Did you ever see a girl brought into the temple? Recently, perhaps? Say in the past week?"

He hunched a shoulder.

"It's important, or I wouldn't ask."

An eye gleamed up at her from the crook of his arm. "It's why you brought me out of there, isn't it?"

She took a deep breath. "Partly. But only partly, Tabe. I wouldn't have left a dog behind if I had found him there in your condition."

He gave a laugh that was nearly a sob. "There are so many more like me, lady. Why me?"

"Because you spoke to me. Because you gave me the gift of your name."

There was a long pause. Tetisheri waited, conscious of the presence of Apollodorus at her shoulder, still and silent, trusting her to elicit the information they needed.

"I saw them bring someone in five nights ago, lady." The boy's voice was muffled. "They were carrying her between them, two men I recognized as priests, although they weren't dressed in temple tunics. She was wrapped like a mummy in a cloak, so I never saw her face. But I could tell she was a girl, because, well—"

"Yes," Tetisheri said. She let her hand rest on his shoulder. "Tabe, would you go home if you could?"

He sat up involuntarily, pressing a hand to his bound ribs with a hiss of pain. "I told you, I can't—"

"Tabe." She cupped his cheek. "If it were possible for you to go home, would you want to?"

The longing was clear in his eyes. It was all she needed to see.

15

They gathered back at the Nut that evening as the sun was setting behind the pyramids. The great triangular shapes cast shadows that grew ever longer and more foreboding with the oncoming darkness, until it felt as if the flow of the Nile itself was in their shadow.

"How long?"

"First hour, I think. Or midnight? We want all the workers home and tucked up in their beds."

"What about guards?"

Tetisheri gave her purse a shake.

"Ah," Is said, nodding his head. "The usual."

They ate heartily of a thick bean stew, scooped up with flat bread and washed down with small beer. "Nap if you can," Tetisheri said as they cleared away their cups and bowls. "It's going to be a long night."

The four men had pitched a tent for themselves on shore. Tabe was wrapped in Apollodorus' cloak and lay deeply asleep between two thwarts. He had resisted every attempt to convince him to spend the night on shore.

Apollodorus joined Tetisheri on the bed in the little cabin. "He's afraid to lose sight of you. Afraid this will have been only a dream." He slid an arm around her waist and gathered her to him, her back to his front.

She settled against him with a sigh, his warmth and strength a barrier against the terrors of the night in store. "He will never wake up from this dream if I have anything to say about it."

They lay in silence for a moment. "Do you have any idea where to begin looking?"

She answered his question with one of her own. "Do you know where most of the children of the population of this nome are apprenticed?" She didn't wait for him to answer. "Most of them are apprenticed to the funerary services in some capacity. Stonecutters and bricklayers. Painters and sculptors and carvers and jewelers. Embalmers and priests. Entombing the dead as befits their rank is second only to farming as an industry in the Nome of the White Walls. There are still plenty of nobles and priests and merchants who follow the traditional ways, or will bow to family members who insist they do. Heron, apart by choice, is an anomaly in his family. Natasen, outcast by birth, is not."

She looked across the river. "Cleopatra has good reason not to speak out publicly against the practice, no matter how irritating she might find it in private."

"Has she started building her own tomb yet?"

She elbowed him and was rewarded with a grunt that turned into a smothered chuckle. "At the moment she's spending every drachma she has on rebuilding the city and recruiting and training an army. And I think she wishes more of her more prominent citizens would invest their savings in similar endeavors, rather than in ensuring they see themselves into the next life with more treasure than they had in this one." She sighed. "But she understands that four thousand years of tradition does not change course in a moment, so..."

"When you said you'd visited Memphis before—"

"Yes. The nomarch insisted we visit his family's tombs, there to admire such a hive of industry, employment, and tax revenue."

"And so long as she gets her share—"

"Yes."

"Do you want a tomb, Tetisheri? Inscribed with hieroglyphics extolling your beauty and virtues and good works, with a relief sculpture of Anubis welcoming you into the afterlife?"

"I'd rather my last remaining friend carry me out into the desert and bury me deep in the sand, leaving no marker behind, than I would have a hundred slaves slowly starve building and decorating a tomb for my body to rot inside."

A brief, startled silence. "You've seen mummies. Your body doesn't really rot."

"Desiccate, then." She raised her head for another look at the pyramids. The dark had at last swallowed them whole. The only remaining indicator of their existence was the triangular-shaped wedges of darkness where they blanked out the stars. "Herodotus tells a story of Cheops, the pharaoh who built the largest of those monstrosities we all bow down to with such reverence. He ran out of money, says the great historian, so he prostituted his daughter and finished construction on the proceeds."

"Nothing honorable in that."

"Or humane. But she was tough, that girl. She agreed to it, to the sale of her body for money at her dear father's behest, and added only one condition. That every man who had her, gift her with one stone for her own pyramid."

"Did it work?"

"He says the center pyramid is hers."

"Some comfort there."

"On the contrary. The woman went to her grave knowing beyond any doubt that she held no dominion over her own body. That she could be bought and sold like a camel or a wedge of soft cheese." She shuddered. "A commodity to be sold by her own father, the man tasked by man and god to protect her and defend her."

"So," Apollodorus said after a moment. "No tomb for you, then."

"No."

"And if we have children?"

She was still for so long he said, "Tetisheri? Are you still awake?"

"Do you want children?"

"If you do."

She twisted her neck to glare up at him. "Don't be so damn deferential. I asked you what you want."

"Hush, you'll wake the boy." He gathered her close again and nuzzled his nose into her neck. "If you will and when you will, Tetisheri."

"Should we—"

"Should we what?" But there was a smile in his voice.

She swallowed. "Should we marry?"

"Why, Tetisheri, is this a proposal?" He laughed when, infuriated, she struggled to free herself from his arms. Not very hard, though. "I will speak to Nebenteru on our return."

"A small ceremony, Apollodorus. Family and friends only."

"Well," he said, "you can try for that. But somehow I have the feeling that your household will want a parade to mark the occasion."

She looked once more in the direction of the granite behemoths whose bulk stained the western sky black. "All these wonderful plans are predicated on the supposition that we survive the night."

"Oh, that."

"Yes, that." Her eyes still on the Pyramids, she said, "White Walls tomb-robbers specialize in lesser tombs, not pharaohs, not even nobles or priests, but merchants, scribes, craftsmen, wealthy farmers."

"Those tombs are worth the effort?"

"Pharaohs never saw their tombs, being focused solely on the outfitting of their own. An old scribe told me once that the result was that the tombs of the artists and craftspeople, while smaller in size, were decorated and furnished even more lavishly and beautifully than the tombs of their masters."

He chuckled. "That's one in the eye for the old pharaohs, then. Good for them."

She tried to lie quietly but she couldn't settle, so great was her dread of what lay ahead. She twitched and twisted and turned, snarling the blanket between her legs, unable to keep still, until Apollodorus had had enough and pulled her against him again. His hands slid up to cup her breasts. Memories of the previous night and that morning flooded her senses and scoured her mind clear of anything except the man holding her, of one hand sliding down between her legs, causing her to arch against him in involuntary arousal.

His breath was warm against her neck. "I would like to make love to you, Tetisheri. On the off chance that it's our last time."

Her voice had a languorous, throaty sound she barely recognized as her own. "When you put it like that…" She was already tilting her head back so he didn't have to work too hard. "But we'll wake the boy."

His teeth closed over the pulse at the base of her neck and she shivered. "We'll be very, very quiet."

And they were, removing only the necessary amount of clothing and taking each caress exquisitely, tantalizingly slowly. At the end her body bowed in a taut arch of pleasure and he had to cover her mouth with his hand when she would have cried out. The marks of her teeth were still there the next day.

A touch on her shoulder was enough to rouse her from an uneasy sleep. There were rustling movements nearby, and she got to her feet to feel around for the boots and cloak she had left ready to hand. Her eyes were adjusting to the dark by the time she stepped down to the deck, enough to make out Apollodorus with his arms full of boy move past her to deposit him on the bed. He tucked the blanket around him and stood looking down for a moment before he turned. His teeth flashed and his voice was the merest whisper in her eyes. "I give you good morning, Tetisheri."

She gave a muffled snort in reply but she could not stop the thrill that ran over her body at the sound of his voice. "Are we ready?"

"The others are already waiting for us."

Tetisheri looked over the side of the *Nut* facing the river to see a narrow fishing boat, with Is in the bow and Cas in the stern, both of them with one hand on the *Nut*'s railing. Tetisheri made to climb over and found herself instead being raised into the air and handed off to Crix, who set her gently on her feet. Dub pressed her down onto a thwart as Apollodorus slipped soundlessly over the side after her. The boat dipped beneath his weight.

Still in silence, Is and Cas pushed off. Dub and Crix produced paddles and slipped them noiselessly into the water. The remnants of moonlight washed the horizon in a silver glow, ceding supremacy to the stars, which glittered like diamonds set into a dome of silvered onyx.

She had noticed it before on long voyages, that there was something extra given to those who looked at the stars from the water, even if the water was only a river. On a night such as this, one felt that the gods were watching over them, Isis and Osiris and Horus, Seshat, yes, and even Ptah.

The nudge of the bow into the mud and reeds of the opposite shore brought her back into her body. She saw that two posts had been newly driven into the bank to provide a secure moorage. Packs were passed from boat to bank. Once everyone was ashore they donned them.

They had only traveled the width of the Nile and yet somehow the pyramids seemed twice as high and ten times as forbidding.

"We're a bit down the bank from the landing. It should be deserted at this time of night."

"Except for the guards." No one seemed overly disturbed at the prospect.

The five men and Tetisheri ghosted up through the tall grass, papyrus by its spicy scent, emerging some time later without sound on the cleared area that fronted the dock driven into the bank. Here was where the artisans and craftsmen and -women who lived in the city of Memphis landed each morning to go to work. There was a guard shack with a guard inside it. His snores shook the roof's thatch with every exhale.

Tetisheri, relieved not to be adding to the body count, turned to face west. The path between the landing and the plateau was wide and well trodden and in places even paved over with flat stone. The Nile had changed course many times over the past four millennia. Each time Egyptian engineers had restored river access to the limestone plateau which supported not only the three pyramids but a village housing slaves and freedmen who couldn't afford Memphis rents, plus multiple necropoli and an extensive industrial area that provided work space and materials for the stonework, carving, painting, engraving, embalming, and the sheer muscle power it took for the massive amount of labor that went into assuring an afterlife commensurate with one's status in the here and now.

In the daylight hours it was a hive of activity. At night there were supposed to be guards to make sure that no one took advantage of the dark hours to diminish the dead's afterlife standard of living. If the dock guard was any example, there was a good chance they would pass through unnoticed.

She took a deep breath and let it out slowly.

"Ready?"

The single word spoken in that low, imperturbable voice steadied her. "Yes."

"Is, up front. Cas, on our rear. Crix, Dub, with us."

They passed silently down the path, over small bridges

spanning drainage ditches, around what had been a port a thousand years before and was now only a swamp infested with crocodiles and the occasional and even more deadly hippopotamus, through fields of papyrus and lotus and beans and grain that appeared whenever the river changed course to leave rich layers of silt behind.

In the distance a dog howled, or perhaps it was a wolf. She was less afraid of it than of what lay ahead.

The surface beneath their feet changed, became more hard packed. The first buildings coalesced out of the night. These were the small dwellings made of dried mud that housed those who lived where they worked.

Apollodorus called in Is and Cas. "Where now?"

Her voice was barely above a whisper. "Left and south. Sokar is especially favored by the White Walls tomb-robbers."

"How do you know this?"

"It is generally known."

"Then why haven't they been stopped?"

"The Ptolemies don't care so long as they get their share of the take. It's only when they think they are being cheated that they get irritable."

"Sokar is where you think we'll find it?"

"It is at least where we should look. We may find nothing at all."

"In which case we'll be home in time for breakfast," Is said. Even his whisper sounded cheerful.

"Why didn't we dock farther up the river?" Dub, sounding a little irritated. Dub was never one for the country.

"Because the landing there is much better guarded. We have a better chance of going undetected approaching from the north."

The path was narrower now, less traveled and more overgrown. There were no bridges fording the various streams and ditches, and Cas had a fright from a crocodile that gave a half-hearted snap of massive jaws in his direction. Otherwise the distance between the two necropoli were covered swiftly and for the most part silently.

They paused where the vegetation ended and the sand began. "Are there guards stationed among the tombs?"

"I don't know."

"Is."

Is dropped his pack and disappeared into the gloom. The rest of them shook the sand out of their boots and quenched their thirst with gulps of water.

Crixus blew on his hands. "It's cold."

"Sun's been down a while, and it is Tybi," Castus said.

"What do we call it now? The new name?"

"October, I think."

"October. Octavo? Eighth? But isn't this the tenth month?"

"It was the eighth month by the old calendar." Castus was a bit of a pedant. "The Roman one, not the Greek one or the Egyptian one."

Crixus shook his head and muttered something to himself.

"I brought some meat rolls."

"Good man."

They ate and felt better for it. Is rematerialized. "Two

guards. Both asleep. Give me one of those rolls, you greedy bastard."

"Did you find them that way?"

Is's chuckle was muffled by a mouthful of dolmas but perfectly audible. Apollodorus sighed. "What happens when they wake up?"

Is drained a flask and burped. "They won't until dawn or until their boss shows up, in which case he will find them smelling of small beer, with empty cups in their hands."

"Well done. Tetisheri?"

"Around to the north side, where the newest discoveries were made. Or the ones that were reported to the queen were."

They donned their packs and struck out again. They gave the guard station a wide berth just in case and spent the next half hour stumbling through and into the corners of flat roofs built so long ago they were now level with the sand. Here was a section of broken stairs made of polished granite, there a portico with no roof and only a single standing column remaining of all its former glory.

"A doorway." Castus made a disgusted sound. "It's like they put up a sign. "'Rob me! Please, please, rob me!'"

Crixus agreed with him. "And oh please, let me make it as easy for you as I can!"

"Quiet."

As they progressed through the necropolis, the tombs deteriorated, both in architecture and material, until they left the granite and marble behind for edifices or parts thereof made first of brick and then of dried mud, like the huts they had first encountered. "Everything old is new again," Is said.

Where the sand seemed at last to take over, Tetisheri called a halt. They took a rest and drank more water. Just finding a tomb to rob was thirsty work. "Spread out," she said. "So far as your fingertips can touch the fingertips of the man next to you and no farther. Walk slowly, keeping pace with each other, back in the direction from which we came."

"How long?"

"As long as it takes, or until the dawn chases us back across the river."

Grumble. But they did as she told them.

Working with professionals was such a delight.

16

It was sheer drudgery, wading through thick sand in the dark. The first hour was enlivened only by Dub stumbling over a sleeping snake. It went skittering away into the darkness before they could identify how poisonous it was, and a good thing, too. Later Castus tripped over the corner of the cornice belonging to a tomb and fell heavily, which did not go unnoticed by his comrades. Subsequent excavation proved it had been separated over time from its parent building and was connected to nothing but more sand.

Further commentary ensued.

"Keep going," Tetisheri said.

They did.

More time passed interminably. Tetisheri's thighs were burning when Crixus said, "Tetisheri? I don't think this is quite what you're looking for, but…"

They marked their positions with sticks and bits of broken stone and followed the dim light to where Crix had lit one of their small lamps.

It was the body of a man.

They excavated the dead man from his sand shroud and Dub and Crix rolled him face up. "Well, he didn't die a natural death."

The dead man's skull had been impacted by something long and rounded. It had left an enduring impression of itself behind.

"The handle of a shovel, perhaps?"

"The shaft of a spear?"

"At least he's been out here long enough that he doesn't smell."

"How long, do you think?" Tetisheri said.

Is shook his head and Apollodorus shrugged. "It's cold enough to see our breath tonight. Is this the first night it's been this cold?"

"We could ask one of the guards, I suppose." Dub, very dry.

Apollodorus grunted. "At most a year. More like two."

He raised his head and Tetisheri could feel him looking in her direction. It had been two years ago that Natasen had reinvented himself as a priest of the Temple of Ptah.

"They didn't bury him very deep," Crix said. "His arm was sticking out of the sand. It's what tripped me."

Apollodorus squatted down. "Plain tunic, old but—" He pointed at a neat patch. "Someone took care of his clothing. Most likely married."

"Hard calluses on his hands," Is said. "Dirt under his fingernails."

"Look at his arms and shoulders." Cas raised the tunic to the body's hips. "Thighs, calves. Takes a lot of heavy, repetitive lifting to build that kind of muscle."

"Thick soles on his sandals. Low quality leather and lacing. Mended more than once and a new hole starting."

There was a momentary silence. "Poor bastard," Dub said. "Just trying to improve his fortunes."

"He had a partner," Tetisheri said. "And it's likely they found something."

They looked at her and she spread her hands. "Why else was he killed in a necropolis known to be a prime target of the wrong side of the White Walls family for generations?"

"Or one of the White Walls tomb-robbers might have caught him in the act."

"Or said tomb robber might have brought him along for brute labor." She looked around. "In which case, it won't be far."

"What won't be?" Dub, sounding thoroughly exasperated.

"The tomb they were robbing."

"Some people sure are slow," Cas said.

They found it shortly thereafter. An attempt had been made to bury the entrance, which only served to attract their attention. A section of suspiciously flat sand turned out to be the intact roof of a portico, this one made of brick. They dug down in the direction of the entrance and found a sheet of wood laid up against it. After that, even Dub dug with a will. There was, Tetisheri reflected, an element of the little boy in every grown man who thrilled at the thought of buried treasure.

She would be happy if they didn't find any more bodies.

The wooden barricade was removed with difficulty, and without further ado Tetisheri wrapped her cloak more firmly around her and sat down at the top of the pile of sand that now stood before the twin columns framing the doorway.

"Tetisheri—"

She ignored Apollodorus and pushed off with her hands.

"Tetisheri."

She slid forward a bit. She tried again, pushing harder this time. She gave a third, hard shove and began to slide forward, continuing to gather speed as she whisked beneath the portico and through the door and kept on sliding until her feet thumped into something hard.

"Sheri!"

Apollodorus' voice was a hollow echo behind her. "I'm all right. I'm in the antechamber. Come down and don't forget the lamps. It's blacker in here than it is out there."

A hiss of cloth on sand. She scrambled out of Apollodorus' way in time. Is was right behind him. She heard the crack of flint on stone. The wick of the lamp caught on the first try and the resulting flame, small as it was, lit the small chamber.

Apollodorus went to the door and spoke in a low voice. "Crix, Cas, Dub, on the watch. If someone shows up, one of you come tell us. The other two stay out of sight unless and until it looks like we need help. If there is someone to follow, follow them."

"Understood. Don't take any wrong turns or fall down any shafts."

Is raised the lamp, staring about him. The walls were covered closely in drawings, floor to ceiling. Many of them featured the goddess Seshat and a gentleman in an old-fashioned kilt and an elaborate wig offering her a parade of gifts. They would probably be very colorful but it would take a great deal more light to be sure. "So what do we have here?"

"It's one of the older tombs," Tetisheri said. She caught Apollodorus' look. "We studied them under Sennefer."

"Oh. Him. The old scribe you mentioned?" She nodded. "Yes, I remember. He smelled. Even from the back of the room."

She winced. "True, but he was a good teacher." She gestured. "This kind of tomb is called a mastaba, a house of eternity. It's a lot smaller than the later tombs, obviously, and much simpler in design and construction. The engineering technology wasn't up to building pyramids yet."

"Any traps?" Isidorus said. He was visibly sweating.

"Not usually. The room we are in is a chapel. That is an offering table."

"Swept clean."

"Do we have enough lamps to leave one behind?"

"Yes." He set the lamp down on the table and lit another from it. "Oh."

"What?"

Is picked his way around the table to the space between it and the wall behind. "Someone has been here. Recently, too." He stood up, holding a rough canvas bag, which he upended on the table. A short-handled shovel, half a round of very crusty bread, a piece of moldy cheese, and some wizened apricots. He raised his head. "Oh, and look over there."

They followed his pointing finger to a ladder resting on its side against the far wall. He came around the table to examine it. "It's tied together with leather strips. The leather hasn't dried out yet."

"Well. If they needed it, we probably will, too." Apollodorus looked at Tetisheri expectantly.

"There should be another room behind this one—" She accepted a new lamp from Is and walked around the end of the offering table and through the opening in the wall behind. She held the lamp high, and out of the gloom of this second room coalesced a seated figure whose head was higher than Apollodorus. Is gasped audibly.

In a voice she was proud was steady, she said, "This would be the man for whom the tomb was built."

"You mean his body's inside that thing?"

Isidorus' outrage forced a choked laugh out of her, or perhaps it was the dark and the suffocating nature of her surroundings having their effect. "No. Just his spirit. See the hole?" She pointed at the rectangular slit in the wall just beneath the ceiling. "This room and the chapel would have been above ground. That hole lets the spirit circulate outside."

"And lets the fresh air in," Apollodorus said.

"Yes, then, before a thousand years of wind buried the tomb in sand."

"What's next?"

The air was close but there was plenty of it and she was in no danger of not being able to breathe. Or so she told herself. "Behind this room should be the shaft that leads to the burial chamber."

The wall between was navigated, not without blasphemy when the ladder proved recalcitrant, but eventually the three of them—and the ladder—were in the room behind the seated statue.

It was square, as were the chapel and the serdab, but smaller. The interior was almost entirely taken up by a vertical stone enclosure that rose from floor to ceiling. It had already been breached, as witness the jagged, man-sized hole knocked into its side. Apollodorus braced a hand against it and pushed. Nothing moved. He rearranged his stance and pushed again. Still nothing.

"What are you doing?"

"We are not going down that thing if it's the least bit compromised." He rummaged in his pack for a coil of rope. Is was lighting another lamp, and set it carefully in the corner near the doorway.

"Torches?" Tetisheri said. She carried the torches in her pack.

"They're shorter burning. We'll use them below." He pointed. "Look. Someone managed to get across there to gouge holes in the opposite wall. Is, the ladder." Is brought the ladder forward and Apollodorus muscled it across the shaft. The two far ends of the ladder fit neatly into the holes. The two near ends rested comfortably on the broken edge of the hole.

"I don't see—oh."

Apollodorus was busy tying the rope to the uprights of the ladder with some complicated and, she devoutly hoped, absolutely dependable knot.

"I thought that ladder was too short at first, but it turns out they knew what they were doing." He looked up and saw her face. "You don't have to come down there with us."

She swallowed. "Yes, I do."

"Very well." He gave the rope a yank. It held. "Put some of the torches in my pack." He turned and she did. Without further ado he swung his legs over the broken wall and let the rope take his weight. The ladder gave a protesting groan but held. He grinned at them, his teeth white in the dim light of the lamp. "One person only at a time on this rope."

"Oh right, because before you said that we were all going to climb down together."

"What was that, Is?"

"One person on the rope at a time, Apollodorus."

"That's better."

And then Apollodorus disappeared. Tetisheri leaned over the edge to watch, and felt Is's hand clutch the back of her tunic. Apollodorus descended the rope easily, hand over hand, before he vanished into the dark. "Be careful!"

A brief chuckle was her only answer.

She waited in an agony of tension before the rope went slack. "I'm on the bottom," he said, sounding very far away. There was a thump and an oath.

"Are you all right?" Is had lit another lamp and was holding it out over the shaft in a vain attempt to cast some light down.

She could have sworn she heard Apollodorus sigh. "I'm fine." His voice echoed up the shaft.

"The gentleman with me is not."

They stood in a circle, gazing at the crumpled body revealed by the leaping flame of the torch Apollodorus had lit and placed in a wall ring.

"Doesn't smell," Is said. "Been here a while."

Apollodorus nodded. "Before or after the body outside?"

Is shook his head. "No way to be sure. They're at about the same stage of decay, but one inside, one outside?" He shrugged. "Impossible to tell."

"We're agreed that the man outside was murdered," Tetisheri said.

Both men looked at her.

"It doesn't help us to assume that this man wasn't." She looked up, and they mimicked her. "He fell, obviously. The broken arm, the fractured leg. And look." She pointed at a dark smudge on a large rock that had rolled free of the broken wall. "He hit his head when he fell."

"It couldn't have been an accident?"

"If both men came here together, it makes some sense to reason that both were murdered, and by the same hand. It gives us a place to start."

The three of them contemplated her words in thoughtful silence for a few moments, and then Apollodorus caught the dangling end of the rope and looked around him. There was a stack of long poles in one corner of the shaft. He selected one and brought it further into the light, where it resolved itself into an oar, an incongruous object in such a setting until one considered that the tomb's inhabitant might have wished for a boat to take with him into the afterlife. Apollodorus took a few turns of the rope around the oar and wedged it between two of the walls. "Stand on it," he told Is. "If someone tries to untie the rope or throw the ladder down the shaft, give us a shout."

Is, sweating even more freely now, said tightly, "Will do."

Tetisheri knew better than to offer sympathy.

The horizontal shaft took off from the vertical shaft at a right angle and was almost immediately blocked with the ruins of what had been a thick wall constructed of stone. The small chamber revealed had been stripped bare, so knowledge of what had once been in it was reserved for the first robbers to pass this way.

There was a second wall of stone beyond the empty room, also pulled down. The stones of the first wall had been somewhat cleared away. The stones of the second had been left to fall where they might, which made for an obstacle course on the way to the next burial chamber. The torch

Apollodorus had lit changed hands a number of times as they approached the broken opening, allowing one to light the way while the other scrambled. Her hands were scraped and probably bleeding and her knees and back ached by the time they finally achieved the hole. It had been opened wide enough to admit one person at a time.

Apollodorus lit another torch set it into another conveniently placed wall ring. "All well, Is?"

"All well. Let's get whatever the hell it is we're down here to do, done." Is had both hands on the rope and his gaze fixed firmly upward.

"You heard the man." Apollodorus lit a third torch from the one he had mounted on the wall. Holding it before him he ducked into the hole, Tetisheri close on his heels.

They halted just inside, Apollodorus raising the torch.

The center of this final burial chamber was taken up by a stone sarcophagus, the lid of which had been opened but not removed, probably because it was too heavy to steal. The inner sarcophagus was made of wood. Its lid had been pulled up and shoved down to one side between the outer stone vessel and the inner wooden one, leaving the mummy exposed. It looked disheveled.

"Did the robbers try to unwrap the body? And why?"

Tetisheri swallowed. She knew it was only her imagination but the way the torchlight flickered made the mummy appear to be breathing. "The embalmers sometimes wrap amulets inside the linen bands. They can be made of gemstones. Very valuable."

"And portable, which would be a concern climbing back up a rope." He turned and his foot struck something. He stooped, rising with it cradled in his palm. He looked at it for a moment and then held out his hand. "Like this."

It was a tiny scarab. From its weight it was made of solid gold.

His prosaic comment stiffened her spine as no amount of concern or comfort would. "Yes," she said, and realized her voice had steadied, too. "Exactly like that. I can't believe they left it behind."

"They must have been in a hurry and dropped it. Can't think why."

Her laugh was shaky. "Can we kindle another torch?"

"It's our last." But he did, and also brought in the one he had left in the previous room. By the light of both, the chamber came fully into view. It was lined with shelves and bureaus and bags and boxes and raiment on stands. There were board games and amphoras of oil and wine and swords and spears and a bow with a sheaf of arrows and a gulel with a bag full of polished stones for ammunition and a chariot and animal mummies of a dog, a cat, and, of all things, a crocodile. "We don't have enough of those already in the real world? Who wants to bring one with him into the hereafter?"

"But..." Tetisheri said, and hesitated.

"What?"

She turned in a slow circle. "There is so much left."

"There is, isn't there." Apollodorus paced around the sarcophagus in one direction as Tetisheri paced in the other.

"One could almost imagine the robbers planned a return to clean out the rest of it."

"Or more than one return," Tetisheri said, thinking out loud.

"Like a bank. Making withdrawals when necessary, and leaving the rest on deposit."

"Exactly." Tetisheri paused in front of one shelf that contained dozens of ushabti, some the length of her hand, others as long as her forearm. "Apollodorus?"

"What?"

"Could you hold the torch closer, please?"

She heard him retracing his steps to the entrance, the rasp of the torch leaving its ring, and the sound of his breathing as he came to stand behind her.

The tallest ushabti were made in the image of Seshat, the smaller ones of scribes. They were carved from wood and only painted, but they had been so well made that they were easily as beautiful as the statue now residing with Matan. They would be equally of interest to those people who collected for scholarship or for vanity, and a lot more affordable. "I think you're right about the return visit. They must have meant to come back for these."

"They may already have been here more than once." Apollodorus reached for a sword hanging in a sheath and pulled it free. The sheath disintegrated and he let it fall. He flipped the sword one, twice, three times, ran a finger along the edge, and then tossed it up in the air and caught it neatly again. "Poor balance. No edge. Badly made. If this was his sword this man was no fighter." He propped it against the sarcophagus. "Who was this person, that he could afford to furnish his tomb so richly?"

"A priest. Possibly even a high priest. That's why he would need so many scribes in the afterlife. Someone close to the throne, perhaps?"

"Whose?"

"Matan thinks the craftsmanship could date back to the beginnings of the Egyptian empire."

"So, historically as well as intrinsically valuable."

"Yes." She was silent for a moment. "If we posit that both of the men we found were murdered, the existence of at least one more is indicated."

"Their leader?"

"It would follow, wouldn't it?"

"Two for muscle, one for brains?"

"Exactly."

"And the brain's first object, after locating and looting the treasure, would be to leave no witnesses."

"So as to avoid the necessity of sharing." She was sweating as badly as Is now, and wiped her forehead on the hem of her cloak. "And once he had gained access and knew how, he could have returned here easily whenever he needed another infusion of capital."

He nodded. "Would there have been enough here to pay for that grand extension to the Temple of Ptah?"

"He was sure to take the most valuable items on his first visit, and—" she looked around "—while I'm no expert, I'm guessing Matan would say that there is more than enough remaining to build another temple altogether."

"Apollodorus!"

The tone of Is's voice was enough to draw Apollodorus back to the hole in the wall. "What's up?"

"Someone is tugging at the rope!"

Apollodorus climbed through the hole in the wall and Tetisheri heard him stumbling and cursing his way through the debris field on the other side. She emptied her pack unceremoniously on the ground, snatched up the first of the Seshat ushabti that came to hand, and rolled it up inside, strapping the bundle tightly to her back. She stood on tiptoe to retrieve the second torch—the first was already guttering—and used it to light her way to the hole in the wall and through it to the other side, just in time to see the distant figure of Apollodorus reach the end of the tunnel.

And Is being jerked off of his perch on the oar.

And see the two men dodge out of the way of the rope and the broken bits of the ladder as both came tumbling down the shaft.

17

"Oh well, fine," Tetisheri said, quite put out.

Is managed a smile, his face greasy with perspiration in the flickering light of the lamp.

They allowed the torch Tetisheri carried to continue to burn in regard of Is's sensibilities. The lamps they extinguished and set to one side against a future necessity all three of them fervently hoped they wouldn't need.

"Is there anything else you want from the inner chamber?" Apollodorus said.

She shook her head and unstrapped her pack and produced the ushabti for she knew not what reason. What comfort could there be in an inanimate piece of wood?

She looked again and could swear Seshat was smiling at her.

"How long before the others get here?"

"Depends on how many of them were caught." Apollodorus didn't sound alarmed.

Tetisheri swallowed. "Caught?"

His teeth flashed in the gloom. "One would allow himself to be. The other two will stay out of sight until whoever joined us here leaves. Then they'll come for us."

His certainty was calming, and the air seemed to become a little less close. "Could we move that body into the inner chamber?"

"Sure. Let him keep company with the man the tomb was built for. If there is actually a hereafter, maybe the priest will hound the robber into eternity."

This was done, and they stood looking down at the parched remains for a moment. "He was a soldier," Apollodorus said. "Retired, be my guess. That kind of musculature comes only with wielding a legionnaire's sword for the full sixteen. Wiry instead of bulky, like the farmer up top."

"Because?" Tetisheri said. His dispassionate assessment helped her maintain her equilibrium in the face of all this death. One body, yes, as expected. More than one was unsettling.

"Swordplay stretches out the muscles," Is said from behind them. "He'd seen a lot of action."

"One of Caesar's finest?"

"Or Pompey's, or even Crassus'. Hard to tell for sure but he seems older."

"So physical strength is what the two dead men have in common."

"That we know of."

"But it fits."

"Yes." Is sighed. "Yes, it does. Poor old bastard. He'd

probably run out his pension and was looking for a new source of income. Mostly when that happens a vet will hire himself out as a private guard, but sometimes they choose what they think might be a path that pays better and more quickly."

They climbed back into the room at the base of the shaft and settled in to wait. "Jerky?" Apollodorus shared it around and they washed it down with gulps of water from their flasks. Tetisheri couldn't help thinking they ought to be careful how much water they consumed, and then shook that thought off as defeatist. Crix, Cas, and Dub would not fail them.

Although the top of the shaft showed no light or life. How long had it been since the rope and ladder had fallen? How would they get out if no one came? Perhaps after all this time the mortar holding the stones in place had become porous enough to drive stakes into – stakes perhaps made from bits of the broken ladder – and one of them to climb up carrying the rope and—

She took a deep breath and let it out. The air was not so close as it seemed in her imagination. Was it? The rocks she sat on were sharp and uncomfortable, and she got to her feet to move some aside, smoothing out a better place to sit. She folded the pack and put it in the open space and sat down on it. The eyes of the Seshat ushabti followed her every move. "Did the five of you join the Tenth Legion right out of the ludus?"

Is looked up at that, and he and Apollodorus exchanged a long, expressionless stare. "Not right out of, no."

"When did you leave the ludus? And why?"

The silence deepened. "There may have been talk."

"About what?"

Nothing. She gave an irritated wriggle, and was annoyed when she saw Apollodorus repress a smile. "What's so funny?"

"Cleopatra could not have chosen better for her Eye," he said.

Is laughed. True, it was short and strained, but it was a real laugh, broken off when the lamp began to go out. He rummaged in his pack for the flask of oil and replenished it, taking every care to spill no drop. "True," he said, corking the flask and resuming his seat. "You are the nosiest person I've ever met, Tetisheri."

She hoped her face didn't show how pleased she was to have made Is laugh or the game would be up.

"Agreed," Apollodorus said. "Worse even than Cotta." He nudged Is and both men chortled, although Is's amusement sounded a little forced.

"What do we do when we get out of here?" Apollodorus said.

"I like your confidence that we will."

"Useless to plan for anything but success."

She couldn't help but smile. "Learn what happened from whoever gets us out of here. Return to the *Nut* and regroup."

"And then?"

And then? She felt a great and welcome welling of anger begin in her belly. "We find Herminia."

"You know where she is?"

"Generally. We'll need a guide."

"We'll find one."

"Yes," she said. "We will."

The moments ticked away one by one, as if Nut herself was stretching out the night as long as she pleased. Or perhaps the dawn had already broken and Ra had superseded his royal sister in the sky. So deep in the earth, how would they know? Would they ever know a sunrise again?

In sheer self-defense Tetisheri leaned her back against what she hoped would not become her own tomb and closed her eyes. After a while she became aware that Apollodorus was singing something in Latin. "Every woman's man and every man's woman/Gaius Julius Caesar noster, imperator, pontifex."

It had the cadence of a marching song, and the lyrics were rude enough to have been one. Tetisheri opened her eyes to see Isidorus keeping time as he joined in on the second verse.

He started out early as Bithynia's bitch
Gaius Julius Caesar noster, imperator, pontifex
Wives he had three, then everyone else's
Gaius Julius Caesar noster, imperator, pontifex
Mother of Brutus, his sister too, who can keep count
Gaius Julius Caesar noster, imperator, pontifex

Apollodorus grinned at Isidorus, who grinned back. Both

men's voices swelled into a roar that defied the very dark itself.

Gaius Julius Caesar noster, imperator, pontifex,
Primum praetor, deinde consul, nunc dictator, moxque REX!

The last word was shouted loudly enough to be heard in Rome, where it would have half the Senate scrambling beneath their beds. "Did you sing that where Caesar could hear it?" she said.

"Jupiter, girl, yes," Is said. "What would be the point otherwise?"

"And no one was crucified?"

"Sometimes he rode up and down the lines and joined in the chorus," Apollodorus said, grinning.

Is had stopped sweating, for the moment. "Is."

"What?"

"Remind me. What is my most important weapon?"

A slow smile spread across his face. "Your most important weapon, Tetisheri," he said, his voice falling into didacticism, "is the one between your ears."

"And my first three actions when confronted with enemy action?"

They said the words together. "Disarm, disable, run away."

Is laughed, sounding much more like the training master who had taught her and Aristander and Cleopatra the basics of self-defense. "And?"

"And surprise will always be my greatest strength."

He slapped his thigh. "I taught you well, Tetisheri, indeed I did." He scowled. "Do you think herself remembers any of the drill?"

She gave him a look of mock reproof. "Do you think herself ever forgets anything?"

Apollodorus began humming another marching song. After a few notes Is began to sing along.

She must have drowsed for a time. When she opened her eyes again Apollodorus was looking up the shaft.

From which came a faint cry. "Is! Apollodorus! Tetisheri!"

Is was on his feet in an instant. "We're here! Cas?"

"Crix! Rope coming down!"

A moment later a length of line dropped down the shaft. They sent Tetisheri up first, followed by Is, and Apollodorus came last. The men clasped arms, grinning, and Crix caught Tetisheri up in a suffocating hug.

"Where's Dub?"

"He let himself be taken while we hid."

"And Cas?"

"He followed."

Apollodorus nodded. "Who was it?"

"We think priests from the Temple of Ptah, but they were dressed in street clothes so we can't be sure."

"What gave them away?"

Crix grabbed the hair at the nape of his neck. "Every one of them was wearing his hair in those cute little buns."

Apollodorus grunted. "Not professionals, then."

"Not hardly. There were six of them, and just looking at

the way they carried their darling little swords? Dub could have taken them all on and won, and without any help from us."

Tetisheri looked at the horizon. "How long were we down there?"

"An hour, maybe a little more," Crix said. "They knew what they were doing when they got inside, knew right where they were going and how to get there. It couldn't have taken them five minutes. What did they do, cut the rope?"

"Broke the ladder and tossed both down the shaft."

Crix whistled beneath his breath. "They blocked the door, too, replaced that piece of wood we found and piled up the sand in front of it. If we hadn't already been in place we could have missed finding it again. They meant to leave you down there."

"Thereby committing three more murders," she said, controlling her shudder at the thought. "They are ambitious."

"Determined," Is said with a sigh.

"Terrified," Apollodorus said. They looked at him. "They are perfectly well aware of the queen's attitude toward tomb robbers. They know what will happen to them if they are caught. They will eradicate anyone and everyone from the face of Egypt who might bear witness against them."

Tetisheri thought of Herminia, and hoped she had not been in error when she had so confidently predicted that the singer was too valuable to be harmed. "And Dub?"

Crix smiled. "Dub is gathering intelligence. And Cas is with him, whether they know it or not. He will be fine."

She thought of the farmer, the old soldier, the two dead would-be assassins, and of Karis, sprawled across the floor of her shop, but held her peace.

Dawn was breaking as they crossed the river. Never had first light felt more beautiful to Tetisheri. Markos was visibly relieved to see them, evidently anticipating a return to Alexandria that included a report to the queen that he'd lost her two most trusted agents. Breakfast was brought hot from the fire, tea and fresh rounds of bread and boiled eggs. "And today?" he said, watching sternly to see that every bite went down.

"We remain another day," Tetisheri said. "We have business in the city. But plan for an early departure tomorrow."

He didn't ask after Dub and Cas' whereabouts. A man of discretion.

Tabe roused at the smell of food and joined them to eat, still half-asleep and monosyllabic. A night's uninterrupted sleep had done his appetite a world of good. When they finished, she bullied him into letting her see to his cuts and bruises again. The swelling had gone down and the cuts had crusted over, but the bruises had achieved a spectacular yellowish purple that wasn't going away soon. Arnica was applied once more and she forced another cup of willow bark tea down his throat, ignoring his protests. He was a boy surrounded by big, strong men. He didn't want to appear a weakling in their eyes by having a woman fuss over him. Also, willow bark tea had an awful taste.

"Ghastly stuff, isn't it," Apollodorus said, ruffling Tabe's hair.

"Women," Is said, hand arresting itself in the air as he realized that smacking Tabe on the back might offer more pain than male solidarity. "They never believe a man can heal up on his own."

Tabe brightened at being called a man. When Crix patted the space next to him the boy's shoulders straightened and there might even have been a little bit of a strut to his walk as he took his seat and accepted another egg and a piece of flatbread warm from the griddle. Tetisheri hid a smile as she put away the medical kit and sat next to Apollodorus.

"So," he said, looking at her. "What's our plan?"

18

They waited until just before dusk to infiltrate the city in three separate groups. Tabe was again muffled to the ears, but this time in a cloak more appropriate to his height. Tetisheri had made herself as unrecognizable as possible with heavy kohl around her eyes, smile stained with a cheap red lip dye, a diaphanous scarf tying her hair back in the fashion of Persian women, and quantities of cheap bangles at ankles and wrists that jangled loudly with every movement. When Apollodorus protested at the noise Tetisheri raised one admonitory finger. "Sometimes the best way to avoid attention is to attract it."

"Yes, but you look like—"

"Thank you," she said gravely. "Such was my intention." And she tried to walk as if she meant it, although putting that much sway into her hips required concentration, which was not helped when Is let loose with a loud, unmistakably admiring whistle.

The festival was still going strong but most of the activities had coalesced around the Temple of Seshat and the adjoining neighborhoods. There were booths for food and games and trinkets, and at regular intervals a small stage could be found with actors declaiming from Telecleides to Euripides, without too many literary liberties taken. Of course the players wouldn't dare take too many, as most of the crowd was so familiar with the plays that they could shout out the correct line when the actor stumbled over it in performance. It mattered, especially to what was put in the bowl that would be passed at the end of the performance.

They slipped through the crowd unremarked—although more than a few men did fix Tetisheri with a speculative eye—and moved down the esplanade past other, lesser temples of minor gods (at least in Memphis) to the Temple of Ptah. By comparison with the Temple of Seshat it was virtually deserted. Somehow the dearth of people made it look more like a fortress than ever.

A few devotees stood or knelt in prayer, and one small boy scurried between them with a basket of amulets and another for donations. Like Tabe, he was painfully thin. He brightened when he saw them and broke into a trot. Tabe, who was obviously a born conspirator, waited until the other boy was safely within earshot before pulling the cloak back from his face. "Idu. Idu! It's me, Tabe."

Idu's eyes widened. "Tabe! What are you doing back here?" He cast a frightened look around but, for the moment, the hypostyle was devoid of priests. "If they catch you—"

"They won't catch me and even if they do they can't make

me stay. I have friends." Idu's eyes threatened to pop out of his head at these heretical words. "Are there acolytes passing out today?"

Idu clutched the basket to his chest. He seemed unable to speak, staring at Tabe with his mouth half open.

"Idu! Are any acolytes passing out today?"

Idu gulped and clutched his basket ever more tightly to his chest, but he gave a slow nod. "It's where they all are. You know. They form the line to heaven for the new priests to walk between."

Tabe looked up at Apollodorus, who nodded. Tabe looked back at Idu. "Do you want to stay here?"

His words were quite clear, even to Tetisheri who stood a little way off with Is and Crix, who had drifted up to join them.

Idu shut his eyes tight and slowly shook his head, once to the right, once to the left. When he opened them again they shone with a desperate hope that made Tetisheri want to pull the Temple of Ptah down stone by stone with her bare hands.

"Then you have friends, too. Leave the basket. Come with us."

They stationed themselves around the back entrance to the temple, Is, Crix, and Idu on one side and Apollodorus, Tabe, and Tetisheri opposite. The construction workers had long since downed tools for the day and the site of the new temple was even more deserted than the old one.

"Where is the ceremony held?"

Tetisheri's voice was barely a breath of sound but Tabe heard her. "There is a small chapel next to our dormitory." He pointed. "They're chanting the closing hymn now, can you hear it?"

If she concentrated she thought she could hear a low hum of male voices, but it was difficult to be sure when the rest of the city was alive with the sounds of festival-induced revelry. "And they go from here directly to the house you told me of?"

"Yes."

Barely had he answered when the door opened and out marched a group of men. She thought the figure in the lead might be the novice master who had left such a bad taste in her mouth from her first visit to the temple. She was certain of it when she heard Tabe mutter a curse that would have been easily understood—and applauded—by any sailor of Tetisheri's acquaintance.

The newly ordained priests seemed to be in a great hurry and were admonished for it by the master several times before they were even beyond the temple grounds.

Following them wasn't as difficult as Tetisheri had feared as locals and tourists alike lingered at still more booths Euphrasia in her wisdom had caused to be placed at large intersections. Wine booths in particular were mobbed and everyone seemed to be having a marvelous time. Tetisheri saw more than one young couple vanish down an alley and wondered how much the birth rate would go up in Memphis nine months from now. One solution to Thaïs the dressmaker's concerns.

"If Theo had named Euphrasia general of his armies he would have won the war." Apollodorus said.

The group of priests turned another corner. Their pursuers came up on it just in time to see the men enter a two-story building set back from a quiet residential street. They were admitted at once and the door closed firmly behind them. The windows were heavily curtained but the glow of lamplight could be seen around the edges.

Tetisheri stepped out into the street only to have a hand fasten in the back of her tunic to haul her back. "Wait," Apollodorus said.

"Do you know what's happening in there?"

"I do, and we still wait."

She kept herself from struggling free of his grasp only with great effort. "Why?"

The shrubbery next to the house rustled. A man emerged and trotted across the street toward them. "That's why."

Castus halted in front of them and jerked his head. "Dub is locked up in a shed out back. I spoke to him through the door. They haven't questioned him yet."

"Get him out."

Cas nodded and vanished again into the shrubbery. Not ten minutes later he was back, Dub at his heels.

"The men at the tomb are priests from the Temple of

Ptah," Dub said. The air of the world-weary sophisticate was gone, replaced by a grim-faced man with no sense of humor and less patience. "Do you have an extra sword? They took mine."

They did, of course, and an extra knife as well. Belt and scabbards clattered to the ground as Dub drew both, naked blades flashing in the darkness. "Let's go. Cas and I will take the back." He noticed the two boys huddled together for the first time. They were frightened of his grim ferocity and showed it. "Tabe, but who's this?"

"Another acolyte from the temple. They helped us find the place."

Dub's expression lightened. "Good men. You stay here." He looked at Tetisheri. "They do not need to see what I heard going on inside that house."

"The Memphis Shurta?" This from Crix, drawing his sword in turn, followed by Is and Cas.

Is shrugged. "Ill-funded, badly trained, and few in number. We'll be in and out well before they muster up the courage to respond. Always supposing anyone bothers to tell them we were here in the first place."

"There are only the two entrances?" Apollodorus said.

Cas nodded. "Although some of the windows along the side are wide and low. Pretty easy egress."

Apollodorus' eyes narrowed. "And access. All right. Dub and Cas in at the back, Is and Crix in on either side, Tetisheri and I through the front. We'll hold on a count of twenty for you to get in place. Wait for my signal." He looked at

Tetisheri. "Do you have a weapon?" She did, a long dagger that only missed being a gladius by a hand's width. "Good." He looked them over, found no fault, and looked at the two boys. "This will be noisy. Don't be afraid."

"Will you kill Min?" This from Idu.

"Who's Min?"

"The novice master."

"If he tries to kill me."

"I hope he does, then."

The words were clearly spoken, with fervor. It was Tabe's turn to goggle.

Apollodorus drew his gladius and saluted the boy. Idu stood straight, unsmiling, and made a small bow in return.

"Let's get to it then."

They fanned out across the street, silent as the ka of the man in the tomb. Apollodorus reached the step before the front door and counted down the seconds.

"What's your signal?" Tetisheri said.

Apollodorus kicked in the door.

He charged in roaring something unintelligible at the top of his voice. His first swing shattered all three of the lares sitting on the altar at the door, the next broke a tall vase into many pieces, the third swiped through a tray of pitchers and mugs. Maximum destruction and maximum noise equals maximum confusion. Yet another of Is's lessons.

A guard was posted at the door; it turned out to be the man still sporting the marks of Apollodorus' attention from two nights before. He had just enough time to recognize

Apollodorus and open his mouth to shout the alarm before the hilt of Apollodorus' sword struck the side of his head. He crumpled to the floor. If he weren't unconscious he had enough sense to pretend he was.

From other parts of the house came similar sounds, the noise and the violence sowing sudden terror in the occupants of the house. Half-dressed men began spilling out of rooms, most of them unarmed and none of whose lives had prepared them for what they were about to face. It was all the worse for them that they knew they were in the wrong. This was just the bill coming due whether they acknowledged it or not.

The events of that night would revisit Tetisheri for the rest of her life in images that appeared to her awake and in dreams. The Five Soldiers had been angry going in and become only more angry with every step they took further into that dreadful establishment.

The front door opened into a small atrium with couches and refreshments, but the rest of the first floor was divided into tiny bedrooms, eight by Tetisheri's count. The second floor wasted no space on public areas. Every room on both floors was occupied.

A man came naked out of one of them and was spitted without hesitation on Crixus' blade. A bed in a room with a girl staring up at the ceiling, arms and legs splayed resistlessly, tears tracking down her face, as a man worked over her, so involved he was unaware of their entrance. Dub's hand grabbed the man by his hair and threw him across the room into the wall, which crumbled and broke under the force of his impact. The man slid to the floor unconscious, possibly even dead. Tetisheri hoped dead.

One of the new priests stood in one of the rooms, staring slack-jawed at the girl on the bed. She was naked, beckoning to him with a forced smile on her face. He was not naked and not smiling, which was possibly why Is let him live.

Two men with one girl between them. One man with two girls. Two girls performing for a wizened old man. One man beating a bound girl, so intent on what he was doing that he never saw the blade that took the hand holding the whip, nor that same blade returning to take his head.

Every room had a girl, except for the five rooms with boys. None of them were out of their teens, more than a few were younger than Tabe, and too many of them displayed bruises old and new everywhere.

The High Priest Natasen was in a back room on the second floor, larger than the rest.

With Herminia.

Even though Tetisheri had only ever seen her from tenth row center, she was instantly recognizable. Everything about her was too large, too wide: her eyes, her mouth, her curves, all of which she could and did play for comedic effect to the delight of audiences from Alexandria to Ephesus to Athens to Rome.

The two of them were, oddly, seated at a table spread with an elaborate meal. Natasen had Herminia by one wrist and was staring at the door with an outraged expression that changed to gaping dismay when he saw who was standing there. His grip on Herminia's wrist must have loosened because she instantly pulled her hand free. With no hesitation, almost as if she had planned what to do if the opportunity presented itself, she snatched up a knife and drove it through his other hand, pinning it to the table top.

For a moment he stared at the blood welling up from the wound, too shocked to say anything. When he screamed the sound nearly brought the roof down.

Dub recovered first. "I suppose there's no point in saving all that dramatic talent for the stage, is there?" Natasen shrieked again, tears running down his face, free hand clutching uselessly at the other. "Oh shut up, you filthy, disgusting bastard, you deserve everything you get and—" Dub gave a thin smile "—you definitely deserve everything that's coming."

Herminia had leaped to her feet to put distance between her and her erstwhile captor. Her gaze fastened on Tetisheri as the only other woman in the room. "Karis?"

"I'm sorry," Tetisheri said, and shook her head.

The novice at the door of the Temple of Seshat took one look at the assembly of girls and boys with their five-man guard and ran for Euphrasia. When she arrived, out of breath, Tetisheri looked at the High Priestess and said one word.

"Sanctuary."

19

"Beaten but not raped, or so she says," Tetisheri said.

"You don't believe her?"

"I don't know. I didn't think she would be harmed, because of who—" Tetisheri stopped herself. "If you'd been inside that house, you wouldn't believe her either. The rest of them have been raped repeatedly, offered as a reward to new-made priests after their ordination. They were also given as rewards to local men who showed particular devotion to Ptah by way of offerings, of treasure or of labor." The man first spitted on Dub's sword had been Natasen's builder.

They were in Euphrasia's parlor, Tetisheri, Apollodorus, Is, Crix, Cas, and Dub. Tabe and Idu were off somewhere being cleaned, fed, and put to bed. The girls and boys from the house had been taken into the infirmary to be treated and from there to the baths.

Euphrasia's face was so expressionless as to be blank, reminding Tetisheri of some of the ushabti in the tomb. Had it only been that morning? She felt as if she had lived a lifetime since. Certainly she felt old enough.

"And Natasen has been actively recruiting acolytes," Euphrasia said. "For how long have these children been held prisoner?"

"Some of them a year or more, I think. I asked one and she couldn't remember. Tabe, one of the acolytes, recognized one of the girls. She was taken from his village at the same time he was."

"She might talk to him and we might learn more."

"Perhaps." Euphrasia had had food and drink brought. Tetisheri could only sip at a glass of water for fear her stomach would immediately bring back up anything she ate.

"Shall I send for the shurta?"

"It depends on how deep they were in the High Priest's pocket."

Euphrasia swirled the wine in her glass. "Natasen relies on the threat of divine intervention as motivation to make the shurta look the other way."

Tetisheri took a sip of water. "Relied."

There was a moment of silence. "Ah."

"I'm sure some of that divine intervention took the form of gold and jewels from the priest's tomb." This from Apollodorus, very dry.

"What happens to the Temple of Ptah now?" Dub said. The first among them to laugh, he was the last to let go of his anger. The hours locked in the shed, listening to the sounds from the house, had had their effect, although the others were at least as angry. "We could just burn it down and start over."

Approving noises from the other four.

Euphrasia's voice was gentle but stern. "The senior priests will hold a conclave and elect another high priest from among their number." When they would have protested she held up a hand. "The worship of Ptah goes back millennia in this land, Dubnorix. Their high priests once married into the royal family. Their followers number among the thousands. You can destroy the temple in Memphis but there are many others scattered from Alexandria to Syene. You will never end the cult."

"The followers of Ptah are not so present in Alexandria," Isidorus said, although it could better be described as a growl. "I don't even know where their temple is."

"The worship of Serapis has become predominant in the city," Apollodorus said in a more moderate tone. "He is much favored by the Romans."

"You mean he has become fashionable," Castus said.

"The many-faced, multipurpose, one-size-fits-all god," Crixus said.

"Yes, I can see that you are all devout followers," Euphrasia said.

Her attempt to lighten the atmosphere entirely missed its mark. Dub made a sweeping gesture indicating the temple in which they now sat, and perhaps all the many temples resident in Memphis. "And surely you can see why, lady. Followers of the old gods like Ptah given free rein to rob, kidnap, rape, and murder where and when they will. If no example is made what is to stop them from starting all over again? What is to stop any other temple? Including Serapis."

Another rumble of assent, although Tetisheri did see Apollodorus put a restraining hand briefly on Dubnorix's arm. Dub didn't quite shake it off but he did glare, and there was no apology in his expression. It had taken all of Apollodorus' authority to restrain Dub from burning down the house where the boys and girls had been imprisoned, with any surviving priests and clients still inside.

Euphrasia witnessed the by-play and understood it immediately. "It is true what Isidorus says, that the Shurta of Memphis are not of the caliber of the Alexandria force, but—"

"Perhaps the queen should be made aware of that fact and Aristander dispatched to Memphis to see what can be done about it," Dub said. He knew Aristander. Aristander had daughters.

The High Priestess of the Temple of Seshat could have chosen that moment to make an appearance and remind them in whose presence they sat, but Euphrasia was smarter than that. She was, Tetisheri thought, fully alive to the rage inspired by the events of the evening, and inclined to be respectful of it. She also knew full well how high Apollodorus stood in the queen's counsel. She had seen, as all of Memphis had seen, the other Soldiers disembark from the *Thalamegos* and take up station around her own palanquin.

For Tetisheri, political considerations were the least of it.

Like Dub, she wanted to burn the bordello down first, and then move on to the temple. After that, they might neaten up the city of Memphis itself, whose citizens had turned a blind eye. Many must have known. The High Priestess of Seshat should have known. "A search should be made of the grounds," she said.

Everyone looked at her.

"Those children were sold into slavery," she said. "They would have been used until they died, or until the girls became pregnant, or until they aged out of being attractive to their masters, when undoubtedly they would have been thrown into the street, or, more likely, killed. The neighbors should be interviewed. Some of them must have seen graves being dug."

"Tetisheri," Euphrasia said.

"What?" Her reply might have been a little testy, and this time Apollodorus squeezed her arm.

Euphrasia looked grave. "What is to be done with Natasen?"

The High Priest of the Great Temple of Ptah was at present profaning the Temple of Seshat with his presence, in restraints and under guard. "What do you mean?"

The High Priestess of the Temple of Seshat came to her feet. She clasped her hands before her and raised her chin. When she spoke, her voice echoed off the walls. For the first time Tetisheri noticed that Euphrasia had at some moment that evening changed into her formal robes of office. She looked taller, and somehow older. Or no, not older. Ageless. Eternal.

"I call upon the Eye for justice."

The High Priestess stared at her, her face set in stern lines. Tetisheri looked around the room and found the Five Soldiers regarding her with equally stern and expectant expressions. With a faint shock she realized that this, too, was part of the job of the Eye of Isis, to make this kind of decision when the queen was not by to render it in person.

It was equally clear where her duty lay. Cleopatra would not thank her for hauling Natasen back to Alexandria, there to expose the corruption of one of the storied Egyptian temples—and a scion of one of Egypt's most powerful nomes, no matter what branch—to public view. She was not only the eye of the queen, she was her mouth and, Bast help her, the queen's hand as well.

Never had the weight of the Eye of Isis hung so heavily around her neck. She looked at Apollodorus and thought she detected a hint of sympathy in his eyes but he, too, was silent, awaiting her verdict.

She rose to her feet in turn and adopted her own formal pose. She spoke directly to Apollodorus and the others. "Gentlemen. Please give us the room."

She didn't have to say please and they knew it. Euphrasia knew it, too, and she waited as the five men filed out of her parlor. Tetisheri went to the door to throw the bolt, locking them inside, and then went through to the enclosed garden to make sure no servant or novice was lurking there.

When she returned to the parlor the High Priestess was doing her best to maintain an air of imperturbability, but Tetisheri thought she caught a flicker of apprehension behind her eyes. Well might she be wary. She kept her voice low in case in spite of her best efforts someone was eavesdropping.

"Who is Herminia?"

Euphrasia flinched almost imperceptibly, but Tetisheri saw it. She waited.

The High Priestess looked down at her hands, saw how tightly they were clasped, and loosened them with a visible effort to smooth the skirts of her tunic. To them she said softly, "Why, a singer and an actress of high renown."

"None of that, Euphrasia. You yourself invoked the Eye of Isis. Only Cleopatra could have told you that I now hold that title. In this moment the truth only and only the truth will suffice. I ask you again: who is Herminia?"

Euphrasia fidgeted, shifting on her feet, looking around the room. "Who do you think she is?"

Tetisheri spoke slowly and deliberately, still in that low voice. "I think you are an attractive woman. I think you were a trusted servant and friend to Auletes. I think it is reasonable for me to wonder if you were more."

Euphrasia raised her head. Although she tried to hide it Tetisheri could see that she was shaken. "You think that—"

"I think you left Alexandria in a hurry to take up the position of High Priestess at the Temple of Seshat here in Memphis. I think the position of High Priestess is one that lies within the sovereign's grace, that he can bestow it upon his personal choice instead of waiting for a conclave of Seshat's priestesses. I think the previous High Priestess was pensioned off well before retirement age and now lives in comfort in

Thebes. I think Thebes is far enough away that it will require a journey involving time and expense for anyone to ask her why she was so suddenly out of a job, but not so far that if someone, like, say, Natasen, or Linos, were truly interested in how and why she left her position she could be found and asked. And I think someone did."

"Tetisheri—"

"I think that the queen sent me to find Herminia because the two women are very closely connected, indeed. I think there may be good reason for bad actors to believe that possession of Herminia may be a powerful weapon against Cleopatra."

The High Priestess looked away, out toward the garden. A nightjar gave a short trill, which ended abruptly in a flutter of wings. There was the merest hint of light from the east.

At last Euphrasia stirred. "I can give you no answers, Tetisheri," she said, and raised her hand when Tetisheri would have spoken. "It is not my story to tell. It may not even be Herminia's story to tell, although I will say it is my belief that she knows very little of the story herself. I did not lie to you. She was raised here in the temple from the time she was a child, and in very truth she remained here until she left to pursue a career on the stage. After that? What you know is what everyone knows."

Tetisheri remembered word for word Cleopatra's command. *Find Herminia. Report back to me only. As soon as possible, my Eye.* She had fulfilled the first of the queen's commands.

"Send for Herminia."

"Tetisheri—"

"You have invoked the Eye of Isis, High Priestess. You will do as the Eye commands."

Euphrasia stared at Tetisheri for a shocked moment before bowing her head in submission. "It is as you command, O Eye."

Herminia was inclined to balk. Tetisheri, who had remained standing, pulled the Eye from beneath her tunic and centered it on her breast. "Do you recognize this emblem?"

Herminia, it turned out, wasn't so good an actress that she could deny it.

"You stand in the presence of the Eye of Isis," Tetisheri said, her voice sounding distant and cold to her own ears. "I am the eye, the hand, and the mouth of Queen Cleopatra, Seventh of Her Name, Ruler of Egypt and Alexandria, Lady of the Two Lands. You will answer my questions immediately and without prevarication. Is this understood?"

"It is," Herminia said, her voice barely above a whisper.

"Tell me of your relationship with Natasen, the High Priest of Ptah."

Herminia looked at Euphrasia and away again. "I—I met him here in Memphis, not long before I left the Temple." Euphrasia gasped and Herminia didn't look at her.

"We weren't lovers, not then. Well, never. But he heard

me sing Medea and he was waiting for me at the stage door after the performance. He had a—a certain charm of manner. The attention, the gifts—" She saw something in Tetisheri's expression. "Don't look at me like that. Please don't. I know that by definition acting is only a step ahead of prostitution in reputation, but for me acting truly is about the stage, the performance, the connection I make with the audience. The money is nice, yes, I can pay my own way and live a decent life and save for the time when I can no longer be heard in the last tier. But for me, it was never about money or fame or—or having a succession of rich lovers who would give me anything I wanted." She paused. "Natasen was so handsome, and, well... different."

I'll say he was, Tetisheri thought. And a High Priest, too, a man of power and substance. Any woman would be flattered by attention from such a man. On the face of it. "In what way?"

"He didn't want a mistress, he said. He didn't even try to sleep with me. He declared himself mad with love, he wanted to marry me, for us to have children and be a family." She sent Euphrasia a fleeting glance. "I've never had a family, and I—" Her voice trailed away.

"You were tempted."

"I suppose so, at least at first. But then he became so demanding, so resentful of the time I spent at work, so insistent on marriage. He even resented the time I spent with Heron, his own cousin, and that was by Natasen's own design!"

"How so?"

"Natasen said the followers of Ptah would be shocked by their priest marrying an actor. He wanted to keep our relationship as quiet as possible for as long as possible. When he came to my house he announced himself as Heron, and then made sure that Heron and I were seen in public enough times to fuel the rumors." Herminia sighed. "That was the end of it for me. I do good work and I'm proud of it. If it was a choice between having a family and never singing again—" She raised her hands in a shrug. "And besides, he was proving a lot less attractive than I had first imagined."

"And did he take his rejection well?"

"He didn't take it as a rejection at all. He said I was confused, that I'd change my mind, that he wouldn't give up. He persisted in appearing at the stage door after performances and forcing himself upon my notice. He even sent Heron to my home with gifts to plead his cousin's case."

"The statue of Seshat among your lares and penates."

Herminia looked surprised. "Yes, that was from Natasen."

"You kept the statue. From a rejected suitor?"

Herminia flushed. "Heron wouldn't take it back!" She glanced at Euphrasia. "And, truth be told, ever have I had a fondness for the goddess, so I placed the statue on the altar until I could return it. And I would have."

"And then?"

"And then, this past Sunday, I went early to Karis' shop in the Emporeum. Natasen knew of my habits and two of his men were waiting for me. We fought, Karis and I, but they struck her down. They carried me to a boat waiting on the canal and brought me to Memphis that night."

All the while Natasen took his ease at the Odeum, in full view of a theater whose audience included Cleopatra. An unimpeachable alibi. "You were kept in that house this entire time?"

"Yes." She saw Tetisheri's look. "I was not harmed, lady, other than being held against my will. Natasen—"

"Yes?"

"I did sometimes wonder," Herminia said a little hesitantly, "if Natasen liked women at all. He didn't—he said we would wait until we were married. At first I thought he meant it, and then—well, he never insisted on anything more than a kiss."

"How did he explain your kidnapping?"

Herminia rolled her eyes. "It was all for love of me, he said. It was my fault, my rejection made him do it."

That, and he knew whose daughter you are, Tetisheri thought, and an ambitious man like Natasen wasn't about to let such a prize slip through his fingers.

The sun was just over the horizon when they assembled in a small private courtyard behind a high wall and a locked gate. It held a single olive tree and nothing else other than the square paving stones beneath their feet. And this morning, Euphrasia, Tetisheri, the Five Soldiers, and, of course, Natasen.

Herminia was there, too. Castus had stationed himself

nearby, ready to catch her if she fainted. Tetisheri, but distantly, thought Herminia was made of sterner stuff than that.

Isidorus and Crixus brought forward the last person present, who proved to be Min, the master of acolytes, whose legs did not appear to be working properly. Natasen, his arms bound behind his back, was on his knees in a pool of his own urine. Before his frantic pleas for mercy became intolerable Dub had gagged him.

The expression on the faces of the Five Soldiers was identical; disgust. They could understand and appreciate fear. There wasn't a decent soldier who hadn't experienced it in the face of the enemy and done their duty regardless. Cowardice was something else altogether and in their eyes unforgivable.

Apollodorus looked at Tetisheri. She stiffened her knees and stepped forward. The Eye of Isis lay on her breast, the nacre and the lapis glowing blue-white with an almost ethereal light beneath the first touch of Ra.

"The Eye of Isis summons Min, Master of Acolytes of the Great Temple of Ptah in Memphis, to give testimony."

Natasen had refused to speak but Min had proved only too willing to confess all he knew, first to Tetisheri, and now before the assembled witnesses. It spilled out a second time in a babbling rush of words. The robbing of tombs to finance Natasen's rise to power at the Temple. The betrayal and murder of the men who robbed with him. The conscription of acolytes and their subsequent sequestering from the world. The abduction of girls and boys from villages as far south as

Syene, acquired in concert with the acolytes. The purchase and purpose of the house in Memphis. There were plans for a second in Thebes and a third in Alexandria itself.

Min stopped short of implicating anyone else other than Natasen. There was no mention of any patrons, royal, noble, or common, but one would have to be half blind not to see the fine hand of Philo in this exercise. They had all been students together at the Mouseion when Euphrasia had left for Memphis. It was more than likely that Philo would at least suspect Herminia's heritage. Somehow, he had discovered Herminia's connection with the Temple of Seshat and with its High Priestess, and ferreted out the rest. Ever on the alert for any opportunity to embarrass his sister or weaken her position, that was our Philo. And in Natasen, he found a most willing tool.

And after all, Caesar had his own spare queen, Arsinoë, under house arrest in Rome. Why wouldn't Philo think it a fine idea? He never had any good ones of his own.

It took a full fifteen minutes for the filth to cease spewing from Min's mouth. The circle of people stood silent. Natasen's eyes were screwed shut as if by not seeing them he could not hear the truth. Euphrasia was horrified and showed it. Herminia was silent but attentive. If anything, the Five Soldiers looked bored.

One by one, slowly, inexorably, all of them turned to took at Tetisheri. The light in the east increased, to fall full on her face and on her badge of office. Ra himself was weighing in on the morning's proceedings.

She forced herself to look straight at Natasen, who still had his eyes squeezed shut. Clearly, without a single tremor in her voice, she pronounced sentence. "By the testimony presented here this morning, and by the evidence seen with my own eyes these past two nights, I pronounce Natasen, High Priest of Ptah, guilty of tomb robbing without permit, theft of tithes of same, of abduction, of rape, and of murder."

The High Priest was given no opportunity to refute the charges. If any of them had been willing to do a proper investigation she could probably have added peculation of public funds along with any number of other crimes, but she had no doubt that Cleopatra would want this cleaned up quickly and as quietly as possible. Truth to tell, so did Tetisheri.

"The sentence for any and all of these crimes is death. May it be so."

Tetisheri nodded at Apollodorus and stepped back. Her knees weren't as shaky as she thought they should have been.

Apollodorus gave the signal. Dubnorix had won the coin toss and his gladius nearly sang as he drew it from its scabbard. A gobbling sound came from behind the gag as Natasen tried to curl into a ball. Isidorus and Crixus grasped him by his elbows and drew him inexorably to his knees and Dubnorix brought his blade down in one swift, efficient stroke. Natasen's head separated cleanly from his body and was immediately covered in a gush of his own blood, steaming in the cool morning air.

Herminia's expression did not change. Neither did she look away.

20

They returned to the Nut immediately afterward. Markos took one look at them and they departed for Alexandria as soon as the last man was on board.

Is, Crix, Cas, and Dub sat in a small circle in the stern, playing senet. Tetisheri stood in the bow, watching the rooflines of the temples of Memphis recede into the distance and then disappear altogether when they turned into the Nile Canal.

"Are you all right?"

Apollodorus. Of course. She looked up to see such an expression of understanding on his face that she very nearly lost her composure, something that she was coming to understand was not permitted the Eye of Isis.

Was she all right? Euphrasia had asked for justice, the queen for a solution to the mystery of Herminia's disappearance, and Tetisheri believed she had done both to the best of her ability.

"Was Natasen's death merited? Unquestionably. Am I unhappy to have been the instrument of that death? I don't believe I am." She swallowed. "What I'm wondering now is if that makes me a monster." She attempted a small smile. "I don't want to be a monster, Apollodorus."

Regardless of who was watching he enfolded her in his arms. It was a warm, solid, secure embrace that all by itself kept any number of demons at bay.

They stood that way for a long time, the sound of his heartbeat steady in her ear.

Markos' crew gave it their best effort and the *Nut* made port just after midnight. Tetisheri and Apollodorus went immediately to the palace. In a very short space of time Charmion, looking sleepy but unsurprised, came for them.

They were ushered into the small parlor that overlooked the Royal Harbor. Cleopatra was waiting for them dressed in a light robe over her night dress, but she looked wide awake, as if she had not yet been to bed. Tetisheri knew that the queen slept no more than six hours each night and sometimes less than that. She didn't know if it came naturally or if it was the only way the queen of Egypt and Alexandria could keep up with the monumental amount of work that encompassed her role.

She did not invite them to sit, remaining standing herself, hands clasped lightly before her. "Report."

"Herminia is alive, Majesty, and in the care of the High Priestess of the Temple of Seshat," Tetisheri said.

The set of Cleopatra's shoulders relaxed infinitesimally. "That is very good news, my Eye." She sat down perhaps a bit suddenly on the nearest couch. "You must be tired after your efforts on my behalf. Sit. Charmion, have tea brought."

Tetisheri and Apollodorus sat down on the couch opposite.

"Markos served you well?"

"Markos was very capable and efficient, and the *Nut* is a fine ship with a fine crew, Majesty."

"That is good to hear."

Tea came and the queen poured it out herself. Charmion took a stool near the door and willed herself into invisibility.

"Very well, my Eye. Tell me the whole, from start to finish."

"Some of it will not be easy to hear, Majesty."

"The whole, my Eye, from start to finish."

Tetisheri drained her cup and set it down. When she sat back her hand was enveloped in a warm, strong clasp. She looked at Apollodorus and he smiled at her.

When she looked back at Cleopatra she saw a flash of something in the queen's eyes. Recognition, and... surely it could not have been envy.

Gently she freed her hand, clasped both in her lap, and sat very straight on the edge of her seat. Cleopatra was solemn and attentive and perhaps a little stern. This was not her friend, this was the Queen of Egypt and Alexandria, sitting in judgement. Tetisheri took a deep breath, centering herself, and began.

"Your charge was to discover the whereabouts of Herminia,

a well-known actor resident in the city of Alexandria, after her disappearance on—Sunday?"

"Sunday," Apollodorus said.

"Sunday. At your command I spent the next day interviewing those in the city who knew her. I discovered that few—" Tetisheri corrected herself "—that none of them knew her well, including the members of her household, her neighbors, even her alleged lover, one Heron, a scholar in residence at the Mouseion."

"Alleged lover?"

Tetisheri gave Cleopatra a long, thoughtful look. "According to him, the stage manager of the Odeum, and her servants, yes. But that lover was not Heron."

Cleopatra's face was impassive. "Continue."

"Her servants told me that she left the house early that morning to visit a stylist at the Emporeum. This is her habit on days of first performances, as stage cosmetics must be mixed by hand in small quantities of precise ingredients. There is a woman she favors whose shop is near the Nile Canal. This habit of hers was known to her kidnappers, who waited for her there that morning. She and the stylist both fought them, which resulted in the stylist's death. Her kidnappers then took Herminia aboard a boat and abducted her to Memphis. She was hidden in a house belonging to the Temple of Ptah, under the authority of the High Priest of the Temple of Ptah in Memphis."

"Natasen." The name came out on a hiss.

"Yes. She was not the only young woman beneath that

roof, and there were five boys held there as well. Most were underage and none of them were there of their own volition." Tetisheri struggled to keep any feeling from her tone. The facts, and only the facts. "They were used to reward priests of Ptah newly sworn to their vows. They were—privileges afforded to donors to the Temple, as well."

"I see." Cleopatra's voice was as emotionless as Tetisheri's. "Where are they now?"

Tetisheri's heart warmed a little that Cleopatra had asked first after the victims. "They are residing temporarily in the Temple of Seshat in Memphis, under the personal protection of the High Priestess."

"I see," the queen said again. "I will write to Euphrasia tomorrow. And Natasen?"

"He himself was in no condition to offer testimony—" a gag often had that effect "—but his Master of Acolytes was more than willing."

"Was he."

"Yes, and quite thorough his confession was. He alleged that the High Priest, before he came to his office, had discovered the tomb of Mnenes, a priest of Ptah in the Sixth Dynasty." She glanced at Apollodorus. "We found and visited this tomb ourselves, and in the process discovered two bodies, both victims of murder, which according to the Master of Acolytes had been committed by Natasen's hand."

"How very efficient."

"Indeed. The find went unreported to the Royal Treasurer, and so was not taxed."

Cleopatra made a sound.

"I beg your pardon, Majesty?"

"It is nothing. Pray continue, my Eye."

Apollodorus turned his head as if to hide a smile.

"The contents of the tomb were harvested over time, so as to occasion less comment when the items came on the market. But eventually they were sold and used to finance Natasen's way into the position of High Priest."

"Tcha!" the queen said. "The priests of the Temple had no thought to consulting their sovereign in the matter?"

"This was almost two years ago, my queen. As you will recall, the times then were quite disturbed." Disturbed indeed, by a lengthy war of succession that had Cleopatra herself fleeing for her life, and her father, Auletes, putting his throne up for sale in Rome, if only Rome would once again place him upon it.

Cleopatra pressed her lips together into a thin line. Her memory was every bit as good as Tetisheri's. "I recall. And, yes, before you say so, I am aware that the richest priest or priestess in the temple often succeeds to the highest seat therein. Nevertheless, there are lines."

Tetisheri remained silent. She never offered an opinion on religion. There were too many temples in Egypt and Alexandria, with too many followers. The gods they worshipped were never static, intertwining and melding into new identities with every passing century. They were exorcized on occasion by this or that priest and one pharaoh had tried proselytizing one god, which cult had lasted barely the length of his reign. Gods sometimes evolved on their own into some new deity that looked familiar but was not quite the same. Or were deliberately constructed, like Serapis.

But gods were also excellent vessels for channeling power into unscrupulous hands. A promise of an easy afterlife was always a seductive call for the least fortunate. A miserable existence was more easily endured if at the end of it was promised a hereafter of ease and comfort. For others, like Tabe's parents, it wasn't so much dedicating a son or daughter to answer a calling as it was having one less mouth to feed.

Cleopatra stirred in her chair. "Very well. One of Natasen's priests confessed. Were you able to confirm his evidence?"

"That he murdered the two men whose bodies we found outside and inside the tomb, only if we were willing to take the priest's testimony at face value. The evidence of their bodies shows that one at least was unquestionably murdered. We had her own testimony when it came to the kidnapping of Herminia. We had the evidence of our own eyes and ears to the rape and abuse of the children in that house. Several of the citizens of Memphis apprehended at the scene were, ah, convinced to offer evidence as well, which confirmed that the building was owned by the Temple of Ptah and came under the authority of the High Priest himself. They were all there at his personal invitation, as attested to by the old woman who ran the house."

"Who took this testimony?"

Tetisheri looked at Apollodorus. "In lieu of a shurta

presence, I did, along with Apollodorus, Isidorus, Dubnorix, Crixus, and Castus."

"You deputized the Five Soldiers."

"I—yes. That is exactly what I did."

"Good." The queen meditated briefly. "How long had the house been in existence?"

"A little over a year. This would have been after the tomb in question was robbed the first time and the same time that Natasen began the extension on the Temple of Ptah."

"I see. Yes, that fits only too well." There was a brief silence. "And Natasen?"

"I pronounced him guilty of tomb robbing without permit, theft of tithes of same, abduction, rape, and murder, and ordered him to be put to death. The sentence was carried out immediately following the verdict in a courtyard of the Temple of Seshat."

"How appropriate."

Tetisheri braced herself. If Cleopatra was displeased by her actions, now was the time when she would hear about it. Not only was it the first time Tetisheri had exercised the powers of the Eye of Isis in full and away from Cleopatra's direct supervision, both women were acutely aware of Tetisheri's strong disapproval of Cleopatra's decision not to prosecute the guilty party of Tetisheri's previous investigation. Natasen's summary judgement and execution might in part have been facilitated out of Tetisheri's fear that Cleopatra could imagine some future use for him, and Cleopatra would know that, too. There were benefits to someone knowing you so long and so completely, but there were drawbacks as well. If that someone was your sovereign, who had named you to one of the most difficult positions in a realm beset by threats on every side… Tetisheri waited for the storm to break over her head.

Instead, the queen rose to her feet and crossed to Tetisheri, giving her both her hands. "Well done, my Eye. Well done, indeed."

It took a moment for Tetisheri to comprehend that her work was being praised. She stood up so she could bow her thanks over their clasped hands. "Majesty."

"Now I suppose I must see what is to be done with what remains of the Temple of Ptah in Memphis."

"Euphrasia seems to think the priests will hold a conclave to elect a new high priest."

"Does she? All very well, I suppose, but it won't do to have a radical sect running about Egypt claiming their leader was removed by a queen interfering in religious matters."

Tetisheri dared a smile. "If it were easy…"

She and the queen said together, "…everyone would be doing it. Quite right." Cleopatra looked at Apollodorus. "The Eye will join you outside shortly, Apollodorus. Charmion."

"Majesty." The door closed quietly behind them both.

Cleopatra bent forward to press her lips to Tetisheri's forehead. "Are you all right, Sheri?"

Tetisheri felt tears begin to gather behind her eyelids and willed them away. "I'm all right, Pati. Truly. If ever anyone needed killing, it was Natasen. It may have been done in secret and the true story of Natasen's death and the reasons for it may never be known to his followers or the people at large, but something very like justice was done in Memphis yesterday morning."

"But by your hand, my very dear," Cleopatra said gently.

In spite of her best efforts, Tetisheri's laugh was shaky. "Don't be kind to me, Pati, or I will embarrass us both."

"You have done good work here, Sheri. Never doubt that I know this. Or yourself."

Tetisheri bowed her head, only half mockingly. "I hear and obey, O most high."

"Tcha!"

Tetisheri raised her head to look her friend in the eye. "Who is Herminia, Pati?"

Cleopatra's expression was suddenly unreadable. She dropped Tetisheri's hands and went to stand at the window. Tetisheri joined her, looking out at the darkened harbor, where a few small dim lights, marking crews still awake on the ships moored in the harbor, were a pale imitation of the vast sweep of stars overhead.

"All right, Tetisheri. Out with it." Tetisheri feigned mystification, although evidently not very well, because Cleopatra said testily, "You always did enjoy surprising me with what I don't know. What else?"

Very well then, Tetisheri thought. To the harbor she said, "There was a fourth person involved in the robbing of the tomb, who also benefited. He might not have been present in person but it is my belief he was instrumental in locating it."

"Who?"

"Heron. Son of Timon, Nomarch of the White Walls."

"I know who his father is, Tetisheri."

"I most abjectly beg your pardon for my attempt to patronize you, O most high."

"Stop calling me that. You don't mean it anyway."

"Heron is a lecturer at the Mouseion. His specialty is engineering."

"I am aware."

"Surveying is a part of the discipline of engineering."

Cleopatra was silent for a moment. "Had Heron been helping Natasen find tombs, my Eye?"

"You always were quick, O most high. Yes, in answer to your question, I believe so. For all we know, perhaps not only Natasen. But it fits together in this case. They are both sons of White Walls, if of different branches, and as everyone knows, White Walls has mysterious sources of income. As a Fellow, Heron has free run of the old records at the Mouseion, and privileges at the Great Library. Any source on the location of tombs would have been available to him." Tetisheri shrugged. "If I'm right, and they were already co-conspirators in the locating and robbing of tombs, it would have been natural for Natasen to turn to Heron to help with his wooing of Herminia." She turned to face her friend. "Pati. Who is Herminia?"

A brief silence. "How fortunate indeed that Natasen in dead. Otherwise I might have had to take official notice of his and Heron's activities." Cleopatra's smile was little more than a baring of teeth. "I trust these activities are now at an end?"

"I don't think Heron has either the initiative or the courage to continue on his own."

"Courage?"

Tetisheri thought of the tomb, of the darkness, of the stifling air. "Trust me. Courage."

Cleopatra gave her an odd look. "I have never been inside a tomb."

"You never want to be, Pati."

"I see," Cleopatra said thoughtfully. "So. You and Apollodorus."

Tetisheri hoped her friend couldn't see her blush in the dim light.

Cleopatra nudged her. "Come on. Share."

Tetisheri felt a smile spread involuntarily across her face, and from the corner of her eye saw Cleopatra peering at her. "Ah. I see. Well done, Apollodorus."

"I was there, too, Pati."

Cleopatra chuckled.

"Pati. Who is Herminia?"

A faint sigh. "I have one more task for you before I release you from your duty to the crown and to me in this matter, my Eye."

Tetisheri shifted from friend back to subject. "I live to serve, Majesty."

Cleopatra snorted. "I require you to take the *Nut* back to Memphis, there to collect Herminia and escort her to Syene. Apollodorus will accompany you."

"Apollodorus?" And then she said, "Syene?"

"Yes, where you will leave Herminia in the care of the lady Amenirdis. If Herminia objects, you will tell her it is by my command. I will give you a letter to carry to Euphrasia with instructions, and another letter to Amenirdis."

Tetisheri stared at Cleopatra, who smiled.

"And when you have completed this task, Tetisheri, you will return to Alexandria. You will take a minimum of two of the new weeks to complete your journey, and I will instruct Uncle Neb and the other members of your family not to worry if you don't return for a month. Do I make myself clear?"

Tetisheri was speechless, but only for a moment. She made her best bow to her friend and sovereign. "Perfectly clear, O most high."

When she stood up again Cleopatra winked at her.

EPÍLOGOS

And so, upon the dawn, Apollodorus and Tetisheri did indeed depart again for Memphis, reaching the city late the next day. They were made welcome the morning after at the Temple of Seshat. This time they moored at the temple dock, and they couldn't help but notice as the city passed in review that the Temple of Ptah appeared all but deserted. Construction on the new addition seemed to have ceased.

Euphrasia called for tea and bread and fruit and bade them break their fast while she read Cleopatra's letter, not once but twice. She set it to one side with a sigh. "Excuse me. I must go to Herminia now."

The two women rejoined them an hour later. Herminia seemed subdued, mustering up just enough energy for a greeting. She made no protest at the plans for her near future.

Drawing Tetisheri aside, Euphrasia said in a low voice, "Herminia has been through a very traumatic experience.

Whether she was raped herself or not, she had to listen to it happening to others in that house for days. I don't have to tell you to treat her kindly. If she wants to talk, let her. For heaven's sake don't try to cheer her up. I promise you that she is going exactly where she needs to go, and where she will receive the care of which she is most in need of."

She would say no more than that. When Apollodorus asked her how the other survivors were doing she would say only, "Time will tell. Some of them were prisoners in that house for over a year. Others of their kind thought by Natasen to have outlived their usefulness—" she spat out the word "—were disposed of before their eyes. That is not an experience one recovers from in a day, or a year. Perhaps ever."

Markos had the gangway up, lines in, and oars in the water within minutes of their being back on board. None of them wanted to linger in Memphis.

It was a swift voyage south, in motion from dawn to dusk, the oars eating up the leagues. They paused only once, at a village some few miles south of Memphis. Tabe jumped into the water before they were fully moored to the bank. "Mother! Father! I'm home!"

The tears with which he was greeted reassured Tetisheri as to his welcome there. The heavy purse she had coerced from Cleopatra went a long way toward easing the worry lines in Tabe's father's face, and when Tabe brought Idu ashore they welcomed him, too.

For the rest of the journey the black banks of the Nile slipped by as they moved steadily upstream and farther south. They stopped only after sunset and were off again before dawn. Oats, rice, flax, and fields and fields of beans were beginning to create a green carpet. Farmers waved their hoes from the fields, naked children begged from boats the shape of almond shells, women slapping their washing against flat rocks arranged at the water's edge blushed and giggled when the crew whistled and catcalled. The eyes of crocodiles and the nostrils of hippopotami lurked in the grassy edges of swamps, ever alert to the possibility of an unwary boatman tripping over a line right into their open maws. It was enough to make every man on board be very mindful indeed of where he put his feet.

Beyond the river banks always was the omnipresent red of rock and sand stretching over the horizon. "It's a threat," Tetisheri said to Apollodorus one afternoon as they leaned against the railing, staring into the west.

"What is?"

"The red land is what the black land could look like if the Nile never flooded again."

"That's why we fill the granaries."

"So long as we can."

The black silt that washed over the river's banks every year was the lifeblood of Egypt and Alexandria. Nile grain fed the world. It was easy to point fingers at Auletes for improvidence but had Rome not needed Egyptian grain for their legions, Auletes would have had nothing to bargain for with Pompey. Lovely as Cleopatra was alternately praised and condemned for being by everyone from Herod to Cicero, Caesar's attention had very little to do with her looks, and everything to do with the tithing of grain and treasure to Rome. It was why, as Tetisheri had said, that Arsinoë was still living. Keeping a spare queen handy was never a bad idea, and Cleopatra knew that as well as Caesar did.

As had Natasen. If Herminia hadn't refused him, she wouldn't have been kidnapped. If she hadn't been kidnapped, Natasen's activities might never have come to the attention of the authorities.

By such slender threads do the fortunes of entire realms hang.

When, she wondered, would Natasen have produced Herminia as his blushing bride? And what would have been his object in doing so? A place at court? A title of his very own? A throne, even?

But if Natasen had thought that Cleopatra—or Philo for that matter—would have stood by as yet another claimant for the throne of Alexandria and Egypt appeared…Well.

Herminia spent most of her time asleep on the bed in the little cabin, said very little, and ate less. Tetisheri and Apollodorus curled up in a nest of blankets in the bow and respected her privacy. There was that air about their little group that the crew left them strictly alone and bent to their task, to such good effect that they arrived at Syene eight days after leaving Memphis.

This ancient, storied settlement, written of by Eratosthenes and Herodotus and too many other natural philosophers, historians, soldiers, and wanderers to count, was the site of the First Cataract, a boulder-strewn ledge that interrupted the Nile from bank to bank, interspersed with narrow bursts of white water that roiled and boiled the otherwise serene surface of the river. It was the first to interrupt the flow (and the navigation) of the Nile, from Syene to Agartum, three hundred leagues to the south.

Syene changed back and forth between being a large town and a small city depending on whether or not it was under siege by whichever Nubian prince was in the mood for plunder and by how many troops were stationed there as a result. It came under the authority of the Nomarch of the Bow and its location was directly responsible for the fame of its bowmen, who were said never to miss. They had had plenty of practice.

A low island sat downstream of the cataract, called Elephantine. It served as a port through which all the riches of Nubia flowed north: gemstones, gold, ivory, dates, and hardwood, among other things. It was also, vitally, one of three local sources for the black, gray, and red granite of which most of the temples and monuments of Egypt were built. An eastward track connected Syene to Berenike, the coastal port that served as the conduit for goods from the east, including the fabled lands of Punt and Sinae. Traded south were, of course, grain, but also oil, wine, beer, linen, and papyrus.

Most importantly, the island was a naturally defensible position to which the sprawling communities on either side retreated in the event of an attack. In later years the attacks had been mostly half-hearted and the retreats therefore short-lived. The Roman legion recently garrisoned there probably had something to do with that.

On both banks communities spread in an ever-growing swarm. Small temples sat next to hovels. Mansions small, medium, and large attested to the success or failure of the traders who had built them. Neighborhoods formed conclaves behind low walls and daring farmers planted fruit trees farther out every year. The brothels vied in number with the tavernas and it was a rare case indeed of either failing with such a large military presence in town.

In short, the city was a dirty, noisy place of quarrels and rivalries that sneered at silly concepts like law and order and civic responsibility. They paid their taxes not out of respect or duty to the crown but because they wanted to be left alone to go their own way, and for the most part they were and they did. As a result their streets were narrow and littered with refuse, their shurta were underfunded and woefully understaffed, doctors and hospitals were virtually non-existent, and such a thing as, say, a park was unheard of. When Cleopatra spoke of Syene, she did so with a rueful smile. She had cause, for both the rue and the smile.

The house of Amenirdis occupied the top of a hill on the right bank facing north, surrounded by a veritable plantation of flourishing date palms, struggling vines, and a market garden overrunning itself with cucumbers and melons. The house itself was a single story, square in shape, and of a goodly size, painted a white that was blinding in the midday sun. A broad path the width of a donkey-cart wound its way up the hill, and by the time they had toiled to the top their approach had been noticed and the door stood open. In it stood a sturdy woman in her early forties, who was flanked by two very capable-looking guards. The woman shaded her eyes with one hand. "Apollodorus?" And then on a more joyful note, "Tetisheri? Tetisheri, is that you?" Followed by a small shriek. "Herminia!"

Herminia started forward, almost stumbling in her haste but catching her balance at the last moment and rushing forward with her arms spread wide open. "Mother!"

She was met by an equally comprehensive embrace that swept her up off the ground. Herminia's back was heaving with sobs. Amenirdis ushered her into the house.

Tetisheri and Apollodorus waited for her in a small parlor. They were attended by a bland-faced servant known to both of them as Hypsicles, a gentleman of impeccable dress and august demeanor who never by so much as the flicker of an eyelash betrayed that he knew them both of long acquaintance.

"So that business about her not having a family," Apollodorus said.

"Yes, I do believe she has been deceiving us," Tetisheri said.

"I think she has been deceiving everyone, Sheri, and I would guess by royal command."

"Oh, would you guess that?" Tetisheri's mouth quirked up at the corner. "I can't imagine why."

"Well. She is an actor, after all."

Tetisheri laughed.

Amenirdis joined them after an hour had passed, her hair ruffled and her expression grave. Of medium height, with skin the color and texture of polished ebony, her eyes were large and dark and slanted toward her temples and her hair was a joyous riot of black frizz rivaling even Nike's. Like Nike, she bound it back with a colorful swatch of fabric. There were tiny creases at the corners of her eyes and mouth. Both were made for smiling but she wasn't smiling now. "Herminia has told me the whole," she said, taking her seat in the same way Herminia moved, as if Aphrodite had laid a gift of particular grace upon this woman of all women on earth. "I—"

Tetisheri had been staring at her since she came into the room. The mouth, the eyes—Herminia's skin was more blanched almond than polished ebony but the cheekbones, the grace of movement, above all the warmth that Herminia could project all the way back to the cheap seats. Herminia and Cleopatra did not look alike, but somehow they both looked like their mother. "You were married before," she said, blurting out of the words.

Words arrested, Amenirdis stared back. "She never told you?"

Tetisheri, dazed, shook her head. "I thought—Euphrasia left the court so suddenly, and admitted to raising Herminia in Memphis, so I—"

"You thought Herminia was Euphrasia and Auletes' child?" The smile became more natural. "Understandable, but no. Herminia is mine. Varro was her father."

"Varro?"

A trace of remembered sorrow echoed in Amenirdis' voice. "He was an officer in Auletes' army, one of the few, I might add, with any sense. He came to Auletes' admittedly scattered attention, and was commanded to court. I went with him. Varro was killed in some stupid little skirmish when Herminia was three. I was heartbroken, and Auletes was kind, and he was the king, and..." She shrugged.

"Why?"

"Why did Euphrasia have the raising of her?" Amenirdis sighed. "You know what court life is like, Tetisheri. You had your own troubles there yourself. Your mother, may Sobek eat her beating heart—" Tetisheri's upraised hand stopped her. "Well. When I became pregnant with Cleopatra, Herminia became an object of far too much attention. Auletes named Euphrasia the High Priestess of the Temple of Seshat in Memphis and Herminia went with her. I visited as often as I could, but it was much safer for her for people to believe she was just one of many orphans raised in the temple. Lately, she visits me here."

Tetisheri couldn't stop staring at the other woman. Philo had made the same mistake she had in assuming Herminia was Auletes' child. If that had been true and Natasen had managed to secure Herminia as his wife, they would have had a faint but legitimate claim to the throne. It had evidently never occurred to Philo that a rival to Cleopatra would also have been a rival to him.

Not that Auletes had ever formally named Amenirdis

as Cleopatra's mother. So far as the public was concerned, Cleopatra was the daughter of Auletes' sister of the same name, and Cleopatra went along with that fiction to avoid offending the delicate sensibilities of her Greek subjects in Alexandria, who found her trying enough already.

It was so obvious when one knew. Auletes had taken a Nubian to his bed and got upon her a child. Worse, he had named that child his heir. A mongrel, as Philo was so fond of calling her, instead of one of his pureblood children. Greeks being the master race that they were, and as such the only truly worthy inheritors to the throne of Ptolemy. Never mind that those true-born heirs were wholly lacking in wisdom and judgement and some of them even a modicum of sanity. "Does Herminia know?"

"Yes. I didn't want her thinking her father was anyone other than who he was." Amenirdis shook her head. "Dangerous, as we have just seen demonstrated. Cleopatra knows, too, of course. Auletes told her everything. Now." She smiled radiantly at the two of them. "Give me news of my younger daughter, and of my grandson. When am I going to meet him?"

They didn't see Herminia before they left, but took a fond farewell of Amenirdis, resisting her attempts to have them to make a longer stay in Syene. "We are faces Herminia associates with her recent trauma," Apollodorus said. "Best we absent ourselves as soon as possible so she can get on with healing."

"If she ever does," Tetisheri said once they were back on the boat and underway downriver.

"No one gets to the top of that profession without a layer of rhinoceros hide over their hearts, Sheri. And Amenirdis is with her, and it's obvious she loves her unconditionally. She is absolutely safe and she knows it. Give her time." He smiled down at her. "Now what was it that our queen commanded we do after we had delivered Herminia to her mother?"

She smiled at him, a little shyly. "That she didn't expect to see us back in Alexandria for at least two weeks."

His eyebrow went up. "Or a month."

"Or a month."

If they didn't use up the entire month they certainly did their best. They stopped at every temple along the river— although none of Ptah—to make offerings. It was surprising how little umbrage the gods took when their thoughts were obviously only of each other and not at all of Sobek or Horus or, horrors, even Isis. They spent a dusty week in Thebes, exploring hidden caves and crumbling tombs of rulers past with no thought of riches, only adventure. They found a mound of sand that might have concealed a door. They did not attempt to uncover it.

They climbed the highest peak above the Valley of the Kings, arriving breathless at the top. Apollodorus had providentially provided them with a blanket and they christened the peak with their love, Tetisheri's cries of pleasure echoing off the hard surfaces of the mountains surrounding them, so many she would later blush and wonder at them and at herself.

They left the *Nut* moored on a lonely bank and walked a day into the desert to pitch a tent at a tiny oasis with an even tinier spring, and spent the night there in laughter and love beneath the stars.

She became attuned to his every expression, his every gesture, his every mood in a way she never had with anyone else in her life. Marveling, she realized it was the same for him.

Markos and his crew pretended they were invisible and so they were to Tetisheri and she thought even to Apollodorus. One evening toward the end of their journey, as the pyramids at Saqqara and Dahshur slipped past and the turn into the Nile Canal threatened, she said, a little daringly, "So this is love?"

He raised her hand in his and kissed it. "It is for us, Tetisheri."

She found he had left something behind in her hand. "What is this—Apollodorus!"

He laughed. "Don't sound so scandalized."

"If she finds out—" The setting sun illuminated every exquisitely formed feature of the tiny golden scarab beetle, holding the sun in his delicate pincers. Matan would expire with envy if she ever showed it to him.

She looked up at Apollodorus. The sun turned his fair

hair to gilt and made his eyes an even deeper green. "You shouldn't have."

"She owes you. She owes us."

"She might have different ideas about who owes who."

"Too bad." He looked down at the bit of gold in her hand. "Do you know what the scarab beetle meant to the old pharaohs, Tetisheri?"

"Something to do with Ra, wasn't it?"

"Yes. The beetle is Ra, who is meant to be pushing the sun up over the sky each day. It's light. It's life."

He drew her in for a kiss, the sun a divine blessing on their faces. He pulled back. "For me, life hasn't been much more than one continuous exercise in staying alive."

He smiled down at her. "Until now."

NOTES AND ACKNOWLEDGMENTS

The original quote from Horace is "Nothing's beautiful from every point of view." Herminia defies all aphorisms so I paraphrased it for him.

Gaius Julius Caesar noster, imperator, pontifex

Primum praetor, deinde consul, nunc dictator, moxque rex

In English it reads as follows:

Our Gaius Julius Caesar, emperor, pontiff

First praetor, then consul, now dictator and soon king

Scans better in Latin, doesn't it? Rome's legions had

some very rude marching songs concerning Caesar's sexual exploits. By all accounts he took them in good humor. I'd be willing to bet he did join in on the chorus now and then, too.

Heron of Alexandria was a real person and a brilliant engineer. He imagined the first wind-powered machine and the first steam-powered engine (which last he may have appropriated from Vitruvius' *De architectura*). In reality he lived a hundred years after the time of this narrative but what's a century more or less in a story set two thousand years in the past? Vitruvius we met in *Disappearance of a Scribe* and as soon as I read about Heron the notion of putting the two men together became irresistible. After all, the Great Library and the Mouseion were the MIT of their day, the lodestone of every practical and theoretical physicist for five hundred years, give or take. The real tragedy is how the Dark Ages swallowed up so much of their work for so long.

The Nile is a river and as such a living thing that changes course over time, or did before the dams at Aswan. Ancient Egyptian engineers took full advantage of this in building canals and ports near the Giza Plateau so as to facilitate landing the necessary materials as close to the site of the Great Pyramids as possible. It's easy to imagine watching the sun set behind them in Cleopatra's time.

Syene is the ancient name for Aswan. I had to dig down to find an ancient name for Khartoum, a city founded only two centuries ago and the site of the Sixth and final Cataract, but there is a scholarly rumor it was once called Agartum, or "the home of Atum," who was the god of creation for both Egypt and Nubia. Close enough for government work.

I managed to skate through Egypt just before COVID in December 2019. At Giza I stood in front of the Sphinx and looked at the jumble of houses a hundred feet from its paws while the guide told us that such real estate was very valuable in that the people who lived in those houses were probably deep under our feet looting tombs as she spoke. They have resisted every attempt to clear out their neighborhood, she told us, defying even President Al-Sisi himself.

In Merenptah's tomb in the Valley of the Kings I saw his sarcophagi: the inside one, the outside one, and a third enormous piece that is found twenty feet up the tunnel leading to the burial chamber, where the tomb robbers dumped it when they decided it was too heavy to steal. And of course anyone who has ever read Elizabeth Peters (and if you haven't I urge you to find a copy of *Crocodile on a Sandbank* immediately) is wise to the nefarious ways of tomb robbers. Her real name was Barbara Mertz and she was a renowned Egyptologist who was also the author of the invaluable *Red Land, Black Land*, wherein she wrote:

> *Of course Khufu could not know that his pious undertaking would survive forty centuries in safety, but it is surprising that he should have sought such secrecy for his mother, and then have himself buried in a monument that was visible for miles in every direction. It was almost a millennia [sic] later before the kings of Egypt learned the painful lesson, that secrecy*

was preferable to bombast in tomb-building. Even the earlier private rock-cut tombs sometimes defeated this advantage by adding porticos and courtyards and chapels—an "X marks the spot" for any interested tomb robber, of whom there were multitudes.

At Dahshur, Barbara Peters and I climbed down inside the Red Pyramid, a 4,500-year-old pile of rocks in the heart of earthquake country. What could possibly go wrong? My description of Isidorus's claustrophobia was written from the heart, believe me.

I see Cleopatra as a forebear of Elizabeth I of England, insofar as both inherited their thrones from an improvident parent who left behind economic and political messes that their daughters had to clean up. It follows that my Cleopatra would take very personally indeed any attempt to defraud her of monies she felt were rightfully her due, including anything realized from the undisclosed theft and sale of tomb treasure, and including summary justice as, ah, executed by her Eye.

Astute readers will have noticed that I have begun each of the first three Eye of Isis novels with the same quote from Josephine Tey indicating our shared opinion of historians, who have a positive knack for ignoring normal human behavior, something I have run into too many times in reading biographies of Cleopatra and her contemporaries. A recent biography of Julius Caesar imagines that Cleopatra went to Rome in late 46 BC.

A month after Caesar went to Hispania to put down yet another Pompeian rebellion.

So we are meant to believe that Cleopatra, in the full knowledge that her Egyptian subjects had rebelled against every single Ptolemaic king and queen who preceded her and whose first recorded public act was to ingratiate herself with those Egyptian subjects by escorting the new Baucis bull to its temple in Memphis arrayed as the Egyptian goddess Isis, went tarryhooting off to Rome in pursuit of a boyfriend who had just left for Spain, and stayed there for two years, until Caesar's assassination in 44 BC.

Honestly. All historians *are* mad.